a simple thing

Also by Kathleen McCleary

House & Home

a simple thing

KATHLEEN McCLEARY

wm

WILLIAM MORROW
An Imprint of HarperCollins*Publishers*

A SIMPLE THING. Copyright © 2012 by Kathleen McCleary. All rights reserved. Printed in the United States of America. No part of this book may be used or reproduced in any manner whatsoever without written permission except in the case of brief quotations embodied in critical articles and reviews. For information address HarperCollins Publishers, 10 East 53rd Street, New York, NY 10022.

HarperCollins books may be purchased for educational, business, or sales promotional use. For information please write: Special Markets Department, HarperCollins Publishers, 10 East 53rd Street, New York, NY 10022.

FIRST EDITION

Designed by Diahann Sturge

Library of Congress Cataloging-in-Publication Data has been applied for.

ISBN 978-0-06-210623-0

12 13 14 15 16 OV/RRD 10 9 8 7 6 5 4 3 2 1

For my father, Thomas R. McCleary, with love and gratitude

a simple thing

The first escape fantasy Susannah ever had came when she was thirteen, sitting in the backseat of her parents' gray Buick with her younger brother and sister, watching the trees zoom by the windows. The road wound through uplands of pines and aspen and into lowlands thick with swamp grasses and orchids and along the edge of a river whose waters tumbled clear over stones as smooth and clean as bones. A small island stood in the middle of the river and a lone white pine grew on the island, and Susannah looked at it and thought how nice it would be to live there. She envisioned a little house built of branches, with a roof of moss and chairs of twigs and pine. Maybe she'd let Jon and Janie live there, too—just the three of them, climbing the laddered branches of the big tree, swimming in the river's cold waters, sleeping next to a fire on beds of balsam fir.

Later that summer, after the accident, they passed the island again on the way home. And this time Susannah looked at it not in idle fancy, but in desperate longing. If only she could live on that island, in the middle of that remote, lonely river. Alone. Forever.

Chapter 1

Susannah 2011

I'm not running away, Susannah told herself. After all, what she was doing could hardly be called "running away" when she was bringing her kids with her—including the child who, to be honest, she'd rather leave behind. She wasn't leaving Matt, even though half the town thought so. This wasn't about Matt, although he could have been a little more involved—okay, *a lot* more involved. She was doing exactly what she had sworn to do from that moment fourteen years ago when the nurse had first placed fierce newborn Katie into her arms: she was protecting her children.

The ferry began to move, and Susannah gripped the green iron railing with both hands and tried to still the fear rising in her chest. The blue-gray water rose in soft swells around the boat, and small whitecaps crowned the waves. *It's going to be okay*, she said to herself. The breeze caught her hair and whipped it around her face, and for a moment she forgot her fear and felt a sudden sense of freedom. *I'm really doing this. I'm leaving all that behind.* She put a hand up to pull her hair behind her ears.

Quinn, her son, stood next to her, his long blond hair blowing back in the wind, gazing at the water moving below them. Yards away the pebbled beach and fir-covered hills of Anacortes basked in the October sun. Giant driftwood logs, the bleached bones of some faraway forest, lay scattered along the uppermost edges of the rocky shore. The ferry chugged forward.

"Is this the ocean?" Quinn said.

"Yes," Susannah said. She focused on keeping her voice steady and calm, for Quinn. "I guess so. We're in a big bay here, but on the other side of these islands is Vancouver Island, and then the Pacific."

She had pored over the map their new landlord had sent to her, memorizing the names and shapes of the islands, the straits, the bays. Now she knew the large masses of Orcas and San Juan, tiny little Patos and Sucia, funny H-shaped Henry Island, and, of course, Sounder, their destination, six square miles of deep forests and rugged beaches at the northern tip of the San Juan Islands.

"Look." Quinn pointed to the sky, where a large bird wheeled in sweeping circles above the boat.

Susannah put up her hand to shade her eyes against the sun and saw a black silhouette against the brightness.

"It's an eagle!" Quinn said. "I've only ever seen one before."

"How do you know it's an eagle?"

"By the way it flies," he said. "See how it holds its wings out really flat and straight? That's how you can tell it's an eagle and not a hawk."

He loved his animals, her boy. He'd left more than six pets behind at home, including two cats, a rabbit, and a salamander. "You can bring *one* creature along with us," she'd told him, and he'd chosen his beloved box turtle, Otis, who was in a plastic pet carrier at his feet.

Susannah watched the eagle soar until it flew off behind

them, back toward shore. When was the last time she'd had even a minute just to watch the sky? Back home in Tilton, their lives were a full catastrophe of work, school, soccer practice, dive team, flute lessons, drum lessons, basketball, Little League, Ecology Club, and, not to be forgotten, Young Zookeepers Club. There, in their lovely little suburb in the northernmost corner of Virginia, the craziness started in September when the leaves on the cherry trees turned rusty red, and ran right through July when the first tomatoes ripened. With the first day of school the whole family was suddenly hurled into an endless sprint of constant activity, like sinewy greyhounds running after a lure they could never quite catch.

Susannah had to paste little pink sticky notes on the dashboard of her car to remind her where she was supposed to be when. "Quinn Zoo 3:00 bring boots" and "Mr. Mumbles to vet 4:30" and "granola bars juice Adams soccer field 6:00." Like everyone in Tilton, Susannah spent her afternoons and evenings and weekends driving from one lesson or game or practice to another, the children flicking crumbs from their laps as they ate in the car. "We're so busy," the parents all said. "The kids never get enough sleep. My family thinks a home-cooked meal is a grilled cheese sandwich."

But for Susannah, of course, a home-cooked meal *wasn't* a grilled cheese sandwich: it was homemade pizza and soups simmered for hours and biscuits made from scratch. She'd quit work the year after Quinn was born and devoted herself to giving her kids the childhood she never had, being the role model she never had. So in addition to managing the kids' packed schedules, she also volunteered at the school library twice a week, served on the board of the Tilton Arts Foundation, cooked meals for the Tilton homeless shelter every month, and served as secretary for the PTA. It was exhausting, being that responsible and good all the time.

"Not anymore," Susannah said.

"Not anymore what?" Quinn said.

"Nothing." Susannah smiled at him. "I was thinking out loud. Thanks for showing me the eagle. I'm going to check on Katie. Don't lean too far over the railing." Fear rose again from her stomach into her chest, and she felt slightly sick.

"Mom. I'm eleven, I'm not a baby," Quinn said, but he smiled at her.

The thought of going to find Katie also made her feel slightly sick. For the past year, thinking about Katie and worrying about Katie and checking up on Katie had crowded every moment of her waking existence, and haunted most of her dreams, too.

" 'You can only be as happy as your unhappiest child,' " Matt would quote to her, but Susannah didn't believe that. If anything, she herself was *unhappier* than Katie, because of Katie. The ferry could not pull them away fast enough from that life.

Susannah took a deep breath and pushed open the wide swinging doors that led to the main cabin. She looked around, past a toddler rolling on the gray linoleum floor, past backpacks and briefcases and people clutching their coffees, until she spotted her daughter slouched in the corner of a booth, her back against the window, feet up on the brown vinyl banquette, her eyes glued to a magazine in her lap.

"Hey," Susannah said, slipping into the booth next to her.

Katie didn't look up. "My cell phone doesn't work here," she said.

Susannah ignored her comment. Of course she couldn't expect Katie to be happy about this move. She just hoped Katie understood the *necessity* of it.

"Quinn just spotted an eagle," Susannah said. "Do you want to come outside and see what it's like here?"

"I know what it's like," Katie said, her eyes on the magazine. "Water, island, water, island, water, island. Living with the whales is going to change my life. I'm the Free Willy poster child. Woo-hoo." She raised one finger in the air and spun it in a circle.

"We're still hours away," Susannah said. "Give it a chance."

Katie put the magazine down, slid her long legs underneath the table, and turned away from Susannah. Her thick dark hair was pulled back into a ponytail, and Susannah could see the delicate curve of her ear just above the lobe. She remembered poring over that space when Katie was a baby, her shell-like ear tilted toward Susannah's face as she nursed. She had a sudden impulse to lean over and brush her lips along her daughter's lobe, as she had then, to inhale the wonderful warm scent of her neck. *This is that child. She's still here, somewhere.* And just as she bent forward, almost mesmerized, Katie jumped and said, "God, Mom, how about some personal space?"

"Katie—," Susannah began.

"I'm *here*," Katie said. "But I don't want to be here, and I'm not going to go out on the deck with you and Quinn and do some happy dance about the trees and the eagles. Can you please just leave me alone for now?"

"Katie! Come on. It's an adventure."

Katie turned her head and leveled a look at her mother. "Going to live on an island without *electricity* is not an adventure. It's crazy."

"It's different. It's a change. It's a chance to get out of the rut we were in."

"I was not in a rut."

Susannah's stomach clenched with a familiar fear. *She's okay,* she told herself. *She's safe now.* "Rut is a polite word for it," Susannah said.

"Polite?" Katie said. "Why? Because really it was 'a total disaster' or something?"

"No," Susannah said. "There's no need to be all melodramatic about it."

"Right!" Katie said. "Because there's *nothing* melodramatic about ripping me out of school and taking me to an island. Nope. Completely normal, that."

Katie did have a point, although Katie was too young—and too fearless—to understand the big picture, to know how quickly and easily something fun and simple could turn dark and ominous, slide into a life-altering disaster.

"All right. We're making a very big change, I'll grant you that," Susannah said. "But that Zach—" She stopped. "The party that night—"

"Oh, my God," Katie said. "I'm so glad we're here, moving on to our new life, where you can still nag me about everything I've ever done wrong."

As things had started to unravel this year, Susannah had realized that no matter how many activities she organized and coached, no matter how many parenting books she read and therapists she consulted and problem-solving talks she had with Matt, none of it would change a damn thing. Their crazy schedule, the endless round of activities, was supposed to be the antidote to the insidious influence of something Susannah couldn't even name, but that was seeping into her family anyway.

"It's not just you," Susannah said to Katie. "Quinn needed a break, too."

"Quinn's a freak," Katie said.

Susannah stifled an urge to grab her by both shoulders and shake her. This child, whose every heartbeat Susannah had felt as her own, was now someone she didn't even know. Sometimes, lying awake in bed at night while Matt snored gently next to her, she wondered if she had reached the supposedly boundless limits of mother love, like rocketing into space only to slam into a big black concrete wall, to find there *was* an end to the universe after all.

Susannah remembered the first few weeks after Katie was born when, crazy with hormones and sleep deprivation, she had sat staring at her baby for hours at a time, weeping with awe and gratitude. *This will be the greatest love of my life forever,* she thought. *No matter what other children I have, no matter what happens with Matt. This.* And Katie was the kind of child who inspired deep emotion. As an infant she would cling to Susannah, put her gummy mouth on Susannah's chin and suck wildly, as though she wanted to draw the very essence of Susannah's soul into her fierce baby self.

She continued to grow into her fierceness, becoming a little girl who cared—deeply, too much—about everything. In elementary school she organized a protest against the aide who oversaw lunchtime recess. She drew up a letter detailing the aide's transgressions, which ranged from the understandable (no standing on top of the monkey bars) to the outrageous (pinching kids in time-out). More than fifty kids signed Katie's letter, and the aide resigned. The storm of feelings that swirled around Katie—children's savior, principal's bane—never settled, like tumbleweeds spinning endlessly across the plains.

But when she started seventh grade, more than a year ago, everything changed. The girl who used to spend hours writing plays for Quinn, casting him as the gentle king or brave prince; who once stayed up all night to help him care for a baby bird he'd found limp in the grass; who used to crawl into Susannah's bed and hug her and whisper, "Don't ever die, Mommy, because I couldn't stand to be without you"—that girl had become sullen and wild and sometimes downright mean.

She started to tease Quinn—sweet, sensitive Quinn with his skinny legs and wide smile—about horrible viruses like Ebola and Marburg, until he started wearing a bandanna over his mouth and nose at recess to avoid germs. She told a racy joke on-air during school announcements. She climbed onto the school roof on a dare and took a photo of herself next to the bell tower, hundreds of feet above ground. She was suspended for two days after she distributed two hundred copies of her own version of the school newspaper—complete with a scathing story about popular Abby Whittle, who, according to Katie's paper, had plagiarized the essay on good citizenship that had won her a hundred dollars and a byline in the *Washington Post*.

Then the Troubles with Katie, as Matt called them (as though it were a book or a movie and not something they had to *live* through every day), gained momentum, a swirl of thick warm clouds gathering strength before a hurricane. There was the day Susannah came home early to find Katie on the couch kissing some boy; the day Katie skipped school and went to the mall with that girl who had been arrested twice for selling pot; the night Katie climbed out her bedroom window and shimmied down the cherry tree and met some friends in the park at midnight. One of the kids had beer, and Katie came home tipsy—at age fourteen. Within a month came the final incident that unraveled everything. Susannah felt sick thinking about it—the terrifying trip to the emergency room, with Katie pale and cold and limp in her arms while Matt gunned their old Subaru through red lights and asked over and over, "Is she breathing? Is she still breathing?" She remembered counting Katie's slow breaths—ten a minute, then eight a minute—and trying to keep Katie upright so she wouldn't choke if she vomited. She remembered the look the nurse in the emergency room had given her after checking Katie's pulse and reflexes—a look of pity that scared Susannah more than anything that had happened yet that night.

"We had to do something," Susannah said. Katie was still turned away from her, toward the big window, looking down at her magazine.

"You overreacted," Katie said.

"I overreacted?" Susannah said. "My *father* was an *alcoholic*. You're fourteen. You drank so much you were unconscious—"

"Stop it!" Katie said. "I know! I could have died! I've had the lecture a million times."

Katie threw her magazine down, pulled her knees up to her chest, and wrapped her arms around her legs. All at once she looked young, wounded.

"Katie," Susannah said, her voice soft, "it scared us. If Annie hadn't called . . ."

"It was one time, Mom," Katie said, her voice muffled against her knees. "*One time.* I told you. We were just messing around and didn't know we were drinking too much. It's not like I was doing that every day, or was about to. It's not like other kids don't experiment, too." Her voice was thick now, on the brink of tears. "But *their* parents don't use that as an excuse to pull them out of school and exile them."

One time, Susannah thought. That's what Susannah's father used to say, too, at first—until it became such a clear and obvious lie that even he couldn't choke it out anymore. She could picture him standing in the kitchen, his back to the sink, looking at her mother—first pleading, then angry—while she and Jon tried to disappear into their chairs, heads pulled down, shoulders hunched, curling over and into themselves like snails.

"It's not exile, Kate," Susannah said.

"Right." Katie turned her face to the glass, her back to Susannah. "It's just pulling me away from all my friends and dragging me someplace where no one can even come visit me. Where even *Dad* can barely visit us."

"Mom." Quinn materialized at her elbow, his face flushed with wind and cold, his nose dripping.

Susannah put a hand on Katie's leg, a touch meant to comfort, to reassure. But Katie pulled away like she'd been burned.

"*Mom.*"

She turned to Quinn. "What is it? You look frozen."

"It's just windy." Quinn rubbed his nose on the sleeve of his orange sweatshirt. "Mom, I met someone who lives on San Juan Island. He said he's lived up here twenty-five years and he's never been to Sounder. He said the people on Sounder don't like outsiders. He said one time he went over to take pictures because there were some cormorants nesting there, and the people there wouldn't even let him step off the dock."

"That's one person's point of view, honey. Our landlord was very friendly when I talked to her."

Katie lifted her head. "I knew it," she said. "I knew it was crazy to come to Little House on the Stupid Island."

Susannah saw the crease between Quinn's brows, the concern in his bright blue eyes. Over the past months he'd become more and more of a loner. Susannah and Matt had talked to his teachers, talked to the principal, but the bullying had been subtle, insidious—taunts hissed in low voices on the playground, accidental bumps in the hallways when the teacher's head was turned. They'd taken him to a therapist about his germ phobia, but the social damage had already been done. Sure, he'd stopped wearing bandannas around his mouth and nose, but he was still the kid who loved turtles, the kid who could (and all too readily would) quote a million obscure facts about everything from earthworm digestion to rabbit reproduction, the kid who felt things so keenly that tears sprang to his eyes too often to allow him to fit in. Two weeks ago he'd come home bloodied from the bus stop, the day before Katie's drinking binge. The last straws.

"What if no one on Sounder likes us?" Quinn said. His eyelashes were so pale they seemed to disappear, giving his face a look of wide-eyed innocence.

"It's not going to be like that, sweetie. You'll see. You're going to make some great new friends."

"Yeah, if they don't burn you at the stake first," Katie said. "Did you ever see that movie *The Wicker Man*, about the police officer who went to that remote island and it turned out all the people there were involved in some bizarre cult and they made him a human sacrifice and burned him up?"

"Kate! Shut up!"

"Fine," she said. "I'm just saying." She took her iPod out of her backpack, put the earbuds into her ears, and turned it on.

"Mom?" Quinn said. "Is that true? Did you see that movie?"

She looked at the two of them and recalled snapshots of other Katies and Quinns: four-year-old Quinn at the park, filling her pockets with his gifts—a stone, a maple seed pod, the cap of an acorn. Katie, not yet one, taking delighted baby steps with her bare feet in the new grass on the first warm morning of spring, crowing with delight. These were her children, and yet not her children; she loved them as much as she ever had, but also, at times, felt almost like she couldn't stand them. The things that had happened this year had required so much attention and vigilance—not to mention raw emotion—that she felt completely spent.

Susannah looked out the window of the ferry. The skyline was sharp, pointed with the tips of the firs—unlike the soft, rounded skyline of the deciduous trees back home in Virginia. The snow-capped summit of Mount Baker floated on the horizon. Friday Harbor, the ferry's destination, was the biggest town in the San Juans, yet it didn't even have a traffic light. From there they'd have to travel another hour and a half on a small boat to Sounder, where there were no paved roads, no landline phones, no electricity, and just seventy-five people.

Susannah glanced at her daughter, curled in a ball of anger in the corner of the booth, at her son standing next to her, wide-eyed and afraid. She thought of her husband, all alone in their big house three thousand miles away. She thought, with some guilt, about the relief she felt in leaving him behind.

She hoped she wasn't making the biggest mistake of her life.

Chapter 2

Betty 2011

Betty Pavalak stood at her kitchen sink and gazed out the window, although she could see nothing but her own reflection. Dusk came early now. Night up here in the San Juans was dark and blacker than anything she'd ever known. She had hated that at first—the nights so dark you couldn't take a step outside without stumbling, unsure of where the ground began beneath your very feet. After the bright lights and wide skies of Seattle, those early nights tucked in here at the edge of the woods had pressed in on her like a crowded elevator. More than once she had gotten out of bed, ripped open the buttons at the neck of her nightgown, and stumbled onto the porch to breathe, facing the ocean, the escape.

Betty lit a cigarette and took a long drag, watching the tiny red glow light up her reflection in the window. Funny, this new tenant, Susannah, was coming here because she *wanted* to. Betty had wanted to come here, too, for about six months, until she realized that living on a remote island was not going to change one good goddamned thing about Bill Pavalak, and that she had just signed herself up for the kind of lifestyle you couldn't pay someone to do—up at the crack of dawn to feed chickens and goats, chopping wood to feed the hungry stove, boiling and washing and tending things all day long, all without even a decent light bulb to make it *that* much easier. But after six months she was pregnant, and the only thing she wanted more than going back home to her family in Seattle was a baby. So she had stayed.

She liked the nights now, found the darkness soft and comforting. When she went to the mainland to see her sisters in Seattle or the doctor in Bellingham, the glow of light everywhere seemed harsh and intrusive, a visual cacophony. She didn't remember at what point the darkness here had become friendly to her, just as she couldn't remember exactly when the sound of the rain beating against the roof had taken on a soothing rhythm, no longer the steady, insistent patter that had threatened her very sanity that first year. It was all how you decided to look at things.

Betty took a last swig of coffee and put her mug down on the counter. She stubbed out her cigarette in the mug and picked up her parka from the hook by the back door. Did she need to bring anything? She opened the door and peered out at the sky. The sun wouldn't set for another hour yet, so if the ferry had been on time and the waters in Governor's Channel were not too rough, then Jim should be at the dock in ten minutes and they'd be able to get this new family settled into the cottage while there was still some daylight. But she picked up the flashlight from the counter to bring with her, just in case.

"Hey, Grim." Hood, her oldest grandson (if you wanted to count the two minutes he was in the world before his twin was born), appeared in the doorway. "Ready to go?"

Even in the soft light she could see his green eyes, exactly like his father's and grandfather's.

"Yes, I'm ready," she said. "Let me give the stew a final stir."

Hood rolled his eyes. "Come on. We want to be there when they get in."

"You'll be there," she said. "Here." She handed him the flashlight and looked around the kitchen for her wooden spoon until she found it in the sink. She knew the twins were excited; there hadn't been a child their age on Sounder since Sally Lewis moved away three years ago.

"Where's your brother?"

"Waiting in the truck. Let's go."

Betty lifted the lid from the cast-iron skillet and gave the stew a slow, careful stir. She planned to feed this Susannah and her kids tonight, and give them some supplies for breakfast tomorrow. She was willing to bet that Susannah—used to all-night grocery stores and convenience stores and restaurants—hadn't even thought about bringing a day or two's supply of food with her. Ah, well. Betty hadn't thought of that, either, her first night on Sounder. She and Bill had arrived on the dock with two sandwiches and their duffel bags and their mutual resentments and not much else. Susannah would learn soon enough that you could take nothing for granted when you lived in a place like this.

"*Grim*," Hood said. The boys had called her "Grim" since they could talk, a term of endearment coined by Jim, her clever son, when she'd objected to being called "Gram." "Can we go now?"

"What's the rush?" She dipped the spoon into the stew, ladled up a small taste of the broth, brought it to her lips, and blew on it to cool it off. She was teasing him, and he knew it. She was almost as excited about the new tenants as he was. Susannah's rent would add a comfortable amount to Betty's small income, and, to be honest, Betty was a bit lonely since school had started, with Jim teaching and the boys at school all day and Fiona, her daughter-in-law, away. It would be good to have

Susannah around. And since Susannah would be here without her husband, she'd likely be lonely, too.

"Okay," she said to Hood. "Let's go."

They climbed into the truck. Hood drove, even though he was only fourteen, because that's the way it was on Sounder. Betty didn't like to drive much anymore, and Hood and Baker were both competent enough.

The truck bumped along the dirt driveway. Three gates stood between the cottage and the main road, although the main road itself was little more than one lane of hard-packed dirt filled with gravel in the low spots. At each gate, Hood stopped the truck and Baker hopped out and opened the gate, then Hood drove slowly through and stopped on the other side until Baker had closed and latched the gate and climbed back in the truck. It was so routine to the boys that neither of them complained, even though they were in a hurry. They didn't want to end up hunting goats or alpacas through the woods if the gate were left opened.

"So do you know if she's hot?" Hood asked, as they turned onto North Shore Road. Even after fifty-five years here, Betty was amazed by this paradox, the contrast between the magical beauty of the Sounder roads and their prosaic names. The dirt road that cut through a meadow of blue camas and yellow prairie violets that blazed with color every spring was called "Gravel Pit Road." The road that wound alongside a stream and past bigleaf maples that turned golden in the fall was "Hill Road." And this road, which passed through a forest of ancient hemlocks and cedar and Douglas firs that towered upward like giant arrows pointing directly to God, was "North Shore Road." Sounder pioneers may have had guts, but they didn't have much creativity.

"What?" Betty said.

"The new girl," Hood said. "Is she hot?"

"I didn't ask for photos with the rental application," Betty said, her voice dry. "My mistake. I don't think I can break the lease if the daughter is ugly."

Hood rolled his eyes. "Very funny, Grim."

"Susannah also has a son," Betty said. "I think he's ten or eleven. I hope you'll make him feel welcome, too."

"It's weird they're coming here in October," Baker said. "School's already started. Why are they moving?"

"I've told you everything I know," Betty said. "Susannah said they needed a change, and she's had some interest in the San Juans since she was young."

"It's weird they're coming here at all," Hood said.

Betty didn't add that Susannah had mentioned her daughter had had some "behavior problems," and that she hoped the different pace of life on Sounder might help. Let her come to Sounder with a clean slate, Betty thought. It's what she herself had tried to do when she'd arrived with Bill all those years ago. They'd purchased the farm sight unseen and arrived with all kind of hopes for their fresh start, even though they'd been married four or five years by then.

And Sounder had worked its miracles, for a while. Those first six months, once she got used to the hard work involved in living without electricity or indoor plumbing, she had relaxed deep inside in a way she'd never experienced before. What had undone her then, and driven her off the island for a while, had had nothing to do with Sounder, and everything to do with the man she'd married.

When she returned, it was with a different kind of hope: hope for her child. That's what drew her back to Sounder, and that's what had kept her here over the years, through bouts of loneliness and boredom. Sure, she'd get letters from her sister Bobbie in Seattle about a party she'd thrown or a movie she'd seen or the fabric she'd bought to redecorate her living room, and Betty would think, *I could leave. I could take Jim and go home, and I could see a movie and live in an apartment with a dishwasher and electric light and never have to look at another goddamned chicken as long as I live.*

But then she'd look at Jim, at her sensitive, brilliant boy, and see the ways Sounder nourished him, from the long wild rambles he took alone in the woods to the library of books and comic books he read over and over (since they had no television) to the gang of kids he'd known since birth—and God knows there was a gang of them back then in the early sixties and seventies, when forty-five children had filled the schoolhouse and swelled the old post office (now the Laundromat) almost to bursting at parties. It wasn't just the kids; it was the parents, too, who knew each other's children as well as their own, encouraged them and disciplined them as their own, who were a community in every sense of the word.

When she thought of moving to Seattle and trying to find a job—at thirty-three or thirty-four, with no employment history, and her only skills things like the ability to pluck a chicken in five minutes flat or to stitch up a man's arm with boiled white cotton thread and a sharp needle—she grew afraid. She couldn't support herself and Jim, and even if she did find a job, what then? Who would watch Jim while she went out to work eight or ten hours a day? They'd have to live in a small apartment, and who knew what neighborhood they'd be able to afford. One sister was ill and still lived at home; her other sister was married, with a house and family of her own. No, the best thing for Jim was Sounder, so she'd stayed.

Then, after thirteen years, after the accident, she had little desire to leave. If she'd been out in the world after the accident she might have gone crazy, she thought. On Sounder she'd been someplace where no one judged her for what had happened, and where Jim, who was twelve and a handful, was safe, or as safe as one could be in a world full of surprises.

Betty shook her head.

"What, Grim?" Baker said.

"Nothing," she said. Something about this younger woman coming to the island, to live in the cottage where she herself had raised her child—Betty felt a deep connection to this woman she'd never met. Feelings and thoughts she'd thought long gone arose inside her like the saplings on the forest floor—steady, insistent. Some of them were things she didn't want to think about or feel again. Not now. She shifted her angular body on the front seat of the truck.

"So do you know why they're coming here?" Baker said.

Betty shook her head. "No idea."

She knew. Susannah was bringing her daughter here to keep her safe—that much was clear. But suffering found everyone sooner or later, whether you ran away or stayed in place.

Chapter 3

Susannah 2011

The first thing Susannah noticed about Jim Pavalak was his eyes, which were a muted shade of mossy green exactly the same color as the waters in Lake Michigan in winter. The second thing she noticed was the way he listened, with his head cocked to one side as though he had all the time in the world. He didn't take his eyes off hers as he shook her hand, asked about the ferry ride, and welcomed her to the San Juans. To Susannah, used to the rapid-fire chatter and distracted gazes that characterized conversation on the East Coast, this was remarkable. The third thing she noticed was his absolute confidence behind the wheel of the boat. Her father had been the same way, so secure on the water that driving the boat was as natural as breathing. Jim's nonchalance—one hand resting on the wheel, his body turned sideways so he could look at Quinn while they chatted—reminded her so much of her father it unnerved her.

Jim met them at the ferry dock, and then they walked through the tiny town of Friday Harbor to the marina, under the canopy of broad, ancient oaks covered in bright gold leaves.

The wheels of their suitcases rattled along the wooden planks of the dock. Sharp-eyed Quinn pointed out two sea otters bobbing in the water alongside them.

"So everyone's curious about why you picked Sounder," Jim said over his shoulder, as he backed the boat out of its slip in the marina. He'd already asked Quinn about Otis the turtle, and had also tried to engage Katie, who had smiled at him but kept her white earbuds firmly in place, which annoyed Susannah no end.

"Why Sounder?" Susannah said. She looked out the window of the cabin at the soft swells of the gray-green water and gripped the edge of the seat beneath her with both hands. "I'm a Shackleton fan," she said, turning back to Jim. "I love adventure stories about life under extreme conditions—you know, the Donner party or the survivors of plane crashes in the Andes or that guy in World War Two who survived all those days in a lifeboat and prisoner of war camp."

Jim's eyebrows shot up. "And you think that's what life on Sounder is like?"

"No, of course not," Susannah said. "But it's different, at least, different enough from what we're used to."

She had first read about Sounder in a *New York Times* article years ago, and she had clipped the piece and saved it in a drawer in her desk, in a file called "Things I Like." It made her think of the little island in the middle of the Fox River in northern Michigan, her longed-for escape. Then, when Katie started acting so crazy and Susannah began to think about taking Katie away—to her mother's in Michigan, or to her brother Jon's in Seattle—she remembered Sounder, the anti-Tilton.

"Hate to disappoint you," Jim said, "but we get very little snow, and we have yet to eat the bodies of our neighbors during hard times."

"Not even the fat ones?" Susannah said with a smile.

Jim laughed. "No, not even the fat ones."

"But Sounder is different," Susannah said. "No electricity, no television, no landline phones—so *unplugged* compared to the way we live."

"It was more different before the Internet arrived," Jim said. "And cell phones. A lot of islanders have satellite dishes now that give them a connection to both."

"Yes!" Quinn said.

"Don't get too excited," Jim said. "We lose the connection every time it rains. And it rains a lot."

"What do you do on Halloween?" Quinn said. This was a particular concern of his, with Halloween just a week or two away. He thought eleven was probably the last year he'd go trick-or-treating, and now they were moving to an island with only seventy-five people, who lived in houses miles apart.

"Golf carts," Jim said. "Lots of people on the island own electric golf carts, and the kids drive 'em around from house to house to trick-or-treat."

"Really?" Quinn looked very happy. "But you don't have electricity. How do you charge them?"

"We have generators, and solar power."

"Why does everyone have golf carts?"

"No gas," Jim said. "To fill up a car with gas on Sounder, you have to drive a boat over to Orcas or Friday Harbor, which can take an hour or two, fill a portable tank with gas, haul that tank back in the boat for another hour or two, and then carry it up the dock to your car. Believe me, it makes you think long and hard about any driving you do. That's why we got the motorcycle. It gets sixty miles a gallon. The boys love it."

Katie pulled the earbuds out of her ears. "How old are your boys?" she said.

Susannah noted that Katie had clearly been listening to the entire conversation.

"Fourteen," Jim said. "Twins. Hood and Baker."

"Like the mountains?" Quinn said.

"Yes. Lucky we didn't have a girl, eh? Or she'd be stuck with a name like Saint Helen." He grinned at Katie.

"Or Shasta," Quinn said. "That's in the Cascades, too."

"Or Shasta," Jim said, opening his eyes wide and nodding at Quinn to show he was impressed. "I like a young man who knows his mountains."

"My dad's a geologist," Quinn said.

"How can your boys drive a motorcycle when they're only fourteen?" Katie said. "Don't you have to be sixteen?"

Jim shrugged. "It's Sounder. Necessity trumps legality sometimes." He paused. "There's no traffic. Kids here need to know how to drive young to help with farm work. Most learn as soon as their feet can touch the pedals."

No traffic. Susannah wanted to do a little dance of joy, right there in the boat. If she'd wanted a life as different from Tilton as possible, she was getting it. What could be more different than not spending six hours a day stuck inside a car in endless traffic? Although the idea of Katie riding a motorcycle, her arms wrapped around some teenage boy, gave her pause.

"You have a motorcycle," Susannah said.

"Yes," Jim said. "But it's actually out of commission right now. You can put your *Easy Rider* fears to rest."

"You read my mind."

Jim tilted his head in acknowledgment. "One of my many skills."

Suddenly the water swelled and the waves grew choppy and rough. The comforting shape of San Juan Island to their left had disappeared, and they were in a wide, open channel. Jim put both hands on the wheel.

"Governor's Channel," he said. "Deepest waters in the San Juans. The currents can be a little crazy here."

Susannah tried to choke down her fear. More than thirty years had passed since she had last been on a boat, other than the ferry she had just ridden to get here. But that was the other purpose of this adventure, wasn't it? She wasn't running away. She was running straight into her own darkest fears.

Susannah had tried to explain this to Matt, as they'd talked about what to do after that horrible night at the hospital. Zach, the *seventeen-year-old* Katie had been dating behind their backs, had taken her to a party and plied her with rum and Cokes until she passed out. It was only the quick thinking of Katie's friend Annie—who arrived late at the party and found Katie sprawled on the sofa in a dark corner with Zach—that had saved her from God knows what with Zach, and had likely saved her life. Annie had texted her own mom, who immediately called Susannah, who raced over there with Matt.

A few days later, Annie's mom called with more news. Zach had a Web site, and had been taking bets from other high school boys on whether or not he could get girls to give up their virginity to him. He handicapped them all and posted odds on the Web site. Katie was listed with odds of two to one he'd have sex with her by November 1.

Susannah and Matt talked about legal action, but they lived in a small town. Susannah had already heard the things being said about Katie, about her own parenting. She didn't want to be the subject of endless gossip as the case dragged through the courts and was written up in the local paper. Her urge to leave was intuitive, reflexive.

"I've got to get her out of here," she said to Matt. "Zach—"

"The little fucker," Matt said, his lips clenched. For a moment Susannah saw him as the boy he'd been at twelve, enraged, struggling for control. Then he had shivered, shaken his head hard, and started planning what to do next, in his rational Matt-like way. "Running away isn't the answer," he said.

Susannah was folding laundry as they talked. "It's not just Zach—it's Katie. What makes her decide to go out with a guy like Zach, or go to that party knowing no adults would be there? We have to get her away from here, at least for a while."

"But she's going to be Katie no matter where she is," Matt said.

"There are more temptations here." Susannah could remember the softness of the T-shirt she held in her hands. "And *problems*. It's Quinn, too." She didn't have to explain. Quinn's isolation pained Matt, who had also been set apart as a boy—the kid with cheap clothes, the kid who ate free school lunch, the kid who couldn't play sports because he had to work. But being different had hardened Matt; it hadn't done that for his son.

"We don't know if that fight he got into at the bus stop was the first, or the tenth. Sure, that's the first time there's been *physical* evidence he's being bullied, but . . ." Susannah's voice trailed off. "And Katie—"

Matt looked at her. "It's almost as if you wanted this," he said. "So you'd have a reason to leave."

"What's that supposed to mean?" she said.

"Nothing," he said. He picked up one of Quinn's baseballs from the coffee table and stared at it, turning it over and over in his hands.

But she knew. Their struggles with both kids this past year had revealed gaps in their marriage she never would have imagined, like snapping open the shade to let in a sudden harsh light, exposing flaws in something that had seemed young and lovely in the half dark. With each fresh crisis, Susannah felt herself spin more and more out of control, desperate to restore the neat, careful life she had built for her family. And Matt, the practical problem solver with the scientific mind, didn't understand.

Over the past six months Matt had worked more and more hours, so Susannah was often left alone to deal with making all the phone calls to track down Katie when she didn't come home on time, or talking Quinn through the unlikeliness of getting hepatitis from a school cafeteria sandwich. At least once a week she and Katie would get in shouting matches, and Katie would start calling her the kind of names her father used to call her: Idiot. Stupid. Jerk. And no matter how much she tried to remind herself that she was the adult, Katie's rage called up something visceral in her that she couldn't face.

She wanted Matt to come home and protect her; Matt wanted to come home to a peaceful, happy home. They were like two pieces of a puzzle that didn't quite fit together.

"I need to try this," she said to Matt.

"I guess you do," he said. He didn't look at her.

"Not just for Katie and Quinn," she said, reaching out to put a hand on his knee. "For me. Going away for a while. Being on the water again. Maybe it's what I need to finally get over it."

It. She didn't need to elaborate. For thirty-three years she had lived with what happened the day of the accident. She knew—in the complex equation of her father's drinking, her mother's failure to protect them, the vagaries of wind and water and wake—who was to blame. Yet still she hadn't been able to set foot on a boat, forgive her mother, control her hypervigilance over her own children. It was exhausting.

Finally Matt—the only person other than her father and brother who knew *exactly* what had happened that day—looked at her with those blue, blue eyes, the color of the ice in glaciers, and said, "Maybe you *should* go."

She'd found Betty's ad the next day, and called before she lost her courage. But the image of Matt standing alone in the airport, waving at them as they disappeared through security, haunted her.

Jim slowed the engine as the swells grew. "Bit rough today," he said.

Susannah felt fear rise in her with the waves. *Don't think about it.*

"How long have you lived on Sounder?" Susannah asked.

"Most of my life," Jim said. "I tried some other places. I worked in California for a while. I even spent a year in graduate school in North Carolina. But the mist on the Smoky Mountains reminded me of Puget Sound, so I ended up hitchhiking home."

"What did you go to graduate school for?" Katie said.

"Law. I didn't like that, either."

"Law is boring," Katie said.

"What do you like?" Jim said.

"Writing."

"Ah, an author. You'll be in good company on Sounder. We have several writers. What kind of writing do you do?"

Katie shrugged. "Stories. Poems. A journal."

"Who's your favorite author?"

Katie didn't hesitate. "Harper Lee."

"Good. I was afraid you were going to say either someone I've never heard of, or perennial teen favorite J. D. Salinger."

"I hated *Catcher in the Rye*," Katie said. She allowed herself a small smile.

Jim grinned back. "Me, too. Most overrated book in the history of English class."

"So what do you do if you're not a lawyer?" Katie said.

"Teach," Jim said. "You'll see me at school at eight tomorrow morning. Don't be late. I give detention."

"Seriously?" Katie said. "*You're* the teacher?"

Jim nodded. "Yup. Dropped out of law school, roamed around, then went to the University of Washington and got my teaching certificate. Taught in San Diego and then came home to help my mom with the farm. But last spring our teacher on

Sounder got sick and had to leave. We couldn't find someone to fill the slot, so I stepped in."

"You teach your own kids?" Quinn said.

"Yes. Not ideal. But it's just for one year. They'll live off-island next year to go to high school in Friday Harbor. Our school only runs through eighth grade."

"I would kill myself if my mom was my teacher," Katie said.

"How fortunate for us all that she isn't," Jim said, his voice dry.

Susannah laughed; she couldn't help it. "Don't worry, Kate," she said. "I have no desire to teach."

"And what do you do?" Jim said in his best cocktail-party voice. He turned his head to look at Susannah but then turned back to keep his eyes on the waves.

"I drive. And volunteer. And organize. Before the kids, I was a 'visual merchandising manager,' which is a fancy way of saying window dresser."

She had loved her job. In those early years of their marriage, when Matt was working on his Ph.D., they'd lived in a tiny apartment in Chicago, and she'd worked for Marshall Field's as a design assistant. She had loved the sense of purpose of those days—getting to the store early when it was quiet and still, gathering clothes and shoes, painting backdrops, constructing props. She and Matt had had a sense of purpose, too, the two of them scrimping by on her meager salary and forgoing dinners out and movies and new books, with Matt's Ph.D. their dual goal, their dual accomplishment. In the evenings, while Matt was buried in his books, she'd paint, experimenting with bold colors and large canvases. She painted a series of landscapes they'd seen on their honeymoon trip out west—bright orange canyons, vivid blue rivers, red moons, and black skies shot with brilliant gold stars. They were filled with all the exuberance she had felt then, happy to love Matt and be loved by Matt and work at something creative. She wondered now where those paintings had gone. The attic?

"Window dresser?" Jim said. "Really?"

"I wanted to be an artist," Susannah said. "But that way poverty lies, as my father loved to point out, so I found something to do that at least let me work with color and design, and the occasional male model."

"Oh, my God," Katie said. "I cannot believe you said that."

"I'm kidding!" Susannah said.

Jim started to say something, then stopped and peered forward.

"I'll hold that thought for a moment. Look! We've got company."

Susannah looked ahead. Cutting through the blue-green water in front of the boat she could see sleek black-and-white forms leap above the surface and then disappear. "Dall's porpoises," Jim said. The kids raced outside, climbing along the side of the boat until they knelt on the bow, side by side, peering into the water. Susannah followed them, her eyes on the kids, not the porpoises. She knelt next to Quinn. There, so close she could lean forward and touch them, three porpoises leaped in graceful arcs above the waves. They flipped onto their backs. They swam in undulating, elongated S-curves—flashes of black, the luminescent white of a belly, then black again, leaping, splashing, spinning. Quinn crowed with glee.

A jolt of fear shot through Susannah—the kids were leaning over the railing, so close to that deep, deep water—but she took a deep breath. She looked at Katie. Her face was open, unguarded. Susannah suddenly remembered being thirteen and skimming across the glassy surface of the lake on water skis, her thighs burning, the skis chattering under her feet as she cut across the wake, and how she'd felt a moment of pure joy, pure freedom. It had been so intense she'd never forgotten it, and she felt it again now—the wind whipping her face, the sharp scent of seawater, the porpoises wheeling through the water, and her children, kneeling on the bow, lost in wonder.

If only Matt could see this, Susannah thought. In spite of all the arguments over the last year, she missed him. She could draw every line of his face with her eyes closed, from the scar on his right cheekbone to the lopsided angle of his smile. The feel of his body against hers was as familiar as the feel of her own tongue against her teeth. They had known each other for thirty-nine years, since that first summer at Camp Chingwa, and been married for seventeen. This next month until he came to visit would be the longest they'd been apart in twenty years. She remembered a time early in their marriage when she'd gone away for work and Matt had mailed a postcard to her every day, just as he used to do when they were kids in the week before camp. Matt didn't talk much about feelings or longings, so she was surprised by what he wrote, things like: "It's raining here, and I miss you. Your pillow still smells like you. COME HOME."

She wondered if he was lonely. She wondered, all at once, if he would still his loneliness with someone else in her absence. The thought startled her so much she almost fell off the boat.

The porpoises twisted, dove. The cold spray from the wake splashed against Susannah's cheeks. Then, just as quickly as they had come, the porpoises shot away, disappearing into the darkening water.

Jim popped his head up through the skylight in the roof of the wheelhouse.

"Hey gang," he shouted. "Look up."

Susannah raised her eyes. She could see an island in the distance. It was shaped like the tail of a dragon, low and close to the water on one end, slowly rising to a thick, solid mass on the other end. She saw sand dunes along the low shore, backed by the sharp silhouettes of cedars and firs, and huge, clay-colored cliffs at the other end, with bright patches of orange lichen, and thick moss covering the rocks below. At the top of the cliff, at the end of the island, she could just make out a shape perched there—not a tree, or a cabin, but something else. It almost looked like a boat, although obviously no one would perch a boat on top of a cliff. But before she could figure it out, Jim's voice broke in.

"Thar she blows," he said. "Welcome to Sounder."

Chapter 4

Susannah 2011

Betty Pavalak's skin looked like a piece of paper that had been crumpled and then carefully unfolded and stretched over a frame, so the surface was smooth while all the lines remained. She was tall and slim, with high cheekbones, warm brown eyes, and a shock of wiry gray hair shaped in no particular style. Her wide smile revealed surprisingly even white teeth for a woman who had to be well into her seventies. The man's plaid flannel shirt she wore hung loosely over her jeans, which were tucked into sturdy bottle green rubber boots.

"Hey," Betty said, catching the rope Jim tossed to her to help pull the boat alongside the dock. Her voice was low, gravelly. "You made it." She slipped the rope through and over one of the cleats on the dock, and then held the side of the boat steady as Susannah stepped off.

Susannah held out her hand to Betty. "It's so nice to have a face to put with your voice. Thanks for all you've done for us, in making these arrangements."

"It was nothing," Betty said, shaking her head. "We're happy to have you here, believe me. And if you don't believe me, my grandsons, who are up there at the Laundromat collecting the mail, will convince you soon enough." She eyed Quinn and Katie, who had clambered onto the dock and were standing next to each other, looking around. Susannah noticed that Quinn stood a little closer to Katie than he usually did, and that Katie wasn't pushing him away.

Betty straightened up, dug into her pocket for a cigarette, shook one out of the box, and lit it with a match, also from her pocket. She blew out a long stream of smoke with a satisfied sigh.

"You will have dinner with us tonight, won't you?" She turned to Susannah. "I figured you'd be tired, and you won't have much food in the house, unless you bought something in Friday Harbor."

Susannah put a hand to her forehead. "Oh, my God. I didn't even *think* about food. How stupid can I be? I'll have to go back to Friday Harbor tomorrow. So, yes, thanks, we'd love to have dinner with you. That's very thoughtful."

"Good," Betty said.

Susannah turned to help Jim unload, feeling both disoriented and strangely at home. They stood on a floating metal dock, with a ramp leading up to a long wooden pier that jutted out over the water in a sheltered bay. A small flotilla of motorboats, dinghies, rowboats, and sailboats bobbed around them, tethered to buoys in the bay. Many of the boats were painted bright colors—yellow, crimson, royal blue—in stark contrast to the blue black water, the muted greens and golds of the trees and shrubs, and the pale white driftwood logs clustered along the shoreline. A faded red pickup truck was parked on a gravel road at the end of the dock. Just up the road sat a log cabin with a green tin roof, a wide porch, and two big windows facing the bay.

"That's the one business on Sounder," Jim said, seeing Susannah look up toward the cabin. "The Arctic Laundromat, which also serves as our post office. My wife, Fiona, ran it for a while; now Frances Calvert, one of the other islanders, oversees it. It's the heart of the island. Parties, community meetings, dances, baptisms, weddings, funerals—they all happen at the Laundromat."

"Why the 'Arctic' Laundromat?" she asked.

"I'm a poetry fan. There's a poem I love called 'Anna, washing' about the first woman to open a laundry in Alaska. Her place was called the Arctic Laundry."

Susannah wasn't sure what she had expected of Sounder's residents, but she hadn't anticipated a poetry-loving farmer/teacher and his Lauren Bacall–like mother.

"The Arctic Laundromat," Susannah said. "Those are funny words to say in the same breath. I never pictured *laundry* as a priority in the Arctic. In the tropics, maybe, where everyone sweats so much. A Tropic Laundromat would make much more sense."

"True, that," Quinn said, one of the slang phrases he'd picked up that drove Katie crazy because it had been cool two years ago and Quinn was just using it now. Susannah glanced at Katie, who, indeed, had stepped away from Quinn and looked like she wanted to push the whole lot of them off the dock. Susannah could feel the anger and impatience emanate from Katie like shimmery waves of heat from a hot sidewalk.

Betty leaned toward Quinn. "You know how to fish?" she said.

"A little," Quinn said. "But I always let them go."

"Ah, don't be a sissy," came a voice from the other side of the dock. "If you don't kill 'em, something else will."

They turned to see an old man floating in a bright kelly green wooden dinghy just yards away. He was lean and muscular with weather-beaten skin, bushy gray eyebrows, and eyes of a bright, piercing blue. He had a red bandanna tied Gypsy style over his head. A black Labrador stood in the boat behind him, nose pointed toward the shore.

"Hey, Barefoot," Jim said. He lifted a suitcase from the back of the boat and handed it over the side to Susannah. "Meet the Delaneys. Susannah and her kids are going to be renting our cottage until June. They're here from the East Coast. This is Barefoot Jacobsen, a longtime islander."

"Hello," Susannah said.

Barefoot snorted. "Let me guess. You're here because you want to get back to a simpler life, grow your own food, work the land—another version of all the goddamned New Yorkers who overran Vermont. Only now Vermont's too crowded, so you've come to the San Juans. Do us a favor: if you like it here, *don't* tell your friends."

Susannah saw Quinn bite his lower lip and reach a hand up to twirl his hair with one finger, something he always did when he was nervous.

"For God's sake, Barefoot, you could be a little more welcoming," Betty said. She turned to Quinn. "Don't mind him. Every island needs its resident grouchy hermit." She ground out her cigarette in a bucket on the dock and pocketed the stub. "The Delaneys are coming to dinner tonight. Why don't you come, too? You can tell them about early days on the island and get to know them so you don't have to be so rude next time you see them."

"I'm not rude; I'm honest," Barefoot said. His tone changed, from one of irritation to something softer. "But I appreciate the invitation and I'd like to come, Elizabeth. I'll bring the wine."

The dog started to bark as a gull swooped down and lit on the piling at the end of the dock. He barked and barked.

"Toby!" Barefoot said. "Quiet!" The dog stopped barking and sat down, looking expectantly at Barefoot. "You'd think he'd never seen a gull before," Barefoot said, shaking his head.

"Dog lives on a damn island and sees a hundred seagulls a day. It's the breed. He's a hunter."

"Actually, Labrador retrievers used to be fishing dogs," Quinn said. "The fishermen in Newfoundland used them to help pull in nets and catch the fish that escaped."

Barefoot stared hard at Quinn. "Is that so?" he said. He shifted his body on the seat of the dinghy and looked at Toby as though he'd never seen him before. "This is my fifth black Lab—fifth one named Toby, too—and I've never heard that."

He turned, raised a hand to his bandanna-covered forehead, and gave Quinn a small salute. "We'll discuss it further tonight," he said. He nodded at Susannah and Katie, and then pulled at the oars and turned the dinghy out toward the bay.

"He's a brilliant and interesting guy," Jim said. "Don't let him intimidate you." He leaned closer to Susannah. "But I'm warning you about his wine—it's homemade and sweeter than maple syrup. If you're lucky, he'll bring apricot wine and you can manage a few sips. If you're unlucky—" He shook his head. "*Brussels sprouts wine.* Seriously."

Two gangly teenage boys came running down the path from the Laundromat to the dock, their strides wide and long, their feet pounding on the wooden boards.

"Hah, beat you!" the first one said to the other.

"Who cares?" the second one said with a wide grin.

"We've been waiting for the new kids," said the first one. He was shorter than his brother, with curly reddish brown hair, warm brown eyes, and a broad, open smile like his father and grandmother.

"Thank God!" his brother said. "This is the most exciting thing that's happened here since the washing machine exploded at the Laundromat."

"If an exploding washing machine is exciting, then this place is even more pathetic than I thought," Katie said. She had come up behind Susannah, and was peering over her shoulder at the two boys.

"You got *that* right!" said the taller brother, amused. His thick, straight blond hair fell below his ears and almost covered his eyes. Susannah could see the glint of green irises beneath his bangs, and the faint traces of blond stubble along the lines of his jaw. "I'm Hood, this is Baker. We're about to be your entire social life."

"Not that you should feel stressed about that or anything," added Baker.

"She may decide the orcas are more scintillating conversationalists," Jim said. "Don't scare our new residents off before they've even set foot inside their house."

"Come on, we'll show you our house and the school," Baker said.

"Okay," Quinn said. He was staring at the two boys in utter fascination, as though they were magical creatures arisen from the ocean mist.

Jim lifted the last piece of luggage onto the dock and then turned to face Susannah. "You have to forgive my boys if they're a little excited," he said. "Your brood is going to increase our student population by fifteen percent."

"There are only thirteen kids in the whole school?" Katie asked in disbelief. "You mean by fifteen percent per grade, right?"

"Ah, beautiful *and* good at math," Jim said, turning to her. "You had it right the first time. We have thirteen students in grades kindergarten through eight."

Katie picked up her backpack. "Oh, my God," she said. "This is *so* fu—"

"Kate!" Susannah's voice was a warning.

"Teenagers," Betty said. "Raised one of 'em, now have a couple twerps for grandchildren. I'd be just as happy to skip from twelve to eighteen. That's when they become human again."

"Very funny," Katie and Hood said in unison. They looked at each other in surprise, and then Katie grinned—a big, genuine smile that transformed her whole face from sullen teenager into beautiful child-woman.

Susannah suddenly remembered the first time Matt had kissed her, when they were both fourteen and working as junior counselors at camp. He'd taken a big wad of gum out of his mouth, dropped it on the sand, and then turned to her, his lips firm and insistent against hers, followed by the surprising and exciting feel of his tongue in her mouth, the sugary, sharp taste of peppermint. Her body flooded with the memory—the feel of his lips, the shocking sensation that had electrified her whole being as he had continued to kiss her, run his hands down to her waist, pull her close to him until they were pressed against each other so tightly she couldn't tell where the frantic thumping in her chest ended and his began.

She looked at Katie. She was very pretty, without seeming to know it, or to care. The ponytail she favored for convenience only emphasized the lovely contours of her face—the wide-set eyes, the high cheekbones, the strong arc of her brows. Her jeans outlined the long, lean shape of her legs. Of course Zach had targeted her; of course boys would be attracted to her no matter where they were. A beautiful disaster.

"Mom?" Quinn said. "Can we go see everything with Hood and Baker?"

"Not so fast," Jim said. "Believe me, you'll have plenty of time to explore. Let's get your stuff loaded into the truck and get you moved in. Then you can take off."

Jim untied the boat from the dock and motored slowly to a buoy about fifty yards away where he secured the boat. Hood invited Quinn to row out in a dinghy to pick Jim up, and Susannah watched Hood demonstrate how to use the oars, how to pick a point on shore as a guide for rowing straight. Quinn looked very small in the dinghy, the muscles of his thin back straining as he pulled at the oars. He *was* small, compared to the vastness of the waters around him. Susannah shivered.

Within minutes they were back and loaded up, and Susannah found herself in the front seat of the pickup, wedged between Jim and Betty. "Our place is on the southwest shore," Jim said, as he accelerated up the rutted dirt road that led from the dock to the Laundromat. As they drew level with the Laundromat, Susannah could see a golden meadow behind the little building, then the woods beyond. Ahead, the road stretched away under a cathedral arch of trees. Bright yellow and rust-colored leaves littered the sides of the road, danced from the branches of the oak trees, and lay scattered along the tops of the ferns and huckleberry. They passed two or three small houses, with gardens of varying sizes, from small vegetable and flower beds to entire fields. In one field, the rusting hulks of two abandoned cars rose above the grasses like an outdoor sculpture.

Betty caught Susannah looking at the cars.

"Costs a fortune to haul a car off the island once it dies," she said. "I know some people think they're eyesores, but we scavenge them for parts."

"Does everyone farm?" Susannah asked.

"Not everyone," Jim said. "Many people grow food for their own families. We grow vegetables to sell at the San Juan farmer's market once a week, and we raise chickens and alpacas. And we've just started experimenting with small grains, for bread."

"And you fit this in after teaching?" Susannah said.

Jim laughed. "Right. No. When I took the teaching job, our neighbors, Joel and Bob Baltimore, helped us out with the spring planting. I took over again in mid-June, when school ended. We shared the produce and the profits last summer. Joel and Bob have a small farm, too. Worked out well because they took in more money than usual, and it gave me time to teach and Fiona time to work on her business."

"Fiona has a business?"

Susannah saw Betty draw her lips together in a thin line, but she said nothing.

"Yeah," Jim said. "She started an import business last year, importing yoga gear from India and selling it to studios and customers, mostly in Vancouver and Seattle. She's in India now for a few months."

Yoga. Susannah had tried several yoga classes and it had driven her crazy. Lying there in corpse pose thinking about her breathing almost gave her a panic attack.

They turned onto the driveway, and Hood hopped out to open the gates as they passed through. They drove by two tall windmills, silver blades spinning in the breeze. At last they pulled up in front of a one-story white clapboard cottage, with a black roof and a peaked gable over the front door. To the left of the cottage, a few hardy chrysanthemums, dahlias, and marigolds bloomed behind a chicken-wire fence. A grove of gnarled apple trees and a faded red barn with a sagging roof stood just beyond the garden. On the other side of the barn Susannah could see fields, some fallow, some bursting with winter squash, and beyond that the forest, stretching narrow trunks to the sky. The air had the rich, loamy scent of decaying things and new life all at once.

"My house is right there, over that rise." Jim pointed to a hill just beyond the farm, further inland. "And Mom's place is there, by the water." Susannah saw a small, shingled gray house overlooking the bay.

"It's an estate," Susannah said.

Jim grinned. "Oh, yeah," he said. "Bill Gates, Paul Allen, the Pavalaks—we all have our spreads in the San Juans." He turned to Quinn. "Your house was built in the twenties. Rumor has it the original family ran a bootlegging operation here."

"Bootleggers!" Quinn said.

Jim smiled. "We lived here for years. Then I built our new place three years ago. We wanted something simpler."

Susannah stared at the cottage, which would be considered an instant "tear-down" in Tilton.

"Our new place is six hundred square feet," Jim said. "It's got a solar-powered water pump for the well, wood-burning stove for heat, a combination of solar panels, batteries, and a generator for electricity. Small, efficient, cozy, cheap—we love it."

Susannah looked at him. She couldn't imagine a family of four living in six hundred square feet.

"'Growth for the sake of growth is the ideology of the cancer cell,'" Jim said, as if reading her mind.

"What?"

"Edward Abbey. I'm a fan."

Susannah tried to take it all in. *If he tells me they compost their own waste*, she thought, *I'm leaving.*

She walked to the back of the truck to help unload and caught sight of the bay through the trees, a few hundred yards beyond the house that would be hers for the next nine months. A large madrona tree grew on a bluff above the water, its red bark peeling back in curls from the smooth white trunk beneath. Wooden steps led down to a dock. The late afternoon sun had broken through the clouds and cast a path of brilliant scattered light across the water. She looked up and saw a hawk gliding in effortless circles above the trees at the edge of the bay.

She felt a nudge against her shoulder and looked down to see Quinn.

"This is cool, Mom," he said. "Where are the chickens?"

She put an arm around him, gazing at his sweet, freckled

face. "I don't know," Susannah said. "Maybe behind the house. You go look for them after we unpack."

She walked around the side of the truck, where Katie leaned against the cab, kicking at rocks while Hood and Baker peppered her with questions. "Why did you come here? What was your school like? Do you have an iPhone? Did you see *X-Men*?"

"How do you know about *X-Men*?" Katie asked.

"Duh! We can read," Baker said. "We have the Internet; we get newspapers every week. Did you think this was like *Lost* or something?"

"I don't know," Katie said. "This was my mom's idea."

"'Duh to that, too," Hood said. "Kind of obvious."

"Come on," Susannah said, nodding toward the bags Jim had unloaded from the truck onto the grass. "Let's get this stuff into the house."

Hood and Baker each picked up a bag and headed into the cottage, following their dad. Quinn was already inside. Katie hung back, just outside the front door.

"I still can't believe you brought me here," Katie said, as Susannah reached for a suitcase. "There are only two kids my age, *two*." She paused for emphasis. "I can't even text anyone at home because my phone hardly works. This is totally unfair. You're trying to control everything, even more than you did at home."

"What I'm trying to control, Kate," Susannah said, "is your tendency to do reckless, dangerous things. I'm trying to keep you alive until you have the judgment to make better choices."

"You're trying to make sure I make *your* choices," Katie said. "But I'm not you."

Susannah looked at her daughter, tall and angular where Susannah was short and curvy, outspoken where Susannah was reticent, impulsive where Susannah was cautious.

"Oh, honey," she said, "I know you're not me. And I don't want you to be."

"Yes, you do," Katie said.

Susannah couldn't help but feel a sense of shame when she thought of herself at Katie's age, of what she'd done that year.

"No," Susannah said, her voice firm. "I don't."

Chapter 5

Betty 2011/1950

Betty leaned against the truck, watching the Delaneys unload their gear and her grandsons trot around Katie like prize stallions at a show. She could see right away that Katie and Hood were attracted to each other; my God, you could practically smell the pheromones in the air. She could also see that Susannah was very protective of Quinn, who was an interesting kid but nervous as all get-out, and even more protective of Katie, who wasn't about to let anyone protect her from anything. She wondered what had happened back home that had led Susannah to make the move to Sounder.

The screen door of the cottage slammed, and Jim came out and leaned against the truck next to her.

"She's an attractive girl," Betty said.

"Who?"

"Katie," Betty said. "Who do you think I meant?"

"Well, Susannah's attractive, too."

Betty rolled her eyes. "You're as bad as your sons. Worse. You're married. And so is she."

"I know. All I said was she's attractive." He shook his head. "She has her hands full with Katie, that's for sure."

Betty fumbled for the zipper on her parka and zipped it up against the evening's chill. "I guess that's why she's here."

"Think she'll like it?" Jim said.

Betty turned her head to look at him. "I think she's scared."

"What, of living here?"

"A little. Of her daughter. Of something back home. Of I don't know what. Doesn't she strike you as nervous?"

Jim put both hands in the pockets of his fleece and looked at the sky.

"A little. She's interesting, though. She seems kind of high-strung, but she's tough, and has a good sense of humor. She's got a great smile. I think she'll stick it out."

Betty eyed her son. His boys were not the only males on this island who could use a little female companionship. And this Susannah, in spite of the anxiety that radiated from her, was a pretty woman, with a wide, ready smile that lit up her whole face, thick brown hair, and a curvy figure you couldn't help but notice. She was sensitive, too, one of those people who seemed to intuit the moods and yearnings of everyone around her before anyone said a word. Betty recognized it right away. Jim was that way, too. It made a person very compassionate, but it was a hard way to walk through the world.

That's why Jim had married Fiona, Betty thought, because Fiona was not a worrier and not exquisitely tuned in to the feelings of others and not raw like that, like him. She remembered when he'd first read *The Lion, the Witch, and the Wardrobe*, at age ten, and sobbed for hours when the ogre shaved Aslan's mane. The fact that Aslan had been mocked and tormented bothered him even more than the lion's death.

Betty liked Fiona, her daughter-in-law, who was hardworking and more than competent but, if truth be told, mighty hard to please. Fiona had spent seventeen years on Sounder, and in that time Jim had fixed up the cottage; renovated the Laundromat so Fiona could run it; built that little cabin they lived in now because Fiona wanted a new place that would be less work; and started raising alpacas because Fiona wanted to start her own crafts business with items she knit from the wool. But she'd tired of the Laundromat after a few years and turned the work over to Frances Calvert, the postmistress. Then she'd abandoned the knitting project a few months after she began, and two years later the alpacas still roamed the meadow, eating bales of good grass hay that could be going to the goats, who at least produced milk.

Now Fiona had started an import business, something to do with yoga and yoga mats and yoga clothes, which made no sense at all to Betty, given that Americans had been crazy for yoga for a good thirty years now, leaving Fiona and her yoga bags well behind the trend. Still, Fiona was convinced that the *quality* of her yoga mats and eye pillows was going to set her company apart and bring in some much-needed money as high school and college loomed for the boys.

Fiona's new business required frequent trips off-island, to Seattle and Vancouver, visiting yoga studios and gyms, and now this long trip to India. Betty knew there was tension between her son and his wife, but kept her mouth shut. She knew, too, the kind of longings that could hit women at midlife, as the children you'd nurtured for so long grew into their own people, leaving you with a strange kind of freedom and emptiness that was hard to fill. All the blather about men and their midlife crises—Betty shook her head. In her experience, *women* were the ones who found those middle years most unsettling, who were most likely to make dramatic changes. But then, what did she know? Sure, she'd done some wild things in her forties, but Bill had died two months after she turned thirty-five. Who wouldn't have gone a little crazy under such circumstances?

"Why do you think she left her husband behind?" Jim said.

Betty, her mind on the absent Fiona, was startled. "Who?"

"Susannah. I don't know; it's hard for me to imagine Fiona leaving and taking the kids for *nine months*. It's tough enough having her gone for *two* months, like now."

"Well, keep wondering. What goes on between two people in a marriage is impossible to fathom from the outside," Betty said.

Which she, of course, knew better than anyone else.

Her own marriage had been unorthodox, to say the least. She'd met Bill the year she turned eighteen and graduated from high school. She had never had a boyfriend before. She had lots of friends, boys and girls, because she was athletic and loved to laugh and was great at party tricks, like blowing smoke in perfect round O's whenever she wanted. But she was all legs and angles and frizzy hair. Her sister Bobbie was the beauty, with silky auburn hair and blue eyes and a succession of boyfriends who took her out to dinners in fancy restaurants and wrote her sappy poems. And her sister Mel's wide-set dark eyes and rich brunette hair gave her an exotic look that intrigued men in spite of her grumpiness. The boys who came through the house with Bobbie or Mel or Jimmy, her brother, loved to tease Betty about her wild hair, tell her jokes that were a little too racy, or take bets on how far she could throw a baseball. She was every guy's little sister.

But then one day Bobbie brought home Bill Pavalak, a former sergeant with the U.S. Army Air Corps, and a buddy of Bobbie's current beau, Dick Hudgens. Bill had dark brown hair and green eyes and the whitest teeth she'd ever seen, with a slight gap between the two front teeth that saved him from being comic-book handsome. He wore a leather bomber jacket and khakis and looked at her so intently when they were introduced that she felt a stirring deep in her belly and a sudden dampness between her legs.

Later, when she asked Bobbie about him, Bobbie said, "Oh, *Bill*. He married his high school sweetheart and they got divorced after the war. I don't know what happened, but he's sworn off women for life. So he's always hanging around with Dick."

"What does he do?" Betty said.

"He works for Boeing. But he hates it. He wants to go to Alaska and work on a fishing boat or something." Bobbie picked at her red nail polish. "I wish he'd go. I haven't had a moment alone with Dick in *weeks*."

"I'll go to a movie with him, if you want to do something alone with Dick," Betty said. The thought of Bill's green eyes made her bold.

"Really?" Bobbie looked up from her nails. "That would be *perfect*. You wouldn't have to worry it would be like a date or anything; like I said, he wants nothing to do with women."

"Of course it's not a date," Betty said, her face warm. She dropped her head so her hair hid her face.

A week later, Betty and Bill went to the movies to see *All About Eve*. Afterward, they ate seafood salad and shish kebab at the Northern Lights on Third Avenue and Seneca. They talked about Betty's secretarial job at the lumber company, and then about the All-American Girls Professional Baseball League. Betty had dreamed for years about playing first base for the Kenosha Comets, but now the league had been sold and the teams were starting to dissolve. They talked about crab fishing

in Alaska in the frigid waters of the Bering Strait, the dangerous machinery, the number of men who died on the job each
season—almost one per week.

"Yeah, but at least they don't die sitting at a desk pushing
papers," Bill said.

Betty quoted a line from the movie they'd just seen: "'You
have a point,'" she said. "'An idiotic one, but a point.'"

Bill's eyes widened, first in surprise, then in recognition, and
his face split into a grin and he leaned back in his chair and
laughed and laughed.

"You're a clever little thing," he said.

Betty felt that same warmth deep inside, and a flush of plea-
sure at being called "a clever little thing." She'd been told often
that she was clever, but no one before Bill had ever called her "a
little thing," let alone said something like that in such a warm,
possessive voice. Later that night he kissed her, pressing her back
against the smooth wood of the railing on the front porch of
her mother's rambling old Queen Anne house, his hands resting
gently on her hips. His touch was so electrifying that she forgot
to worry whether or not Mel or Bobbie or one of the boarders
might still be awake, peering through the window, or whether
Grammy might be wandering the house with a rolling pin, as
she often did at night, making sure no intruders threatened, or
whether Smelly the dog would erupt into a frenzy of barking and
start leaping against the windows. Betty kissed him back.

Bill took her out almost every night after that, sometimes
just for walks or a ferry ride, other times to dinner or a show.
He bought her feminine little things as gifts, the kinds of things
she, a confirmed tomboy, had never owned before: a beret in
powder blue to match her eyes, a pair of lace gloves, a rhine-
stone brooch. He listened to her stories and jokes, his eyes never leaving her face. She was smitten.

Bobbie was disgusted. "He's *divorced*, Bets," she said. "He wants to be a *fisherman*. Go dancing with him, but for God's sake don't fall in love with him."

Betty never asked about his first wife. It was his business, she figured, and what's past is past. Then, one June night they were at a Seattle Rainiers game, and Betty was keeping score in the program, marking called strikeouts and wild pitches and an unassisted putout in the third inning. Bill looked over her shoulder at the scorecard.

"You are a hell of a woman," he said. "You know what an unassisted putout is?"

"Sure," Betty said. "My dad was a baseball fan, and after he died I kept listening to games on the radio and going to games with Jimmy. It's something I share with my dad, even though he's gone."

Bill shook his head. "A hell of a woman," he repeated. "You're about as different from Jacqueline as you could be."

Betty was still, her pencil poised over her scorecard. *Jacqueline*. He pronounced it the French way, zhak-LEEN. Betty immediately thought of someone petite and delicate, with dark curly hair and dark eyes and flawless porcelain skin. *Jacqueline*.

Bill put one hand over Betty's, to still her pencil, and the other under her chin, turning her face toward him. "You've never asked about her," he said. "I want to tell you."

"Okay."

"We were high school sweethearts," he said. "I enlisted in the army the day I graduated in 1944 and got my orders two days later to ship out to Killeen, Texas, for training. I was eighteen and I'd never even been on a plane before. I was scared. The day before I left I asked Jacqueline to marry me. I wanted—" He stopped. "I wanted some connection to home that seemed permanent."

Betty heard the sharp crack of a bat making contact with the ball, and the crowd roared around her.

"She was very dependent on me," he said. "Even in high school. She wouldn't go to a movie in case I might call and want to do something. She read all the books I liked. It was flattering—for a while. My mother adored her.

"My unit was shipped over to Belgium the day after Christmas in 1944." He nodded in response to the question on Betty's face. "Yup. Battle of the Bulge. I don't want to talk about that." He paused. "Then the war ended and I came home and there was Jacqueline, wearing my ring, all excited and proud. I didn't want to marry her; I was a different man. But I couldn't exit gracefully."

He shook his head. "So a year later I exited with no grace at all, and had an affair, and broke Jacqueline's heart and my mother's, and moved up here to escape my shame. Now you know."

He cupped Betty's face in his hands. "But you're entirely different," he said. "You're opinionated and strong and your own person. I'm crazy about you, Betty."

Her heart careened inside her chest. The crowd roared again.

"I missed two plays," Betty said.

Bill grinned at her, picked up her scorecard, tore it into pieces, and then threw the pieces up in the air like confetti. The bits of paper floated down over them as he leaned forward to kiss her, his lips warm and forceful against hers.

Six months later they were married in city hall, and she found out she was pregnant a month after that. She was nineteen years old, and green-eyed Bill Pavalak loved her, and she was carrying his baby, and, for the first time in her life, the restless yearning that had always driven her was stilled, and she was happy.

Chapter 6

Susannah 2011

Susannah stood in the middle of her new home and tried not to panic. The cottage itself was lovely, with beamed ceilings and white beadboard walls and French doors at one end of the living room that looked out onto a fading garden. The furniture was clean and comfortable, and the place was filled with homey details—bright braided rugs on the floors, handmade quilts on the beds, even a blue earthenware pitcher filled with late dahlias from the garden on the round dining table in the main room. The kitchen, at one end of the big L-shaped living area, held the biggest stove Susannah had ever seen—black cast iron, with brass handles on the many doors and drawers. Susannah could feel its warmth emanate from across the room. But Katie had just pointed out that no matter how impressive the stove might be, the kitchen lacked a refrigerator—*no refrigerator?*—and with each passing moment Susannah was growing more nervous about what she had gotten herself into.

Susannah took a deep breath. "You always tell me your life is totally boring and we never do anything," she said to Katie, as though the lack of a refrigerator were something not at all unusual. "So here we are; we're doing something."

"Yeah, we're doing something even more boring and stupid than our real life," Katie said.

Susannah sighed. "Did you see the bedroom?"

On the other side of the living area, three steps led down into a utility room, with shelves that held everything from canned food to candles. At the back of the utility room was a small bathroom, with a sink, toilet, and stall shower. A bedroom to the right of the steps held twin beds and two dressers. Someone long ago had covered the bedroom walls and the sloping ceiling with wallpaper, with faded yellow roses blooming against a white background. The other bedroom was off the kitchen, and held a double bed in an old-fashioned wooden spool frame.

"You have two choices about bedrooms," Susannah said. "You can share the room with twin beds with Quinn, or we can move one of the mattresses from there into the utility room, so you can have separate rooms. I talked to Betty and she said that's what Hood and Baker used to do."

Katie's eyebrows rose. "Are you kidding?"

"It's not a big deal."

"Oh, please."

"This is it, sweetheart. Two bedrooms. We have to do the best we can."

"Why don't you and Quinn share the twin bedroom?" Katie said. "I'll take the one by the kitchen."

"Because you're the kid," Susannah said, "and I'm the one paying the rent."

Tears of frustration welled up in Katie's eyes.

"Come on, Kate," Susannah said, her voice softening. *This is my beloved child, mine own.* "This is going to be good for us. Give it a chance."

She thought of all those early years when Katie had been so

attached to her that she would scream whenever Susannah left, crying in gulping sobs for hours. It continued into preschool and even kindergarten. That image of Katie was forever burned into Susannah's mind—the skinny, chestnut-haired girl held tightly in a teacher's embrace, reaching out with both arms toward Susannah, howling with loss. She had outgrown it, but slowly. In some ways Susannah had liked knowing that the fierce love she had for Katie was returned equally. They were a part of each other. While she loved both her children with all her heart, Katie was her first, the one who had revealed to Susannah the almost frightening intensity of her own maternal passion. It was hard not to take Katie's rejection now personally—to see it instead for what it was, the natural growth of a young thing yearning to find its own light.

At that moment Hood and Baker appeared outside the French doors in the living room. Hood pressed his forehead against the glass, furrowed his brows into a deep V, and gave Katie a mock stern glance, beckoning her with one finger. She looked at him and smiled, and then ran over and opened the door to join the boys outside.

Two weeks, Susannah thought, watching as Hood leaned over and whispered something in Katie's ear. *I bet those two are exploring each other in two weeks.* She suddenly saw that all the things that had drawn her to Sounder—unstructured time, freedom from the constant routine of checking in, close relationships with a small circle of people—were fertile ground for an intense teenage love affair. Which wasn't the worst thing that could happen, but for Katie—angry and wounded and mixed-up as she was right now—it wasn't the best thing, either.

Jim walked in, a cardboard box in his arms. "This is the last of it," he said.

"That's not mine," Susannah said.

"Yes it is." He put the box down on the table and took out

a bag of coffee beans, a loaf of bread, a jar of peanut butter, a stick of butter, a carton of orange juice, a bag of sugar, and a Tupperware container holding half a dozen eggs.

"Breakfast," he said.

Susannah shook her head and smiled at her own folly. "Thank you," she said. "I'm usually much more organized."

Betty, who had followed him in the door, said, "You'll get used to planning ahead. Can't run out for a quart of milk at the last minute anymore." She sat down on the arm of the sofa and unzipped her parka. "Warm enough in here for you? Jim lit the stove before he left for Friday Harbor."

"Yes," Susannah said. "It's lovely."

The worn pine boards squeaked beneath Jim's feet as he walked into the kitchen. She looked at him and thought of Matt, thought of moving into the first place she'd shared with Matt. *It should be Matt standing there. Matt should be here.*

She and Matt had moved into an apartment in Chicago two weeks after they were married. The apartment filled the top floor of an old Victorian house, which meant they had to walk up two long, steep flights of stairs to get to their door. The ceilings sloped down to meet pale yellow walls, and four dormered windows let in light all day long. They slept on a foldout couch in the middle of the main living area. A bathroom with a big claw-foot tub and a large walk-in closet with a leaded window completed the space.

Matt had grown up poor in an affluent suburb west of Chicago, in a town of cobbled streets and grand mansions and towering elms, with dappled sunlight on green, green lawns. His family of five—Matt, his parents, and his two brothers—had lived in a two-bedroom apartment in the basement of the upscale building where his father worked as the apartment manager and his mother worked as a housecleaner. His parents had wanted the best schools for their boys, not understanding what it might mean to be the poorest kid in a rich neighborhood.

He'd attended college on scholarship, sharing a dorm room with two guys. After college, he'd lived in an apartment with five friends, the six of them sharing two bedrooms and two baths. Matt had never, Susannah realized, had his own private space. So she decided to create one for him.

While he worked late nights at the library on his dissertation, she emptied out the walk-in closet and painted it a warm, deep orange. She scoured flea markets and pawnshops and antique stores and found a leather armchair and ottoman and an old Oriental rug in turquoise and orange and brown—all the perfect size. She mended the tears in the leather and sewed throw pillows and painted the scratched base of an old standing lamp and bought a new shade for it. Finally, she did a painting of the lake in the woods in northern Michigan where they had met and framed it and hung it on the wall.

She had told him she had his Christmas present hidden in the closest to keep him away. On Christmas Eve, she had opened the door with a flourish and turned to him. "Ta da! Your private study, my lord. I promise not to tidy it or nag you about keeping it clean or enter without knocking. You can hang paintings of dogs playing poker on the walls if it makes you happy. Or naked women." She frowned. "Okay, on second thought, maybe not naked women. But I wanted you to have your own private space, for once." She looked at him eagerly.

He had been speechless for a few minutes. He stepped inside and ran his hand over the leather arm of the chair, studied the painting she'd done on the wall, turned on the lamp. "I don't know what to say. I mean, I love it. I can't believe you did this."

Her thanks came over the next few months, as Matt piled

books on the floor in his "study," spent hours in the armchair reading, often with the door open so he could talk to her as she cooked dinner, and tacked photos and articles and postcards to the walls. He loved it. He was happy. *They* were happy.

"So, a few things you'll need to know," Jim said, interrupting her reverie. "First, maybe you noticed there's no refrigerator."

Of course Susannah *hadn't* noticed, until Katie pointed it out, but then she'd also forgotten to stock up on food, which meant she clearly was not made of the same stuff as Ernest Shackleton or even Laura Ingalls Wilder.

"The electricity here runs on a renewable energy system. The energy comes from wind generators and solar panels. It's enough for running lights inside the house, plus a computer and one or two small appliances." Jim smiled. "And to us, *small appliances* means appliances with a purpose—power drills or electric goat shears, not hair dryers."

"So you're telling me I need to learn to style my hair with electric goat shears."

Jim laughed. "That's not as crazy as you might think. Fiona whips up homemade mayonnaise with the power drill. Works pretty well."

Susannah hoped her expression didn't convey her sudden, gut-wrenching fear. She had no idea how to make mayonnaise from scratch, let alone operate a power drill.

"But, as I was saying, refrigerators suck way too much energy, so there's a cold cellar out back." Jim walked across the kitchen and opened the back door, a wood frame door with a six-paned window across the top to let in the light. Susannah followed him out onto a small covered porch. Faded gray paint covered the railing and floor, and two wooden rockers faced the view of the bay through the trees.

Jim pointed to a pair of wooden storm cellar doors with black hinges, set into the ground at the back of the house. "There's a small cold cellar down there. It'll keep most things pretty cool. And over there"—Jim pointed to a grove of small trees and brush about ten yards behind the house—"that's where you throw kitchen waste. We feed the chickens from the scraps. See that little peach tree? Sprouted from a pit Baker threw out there a couple summers ago."

"I see."

"You *really* have to reuse and recycle here. It may be a slogan for the rest of the world, but it's reality for us. The only way to get garbage off the island is to haul it to the dock, take it out by boat, and pay good money to dump it someplace else."

He walked her back inside and showed her the box in the utility room that controlled and distributed the energy from the solar panels and wind generators, and explained the solar water heating system ("no long showers"). Susannah's head began to ache, and she felt a tiny, ice-cold kernel of terror in the pit of her stomach.

"We use a lot of twelve-volt LED clusters," Jim was saying as they walked back into the living room, "but we find them too dull for lighting a whole room, so we use eight-watt 2D units, which give a nice light with a good color, and small eight-watt strip lights above work areas, like the kitchen counter."

"Oh for Christ's sake, Jim, don't talk her to death," Betty said. "You're scaring the hell out of her, can't you see? She just wants to know how to turn the lights on and off. She doesn't need your whole Al Gore lecture."

Susannah smiled. "Of course, the most important things to the kids are the computer and the cell phone."

"The electricity you have here is enough to charge your cell phones and your computer." Jim raised his thick brows and looked at her over the frames of his glasses. "I'm assuming you have a laptop computer? Most laptops use just fifteen to forty-five watts, versus up to two hundred and fifty for a desktop computer."

Betty rolled her eyes. "Just tell her where to plug the damn thing in."

"I'm getting to that." Jim pointed at the electrical outlets along the baseboard in the living area. "You can plug it in to any outlet. We have a router and Wi-Fi connection at our place. The Wi-Fi works here, so you should be able to access the Internet very easily. I will warn you, our connection for the Internet and cell phones depends on the reception we get from a satellite dish we put up in a Doug fir by our cabin. Sometimes if it's raining hard, or blowing, we don't get reception."

He grinned. "And you can't call the cable guy if it doesn't work. Just have to wait it out."

Susannah's cell phone rang, as if on cue. The noise seemed loud and out of place, and she jumped, startled.

"We'll get out of your way now," Betty said. She stood up. "Dinner's at seven thirty. But you come on down whenever you feel like it."

"*Thank you*," Susannah said, in as heartfelt a voice as she could muster.

She flipped open her phone as the screen door slammed behind them.

"Susannah?"

Susannah's heart clenched. Sweet Jesus, she'd been on this island all of sixty minutes and her mother was already checking in. Just the sound of her mother's voice stirred an undercurrent of anger and irritation in Susannah, something dark and viscous. It had begun shortly after Katie was born, when Susannah had looked at the tiny infant in her arms and been filled with a sudden rage. She could not imagine a mother, any mother, failing to protect her children, as her own mother had. From that moment, Susannah had sworn to herself: *Not on my watch. Never.*

"Mom?"

"Hi. Do you have a minute?"

Susannah took a deep breath. "I'm kind of busy right now. Can I call you back?"

"Of course. What are you doing?"

"Well, we literally just got here, to our house. We haven't even unpacked yet."

"Is it habitable?"

"Of course it's habitable. It's a house, with four walls and a roof and a bathroom and everything you'd expect."

"I wasn't sure *what* to expect."

"It's nice. It's definitely *different* from what we're used to, but it's nice."

"I just wanted to suggest one thing about Quinn."

Quinn was her mother's clear favorite, and he in turn adored "Dida," the name that had stuck after his first, baby attempts to pronounce "Lila," Susannah's mother's name. With Quinn's birth eleven years ago, the hard, protective shell Lila had worn for so many years had cracked, and she'd allowed herself to fall in love with this fair-haired, blue-eyed baby. Little Katie, with her dark hair and dark eyes and stubborn moods, had been too reminiscent of Janie, Susannah's little sister—even Susannah could see that. But Quinn was Lila's second chance. They talked on the phone every week, and took trips together once a year—to Cooperstown, to the Key West Turtle Museum, to the Grand Canyon.

"What about Quinn?"

"He sent me a picture last week that showed him with long hair. I know he was getting teased at school, and that hair can't help. You should cut it so he doesn't get teased at his new school."

"Quinn likes it long, Mom."

"Yes, but it looks terrible." Lila paused. "Can't Matt talk to him? Matt has—"

"Mom? Quinn loves Jered Weaver, and Jered Weaver has long hair. It's *his* hair. And I *really* can't talk right now, I'm sorry."

Lila sighed. "You're *always* too busy to talk. I hope this move changes *that*, at least. You run around from one thing to another like a chicken with its feet cut off."

"*Head*," Susannah said. "A chicken with its head cut off. A chicken with its feet cut off couldn't run."

"You know what I mean."

"Mom—"

"All right. But Quinn—"

"*Mom.* I've got to go. I'll call you tomorrow." Susannah slipped the phone back into her pocket. Three thousand miles and thirty years, and she still couldn't escape.

And what was she trying to escape? A childhood that wasn't, really, remarkably worse than anyone else's, at least before Janie died. Her father yelled. Her mother made excuses and apologies. Yes, her father's rages—irrational, bitter, and well fueled by the vodka martinis he drank every evening—had terrified Susannah. She never wore shoes in the house, so her footsteps didn't annoy him. She buried herself in books, reading upstairs with a flashlight in her closet. At times she was still haunted by the painful self-consciousness of those years—her profound desire to fade into the background, to become a shadow, a branch, a pebble pressed into the soil. Something you'd never notice.

But she'd survived. She'd found Matt. *Matt would never yell at me*, she remembered thinking when she was eighteen or nineteen and the idea of marrying him had first crossed her mind. *My kids would grow up totally differently with Matt for a dad.*

And they had. Matt was a kind and involved dad. While

he didn't quite get why Katie was so difficult, he held her and rocked her through the sleepless nights of her first year, coached her soccer team, taught her to shoot layups, and sat at the dining room table, his graying head next to her glossy dark one, explaining her math problems. He didn't yell.

Yet still Susannah was uneasy. She looked around the room, at the space that would be home for the next nine months—a haven, or, if you were Katie, a jail. She was protecting her daughter from a threat she couldn't name, from all the unseen things that might harm her—or worse, make her feel she wasn't worth protecting.

Chapter 7

Betty 1952

Four months after the wedding, Betty miscarried. Not at all unusual, the doctor said, and nothing to worry about because she was young and healthy and had gotten pregnant so easily. Betty accepted the doctor's reassurances and tried to believe him. Someday we'll have a houseful of children, she told Bill, like the one she'd grown up in, a big old house filled with roller skates and baseballs and a piano and bicycles leaning against the front stoop. Bill had been tender with her about the miscarriage, worried about her health. But he didn't grieve the baby as she did. He wanted kids, of course he wanted kids—they'd talked about that before they got married. But she'd gotten pregnant awfully fast. Why, they hadn't even been *trying* for a baby.

A few months after the miscarriage she was curled against him in bed, her head on his chest, one arm thrown across his flat stomach. They'd made love twice already this afternoon. He stuffed another pillow behind him to prop up his head, and lit a cigarette. "Maybe now there's no baby coming and you're feeling better we could think again about Alaska," he said.

"Alaska?" Betty pulled herself away and sat up, turning to face him. "Alaska? I thought we decided that didn't make any sense."

"*You* decided," Bill said, taking a long drag. "I think it makes plenty of sense. Let's do it now, before we have kids. And if we like it, we'll have our kids there."

Betty felt cold suddenly, deep inside her body. Yes, they had talked about it. Crab fishing was too dangerous, even Bill admitted that, for a man who had a wife. But he'd found out he could get a civil service job on the Fort Richardson Army Base, near Anchorage, and homestead a 160-acre parcel nearby.

"Think of it," Bill had said. "One hundred and sixty acres all our own, for free."

"It's not free," Betty had said, her voice dry. "You have to farm it and live on it for five years before you own it. That's a lot of sweat and hard work. That's not 'free.'"

The debate had ended with the discovery of her pregnancy. Bill had agreed it would be too hard to move and homestead with a new baby. In Seattle he had a steady job with Boeing and she had her family nearby and they had their little apartment, just a ten-minute walk from her family's house on Queen Anne Hill. But Bill was restless.

Now, "Alaska's not even a state," Betty said.

"It will be someday," Bill said.

"And what am I going to do there?" Betty said. She'd given up her secretarial job at the lumber company when they got married, although, truth be told, she itched to work again. She took care of the house and shopped for groceries and cooked, but she didn't enjoy it the way some of her married friends did, or the way Bobbie did. Bobbie had married Dick Hudgens and had a sweet little house near the university, and was forever sewing things for the house or herself and throwing wonderful parties with themes like "An Evening in Hawaii." Betty couldn't operate a sewing machine to save her life, nor could she understand how anyone could think that tiki torches and leis and grilled pineapple on skewers would convince anyone they were in Hawaii and not standing in a soggy, cold, fog-soaked Seattle backyard.

"You can help with the homestead," Bill said. He gave her muscular thigh a playful slap. "You were made to be a farm wife."

"Maybe," Betty said, leaning over to take the cigarette from his mouth and take a drag on it herself. "But I don't want to be a farm wife." She drew in a deep breath. "I want to go back to work, Bill. I liked my job."

He raised both eyebrows. "Your secretary job? Working for the fat guy with the scotch bottle in his desk drawer?"

"Mr. Timmins is a smart man," Betty said. "And he always treated me fairly."

"Look, honey." Bill took the cigarette back and ground it out in the ashtray on the bedside table. "I make enough money. You don't have to work. I know you're disappointed about the baby, but maybe this means we should do something different. Maybe we should wait on the whole baby thing and explore our options."

"I don't want to go to Alaska."

"I told you before we got married that I didn't want to stay in Seattle."

"You also told me you loved me and you'd do anything to make me happy. So let's stay here. I can go back to work, even part-time."

"And how long are you thinking we'll stay here?" Bill said.

"I don't know," Betty said. "It depends. On your work, on kids, if we have them. On us and how happy we are here."

"I'm not happy pushing papers," Bill said.

Betty felt a stirring of unease then, something discordant.

Bill loved her because she was strong, independent. But Bill also wanted her to do what *he* wanted.

"Do you want to have a baby?" she said.

She wanted a baby. She'd had a big family and a happy childhood and wanted to recreate that with Bill.

"Sure," Bill said, but his eyes didn't meet hers. "But you're young—we're young. We can wait."

"And go to Alaska?"

"I don't know." He was exasperated now. "I just know I don't want to spend my life sitting in a windowless office at Boeing." He stood up, got dressed, and then went to the closet and found his bomber jacket.

"I'm meeting some of the guys for a drink," he said. "Don't wait up."

Betty was just as proud and stubborn as he was. "I won't," she said.

"Oh, pooh," Bobbie said. "You don't have to go to Alaska."

Betty and Bobbie were sitting on the back porch of their mother's house, with gin and tonics in hand and feet up on the railing. Betty had walked over after Bill left, where she found Bobbie in the kitchen, fending off Grammy.

"Your sister is ruining my pot roast," Grammy said, when Betty arrived. "She's pouring cups and cups of beef stock in. She's doing it all wrong."

Betty laughed. Long ago Grammy had misread her pot roast recipe and put in two and a half quarts of red wine and a cup of beef stock instead of the other way around. She'd made it exactly the same way ever since, insisting she was right even though the result was a cabernet-colored slab of tough meat that the kids fed to Smelly under the dining room table. Smelly got a little drunk after a pot roast dinner, and would lean against the door jamb in the kitchen and howl, which would lead Grammy to think Smelly was having one of her "attacks" and put her in the bathtub to calm her down.

"Smelly will love you for this," Betty told Bobbie.

"How's married life?" Bobbie said. She grabbed Grammy's yellow flowered apron from the hook on the back of the kitchen door and tied it around her waist.

"Dreamy," Betty said. "Isn't that the word now? Married life is dreamy."

"Married life is dreamy, huh?" Bobbie said. "That's why you're over here at eight P.M. on a Saturday night?"

"*You're* over here. Where's your husband?"

"It's Dick's regular poker night. I come here every Saturday for dinner."

"Bill's out with friends."

"Uh-huh. What was the fight about?"

"There wasn't a fight."

Bobbie lifted the lid from the cast-iron skillet and poked the pot roast with her fork.

"He shouldn't be arguing with you so soon after you lost the baby. No woman is in her right mind for a few months after something like that."

Betty told her about Alaska.

"I'm going to pour us a drink," Bobbie said.

So here they were freezing their asses off on the porch, with the gin burning a path down their throats and Smelly lying at their feet, calm and unbathed.

"You don't have to go to Alaska," Bobbie repeated.

"Well, I don't want him to be miserable."

"Get pregnant again."

"I don't know," Betty said. "I think Bill would rather wait a while. He wasn't really thrilled I got pregnant so fast." She sighed. "Although I may not be able to help it." It was hard to use the rhythm method when they were having sex three or four times a week, and her desire for him was strongest at exactly the time of the month when she was supposed to abstain.

"Then figure out a compromise," Bobbie said. "He wants to go to Alaska, you don't, so think of someplace *you* want to live and convince him he wants that, too."

Betty rolled her eyes. "You read too many magazines," she said. "I'd like to see you convince Bill Pavalak of anything." She closed her eyes and took in the scent of the Douglas firs that towered next to the house, the aroma of pot roast, the slightly musty smell of the old wooden porch. "And I don't want to leave Seattle. I'm happy here."

"You should have thought of that before you got married."

"I didn't really think about much other than Bill before I got married."

"I know," Bobbie said. She was quiet for a moment, rocking on the porch. "He's not the type who's going to be happy in one place, Bets. You've got to indulge his taste for change in some areas, so he doesn't indulge it in others."

"What's that supposed to mean?" Betty's voice was sharper than she meant it to be.

"It means he stepped out on his first wife—don't look at me like that, Dick told me about it. And you don't want him to cheat on you."

"If I've got to move to Alaska to make sure he doesn't cheat on me then I shouldn't have married him," Betty said.

A dog barked down the street. A long silence filled the space between them, and grew until it seemed to Betty almost like a tangible thing.

"So that's what you think," Betty said finally, her voice flat. She adored Bobbie, whose calm optimism had always been a touchstone for her. Bobbie's silence stung.

"He loves you, Bets, I really believe that. I wouldn't have let you marry him if I didn't. But he's a guy who likes adventure and change. He's not going to be happy working nine to five in an office every day for the rest of his life, then coming home to a house on Queen Anne Hill with a bunch of kids. So you have to figure out how to get some of what you want—like a big family—and give him some of what he wants."

Betty said nothing, but rolled Bobbie's words over and over in her mind during the next few weeks. Bill had come home drunk that night, and then apologized the next morning. *He's the kind of guy who likes adventure and change.* Betty saw how hard it was for him to get out of bed on weekday mornings, how he'd lie there long after the alarm clock had rung, flat on his back, staring at the ceiling with his hands on his chest, until he'd roll over with a heavy sigh and get up. She felt the sinking mood that settled over him on Sunday nights, noticed the flatness in his voice when he talked about work.

They talked about it. He wanted, *needed* something more. They debated likely jobs for him. Forest ranger? Fishing guide? Bill kept coming back again and again to homesteading in Alaska. Betty couldn't imagine it: In addition to Bill's job at the base, they'd have to build their own house and farm their land. It seemed impossible. Yet when they talked about leaving Boeing, or leaving Seattle, Bill's whole face changed. His smile widened, the deep vertical crease between his brows softened, the tight muscles around his jaw relaxed. She couldn't kill the hopefulness in him.

He was grateful to her for considering it, and brought home flowers unexpectedly, sometimes twice a week. They made love more often than ever, lingering in bed while Bill sketched out the outlines of a log cabin on a notepad, or read books on farming. "Maybe in two years," he said. "We could save as much as we can for two years, then we'd have something to help us get started once we move."

Betty never agreed, but she never said no, either. The next

spring, when she found out she was pregnant again, she waited three months to tell him, to make sure she wouldn't miscarry, that this one would stick. She saw the hope die in his face as soon as the words were out of her mouth.

"We could still move," she said. "We just have to wait until after the baby comes."

"And then we'll have to wait until the baby is older," Bill said.

Betty saw what he saw, the future unfurling and the relentless grip of responsibility and duty and routine tightening their hold.

He tried to smile. "It's good about the baby. The doctor says you're okay?"

"The doctor says I'm fine. I'm past the point where I might have a miscarriage."

"That's good."

Later that night he picked up his hat and coat and went out for a walk. She assumed he was going out to drink, but he came home sober, his face and hands cold and smelling of the fresh Seattle night air. He got undressed and climbed into bed beside her and lay there staring at the ceiling without saying a word, for as long as she was awake and, she guessed, probably longer.

Chapter 8

Susannah 2011

Susannah loved Betty's kitchen right away, with its warm oak floors and blue tile counters and pale yellow metal cupboards. Low-watt lights cast a soft glow, and the open window above the sink let in the cool night air and the quiet murmur of waves in the bay. She paused several times during dinner—listening, waiting, only to realize at last that what she was waiting for was *noise*. The humming, throbbing, buzzing sounds of home—furnaces, refrigerators, dishwashers, clothes washers, computers, televisions—were absent. No cars or trucks revved outside; no sirens wailed; no phones or radios or televisions blared. The only sign of technology was a laptop computer, sitting in a corner on the counter next to a tin breadbox.

They had eaten at a long pine table with benches on either side, like at a logging camp or a ranch. Katie chatted with Hood and Baker throughout the entire meal, while Barefoot and Quinn talked turtles, and Jim and Betty told Susannah stories about other Sounder residents. Now they'd cleared the dishes away, put them to soak, and sat at the table drinking Barefoot's plum wine, which *was* sweet but also spread a pleasant warmth in Susannah's chest and belly. The kids were in the other room playing cards. And after the long past few months of fear and worry, Susannah felt the tight muscles in her neck and shoulders start to relax. She pushed her empty wineglass toward Barefoot, who refilled it from the bottle at his elbow.

Jim lit a fat cigar and leaned back in his chair across from her. The candles on the table flickered in the reflection on his glasses so she couldn't see his eyes.

"So," he said. "You know us now. We've shared a meal. Want to tell us what really brought you here?"

Susannah paused. She didn't want Katie's past mistakes to haunt her here before anyone got to know her. And Susannah herself didn't want to feel judged the way she did at home, as though the scarlet BP of Bad Parenting were branded into her forehead.

"We're here because Katie was in trouble," she said. She twirled the stem of her wineglass between her fingers, trying to decide how much to say. She trusted the Pavalaks already; surely they wouldn't judge her.

"Katie was dating an older boy behind our backs," Susannah said. She kept her eyes on the purple wine in her glass. She told them about Zach's Web site, about his contest to see if he could have sex with Katie by November 1. Then she told them about Katie's drinking at the party, the alcohol poisoning, the terrifying trip to the ER. She paused. "I had to get her out."

"This is why they should bring the belt back to public schools," Barefoot said. "Or the paddle. Whip the hell out of a little bastard like that boyfriend and he'd be highly motivated to treat young ladies with more respect."

"Amen," Betty said.

"We have our own—" Jim started to say, but he was interrupted by Hood, who came into the kitchen and began to open drawers. "We're going to play flashlight tag," he said. "Where are the flashlights, Grim?"

"Where they've always been," Betty said. "Bottom drawer on the right."

The others came in and began to grab sweatshirts and jackets. Quinn looked nervous. Susannah could see how much he wanted to be part of things, be game for anything, but she could also see his fear—about *what* exactly she didn't know. Baker seemed to sense his hesitation, because he grabbed a large yellow flashlight from the counter and handed it to Quinn, saying, "We'll be partners. Here, you take this one."

Susannah looked at Jim, who sat at the table, puffing away at his cigar. He didn't look at all nervous about the idea of the kids running around in the pitch black of a Sounder night, with the bay so close by. *So it must be okay.*

Quinn twirled his hair with one finger. He looked around the room, and his eyes lit on Toby, Barefoot's black Lab, sleeping on the braided rug by the door. "Can Toby come?" Quinn said. At the sound of his name, Toby sat up and wagged his tail.

"Sure, take Toby," Barefoot said.

Quinn took the flashlight from Baker in one hand and put his other hand on Toby's head. He looked down at the flashlight, then at Susannah. "Do I need hand sanitizer?" he said. Susannah shook her head.

Jim raised his eyebrows as the door closed behind them. "Hand sanitizer?"

"He's afraid of germs." Susannah sighed. "Another reason we came here."

Barefoot snorted. "Because there are no germs on Sounder?"

"No, of course I know there are germs here. But the germs were just part of it. He was afraid of getting sick and throwing up at school, and then having everyone make fun of him.

Quinn's always been different, and so sometimes he's been a bit of an outcast."

"Have you taught him how to throw a good punch?" Barefoot said.

Susannah smiled. "You sound like my husband. The problem in a place like Tilton is that if Quinn punched another kid, even if it was well deserved, we'd get sued by the parents for assault."

"Oh, for Christ's sake," Barefoot said. "I've had my nose broken twice." He rubbed the crooked bump at the bridge of his nose. "And I've broken a few noses myself. I'll give him boxing lessons."

Susannah thought of a fist landing on Quinn's sweet, freckled face and felt sick to her stomach. "Oh, God, no. I don't want him to fight. He's just got to learn to let things roll off him more easily, you know?"

"He won't be an outcast here," Jim said. "The group's too small. And honestly, people who choose to live and raise their kids in a place like Sounder tend to march to a different drummer anyway." He grinned. "We're all different."

"Speak for yourself," Barefoot said. He turned back to Susannah. "Listen, even if he never actually breaks someone's nose, it would be good for him to know that he *could*. It boosts confidence. The boy could use a man's help here, since you're a single parent."

Susannah felt a sudden rush of longing for Matt. For some reason an image of Matt as she'd first seen him arose in her mind—age seven, standing on the sand in his swim trunks, skinny and nut brown, watching her race T. C. McNeely across the beach. "Hey, new girl!" he'd said. "Bet I can beat you." She remembered the tears of frustration in his eyes when he'd stumbled and lost. He avoided her after that, but she kept an eye on him. Wiry and athletic, he was the best at most sports, always team captain, obsessed with fairness. More than once he walked off the baseball field in a rage after a flagrant call. But his wary eyes and quiet intensity hid a tender heart. One year he gave his stash of candy bars to a boy whose parents hadn't sent him a single letter all month. At night, he would sneak out to free the fireflies the kids had trapped in jars.

Growing up in a home where nothing seemed fair, Susannah was drawn to Matt's integrity, his stubborn perseverance. After that first summer, when he'd cried after losing the race, Susannah never saw him cry again. Year after year he worked harder—at sports, at school, at hiding his embarrassment about his family's poverty. He didn't talk a lot, or laugh easily.

Susannah, in contrast, talked and laughed a lot at camp, because she was free. At first camp was a respite from the chaos and unpredictability of home; later it was a respite from grief. She danced under the stars on the beach, made up silly songs, told jokes—all the things she couldn't do at home, in case her father got angry, or her mother was sad. Accustomed to being a caretaker at home—where her father was often drunk and her mother often in bed with a headache or a backache—Susannah naturally took care of others at camp. She cheered Matt on at athletic competitions, teased him about his love of vanilla ice cream, and helped him craft funny, anecdote-filled letters home. To Matt, who'd had to work at odd jobs since age ten and fend for himself while his parents worked long hours for never enough money, Susannah's interest and concern were remarkable. No one had ever had the time to listen to his stories, remember his likes and dislikes, root for him. She saw in Matt someone serious and fair, a champion of the weak or outcast, unlike her father. He saw in her, she realized later, all the feelings he wouldn't allow himself to acknowledge or express. They became unlikely allies, and friends.

The summer of the accident he had written her a letter.

He didn't mention the accident—what adolescent boy would know what to say in such circumstances?—but he had made a little quiz full of silly questions all about Susannah that had let her feel, for a few moments at least, as though she could hold her head up again, as though there was still *something* inside her someone could like.

For years, their constant mutual attraction was like a firefly dance against a dark sky—brief, abrupt, lovely. Then, when they were both seventeen, working as camp counselors, his kisses and his hands and their mutual desire unleashed what had been building for years. They tumbled together late one night in the boathouse, their frantic fumbling evolving into something slow and passionate and so intense that when the first rays of the sun hit the dusty glass of the boathouse window, they were still exploring each other's bodies, hungry for more.

"I'm not going to get all silly about this," she said, as they hurried to get dressed.

"Why not?" he'd said. And he had not stopped loving her from that moment on—even though they lived hundreds of miles away from each other, even though he had other girl-friends, even though she had other boyfriends. As time went on, Matt became the pole around which she centered her life. Her father might divorce his second wife (or third); her mother might withdraw into grief; Susannah herself might transfer colleges or abandon a career or paralyze herself with guilt. But Matt would be the same, smooth and solid as the lake in early morning, with a similar strength underneath that calm surface.

But once Katie was born, something roared forth in Susannah. Matt's easygoing attitude veered sometimes into carelessness, his emotional reticence into indifference.

"I guess I am a single parent," Susannah said. "Although I don't think of it that way because I'll be talking to Matt every day, and he'll be out here once a month." She cleared her throat.

"That was the hardest part in deciding to come here. Matt started a new job last year. He's a geologist—I think Quinn told you—and he took a job with the Department of the Interior. He's teaching, too. He couldn't take a sabbatical, not now."

"I understand," Jim said.

"What kind of a man lets his wife and kids leave?" Matt had said, the day she'd decided to go. The question had hung there between them, along with its unspoken corollary: *What kind of a woman takes her kids and leaves her husband behind?*

"It's okay," Betty said. "This is a good community. You'll have a lot of help."

Silence fell around the table for a few minutes. The call of the kids' voices outside the open window had faded, and now Susannah heard splashing, the sound of something moving in the water.

"Are the kids still playing tag?" she said.

"They probably took the kayaks out," Jim said. "The moon's coming up."

"They took the kayaks out at night?" Susannah stood up. She felt a sudden panic.

"Only on nights like this, when it's dead calm and there's moonlight," Jim said. "The phosphorescent trails behind the boats are pretty amazing."

"I don't want my kids on the water at night," Susannah said. *You'd never find a body in that big bay, even in daylight. And never at night.*

She opened the door, her heart racing. Fear had driven her here to Sounder. But it was like escaping from a wolf by hiding in a cave with a bear. She remembered her longing all those years ago to live on the little island in the middle of the Fox River, her desire to think only about the next meal, the next bit of warmth, the next shelter, like Shackleton. But it was a stupid, childish fantasy, and the reality was that she had brought herself and her children to a remote place surrounded by water, far from medical care.

She felt a hand on her arm. "Whoa, woman. Calm down." Barefoot's hand encircled her wrist in a surprisingly strong grip.

Susannah turned a white face to him. "If they fell out we'd never find them."

"Your kids can swim can't they?" Jim said. "But it's okay. I'll go get them." He went outside and she heard a long, piercing whistle cut through the night, and an answering whistle from the bay. "Come in!" Jim shouted. Another whistle answered him.

Jim came back into the house. "You look like you've seen a ghost," he said. "You're going to have trust that we know what we're doing here. My boys are smart kids. They're pretty responsible, too."

"I was in a boating accident when I was thirteen," Susannah said. "On Lake Michigan. With my father and brother and sister. My sister drowned. I've been afraid of boats ever since. One of the reasons I came here was to try to get over it, finally. I don't know what I was thinking."

Betty looked at her. "I'm sorry," she said. She looked at her a long time, her eyes studying Susannah's face as though she'd never seen her before. "How old was she?"

"Three," Susannah said. "Janie. She was three."

Betty shook her head. "That's heartbreaking."

"It's even harder if you don't deal with it," Barefoot said. He let go of her wrist. "Good God, you're afraid of boats so you decided to move to an *island*?"

"I'm facing my fears," Susannah said, with more courage than she felt.

Barefoot slammed his hand on the wooden counter, palm down. "That's settled then. I have to go to Friday Harbor tomorrow and I understand you need groceries. We'll go in my boat. You can start getting over it tomorrow."

Susannah looked at Barefoot. He looked like a crazy person, with his wiry eyebrows and piercing blue eyes and the bandanna tied around the top of his head. But she was so *tired*. Constant vigilance was hard, exhausting work.

"Okay," she said. "I'd be happy to come with you tomorrow. Thanks."

The kids appeared in the doorway, breathless from running, cheeks flushed.

"What's up?" Hood said. "Why did you need us to come back?"

"Susannah wants to get to know the island a little better before she lets the kids take kayaks out at night," Jim said. "And it's getting late. School tomorrow."

Susannah picked up her parka from the hook by the back door. "Thank you so much for dinner," she said. "For everything. You've made us feel so welcome here. Here, let me help with the dishes." She started toward the table, to clear the mugs and glasses, but was shooed away by Betty.

"It's your first night here," Betty said. "Go home and get organized."

Hood and Baker walked them home across the bumpy meadow to the white cottage. The windows of her little house gave off a warm glow, a cozy cocoon tucked inside the vast dark of the night.

"We moved Quinn's mattress into the utility room," Baker said to Susannah, as they entered the cottage. "I slept there a lot when we lived here because Hood snores like you wouldn't believe." He shot a merry look at his brother and began to snort loudly. Hood leaned over and cuffed him across the back of the head.

"We'll come by at eight to get you for school," Hood said. Then the door closed behind the twins, and, for the first time since they'd set foot on Sounder, Susannah and her kids were alone.

"I can't believe you," Katie said, turning to face her mother. "That was *so* embarrassing."

"What?"

"You made us come in from kayaking because you freaked out," Katie said. "You drag us here, we finally are doing *one* fun thing, and you act like we're some kind of babies. It's just like at home." She began to cry, tears of rage and frustration.

"You guys are not great swimmers," Susannah said. "I have no idea how sturdy the kayaks are. Were you wearing life jackets?"

"No!" Katie said. She stood in the middle of the living room, her hands clenched into fists at her sides. "Because we're not freaks! We had life jackets *with us*, but we didn't have them on. Baker and Hood go out in the kayaks all the time without wearing life jackets."

"That's Baker and Hood."

"And it should be us! I can't stand you. You're crazy!"

"I am not crazy," Susannah said. She could not get over her reflex to defend herself when criticized. "It's my job to make sure you're safe."

"It's your job to ruin my life," Katie said. "If you want to know why I did stuff like go that party with Zach it's because I don't want to grow up to be like *you*."

Susannah pulled her lips together. "That was your bad decision," she said.

They glared at each other. Susannah could feel her heart thumping hard in her chest, a lump in her throat. She was exhausted, and ready to cry herself. "I'm going to unpack," she said, and walked into her room and closed the door.

She took one look at her suitcase and decided to save unpacking for the morning. Instead, she collapsed into the bed, not even bothering to get undressed, and pulled the quilt over herself. She felt heavy and yet hollow, like a leaden pipe, spent with fatigue. She closed her eyes.

Minutes later, a scream from Quinn penetrated the door. Susannah jumped up and ran into the living room, where Quinn knelt on the floor, crying.

"She killed Otis's wife!" Quinn cried. "She killed Otis's wife!"

"What happened?"

"She threw Otis's wife at the wall," Quinn said, wiping the tears from his cheeks with the back of one hand, and pointing at Katie. "I *hate* her!"

"He started it," Katie said. *"He's so dumb! He said—"*

"I don't care who said what," Susannah said. "How could you break Otis's wife? You know how important it was."

Otis, whom Quinn had owned for six years, was a mild-mannered box turtle with one obsession: a ceramic turtle, roughly his own size, that Matt had found on a trip to Mexico. Otis loved this turtle with all the energy in his little carapaced self. He slept next to it at night, returned to it after his outside-the-cage forays during the day, and even made love to it, his shell clanking insistently against the ceramic. Often Quinn would find Otis on his back in his cage in the morning, unable to right himself after a particularly vigorous session of lovemaking.

"Did you know male turtles in the wild sometimes fall backward just like Otis after having sex?" Quinn had told Susannah. "Only they don't have me around to put them back on their feet and they can *die of starvation*. Really."

Quinn loved his bizarre turtle facts as much as he loved Otis, which made it all the more outrageous that Katie had just hurled Otis's wife against the wall.

"I'll pick up the pieces," Susannah said. "Quinn, go get ready for bed."

"Why?" Susannah asked, after Quinn left the room. She stood facing Katie, both hands on hips. "Why would you do that?"

"Like you care why," Katie said. "I don't want to talk about it." She picked up her iPod, inserted the earbuds, and turned it on.

"I'm not finished talking to you," Susannah said.

Katie sat down on the couch and put her feet up on the coffee table.

"How dare you. TURN THAT OFF."

"You never see my side of anything," Katie said, her voice loud because of the music pounding through her headphones. "You assume your beloved little Quinnie would never provoke someone, right?"

"We're not talking about Quinn," Susannah said. "We're talking about *you*. What you did was wrong."

"You're right," Katie said, her voice brittle with sarcasm. "You're always right."

"You're unbelievably rude." Susannah felt her anger rise up, wash over her. "Turn the music off *now*."

"Get off my case," Katie said. "You are such a *bitch*."

Reflexively Susannah raised a hand to slap her, but then brought it down. Instead, she yanked the iPod out of her daughter's hands, turned, and marched to the bathroom, where she dropped it into the toilet and flushed.

There was a scream of pure outrage from Katie. "You're crazy!" she yelled, watching the swirl of water in the toilet. "You're totally crazy. Jesus!"

Susannah was so angry it was hard to breathe, her chest and throat thick. "If you can't show me the respect of listening when I talk to you, you don't deserve an iPod."

Katie turned and ran from the room, and Susannah heard the slam of her bedroom door, muffled sobs. With a sigh, Susannah walked back into the living room and collapsed on the couch. Quinn followed her.

"Do you think Otis will die of grief?" he said.

She looked at him. "No, honey. I'm going to Friday Harbor tomorrow. Maybe I can find a new wife for Otis."

Quinn looked hopeful. "That would be great. But it has to be just the right size."

"I know. Go brush your teeth."

She heard the trickle of water in the bathroom sink, the flush of the toilet.

"Mom? *Mom!*"

She jumped up and ran into the bathroom to find the toilet, clearly rebelling at the recent ingestion of Kate's iPod, overflowing onto the bathroom floor. She looked wildly around the room for a plunger, but didn't see one.

"Shit!" The water splashed over her shoes, onto her ankles. She grabbed towels and threw them onto the floor. She knew nothing about the mechanics of toilets. Was there a water shutoff valve? Had Jim showed it to her when he was explaining about distribution systems and 2D-watt bulbs or whatever the hell he'd been talking about?

Katie appeared in the doorway, walked over to the toilet, reached down, and turned a knob on the wall beneath it.

"That's where you shut the water off," she said. "Baker and Hood showed me."

"Thank God," Susannah said. She sighed. She looked around and spotted a mop in the corner of the bathroom. She reached for it and turned to Katie. "You mop up. I'll call Jim in the morning about fixing the toilet. Until then, we'll just have to go outside."

"Why do *I* have to mop?" Katie said. "*You're* the one who—"

Exhaustion and anger rose in Susannah and she shoved the mop at Katie with such force that the handle almost hit her in the forehead. Katie's eyes opened wide in surprise. "I'm *done*," Susannah said. "Shut up and mop."

Later, alone in bed, Susannah stared into the darkness and listened to something—a bat? a mouse?—rustle inside the wall. She lay on her usual side of the bed, even though Matt's side was empty. Katie wasn't speaking to her. Quinn had finally fallen asleep after twirling his hair so much that a handful of strands lay scattered across his pillow. She drifted into a restless sleep. Three times she thought she heard someone cry out, and each time she got up, made her way in to check on the kids, found them fast asleep, and stumbled back to bed. Finally, she crawled under the covers and lay on her back, eyes wide open, until the darkness began to fade and the day awoke.

Chapter 9

Betty 1954

Betty discovered the affair by accident. She was seven months pregnant, and so big the doctor thought she might be carrying twins. A mid-August heat wave, unusual for Seattle, had caused her to retain water, and her hands were so swollen she couldn't even wear her wedding ring. She woke up one morning and felt even hotter and more out of sorts than usual. Her back hurt. Her abdomen felt crampy. She was bloated. She decided to take the ferry from Seattle to Bainbridge and back again, to be on the water and get the cool breeze. She liked the idea of doing something as frivolous as riding the ferry back and forth just for the sake of the ride. It felt wickedly indulgent, even though it cost only five cents. She tried to get Bobbie to come with her, but Bobbie had a decorator coming and a doctor's appointment and thought Betty slightly crazy for suggesting it.

Betty didn't see them until the return trip. She was sitting on a bench on the deck, on the starboard side of the ferry so she was in the shade cast by the cabin. The dull ache in her lower back had turned into an insistent pain, and she was glad to sit down. The breeze whipped at her skirt, lifted her hair, and cooled her warm, swollen skin. She was gazing at the Seattle skyline, thinking about the baby. If it was a boy, Bill wanted to name him Michael, after one of his war buddies. But Michael was so common. Betty preferred something different, like Grady or Riley. If it was a girl, Bill wanted to name her Roxanne. When he told her, Betty had laughed and laughed. *Roxie*. It sounded girlish and tough at the same time, and she loved it.

Betty was sure it would be a boy. She was much more comfortable in the company of males, even though she was close to her sisters, and found it hard to imagine parenting a daughter. And she was so in love with Bill—she wanted a boy for him, and for her, because a boy would seem even more a part of Bill.

The baby kicked inside her, a thump against her rib cage, and then rolled, a ripple across her belly. She still couldn't wrap her mind around the baby as a person, someone she would caress and nurture and love. And she couldn't imagine, in her wildest dreams, loving the baby more than she loved Bill.

For a few weeks after she told him about the pregnancy, he was different. Not angry, not sad, just different. He got up and went to work in the mornings and came home and ate dinner and smiled at her and read the paper and drank a beer and went to bed. She went with him, of course, but even then he would put a hand on her hip, lean forward to kiss her on the cheek, and then roll over with a yawn to face the wall. The passionate kisses and eager sex that had characterized the early days of their marriage were gone.

He hadn't made love to her since she'd told him she was pregnant. That was normal, the doctor said, and probably best for the baby. But Betty missed the feel of his smooth skin against hers, and missed him. He hadn't mentioned Alaska once in the past few months, either, and had put away the topographical map of Chugiak that had laid stretched out on the coffee table for weeks and weeks.

A light, bubbling laugh caught her attention and she turned her head. A woman in a yellow dress leaned back against the green iron railing of the ferry. The dress was nipped in at the waist with a white belt, and her waist was so small that the man who stood opposite her, with his back to Betty, could have spanned it with his two hands. She had red hair and wore a jaunty little green hat, and she was laughing and looking up at the man as he bent to kiss her. And something about the set of the man's shoulders, the angle of his neck as he leaned in to the woman in the yellow dress, sent a shock of recognition through Betty.

"Bill?"

He didn't hear her.

Betty struggled to stand up. She was so big now she couldn't stand without pushing herself up off the arms of a chair, or giving both hands to Bill to pull her up. But there were no arms on the bench she sat on now, and Bill was there with his back to her. She braced both hands on the bench beside her hips and tried to stand, but the rolling motion of the ferry caught her, and she lost her balance and fell backward awkwardly. She hit her tailbone hard against the metal bench.

Bill turned and saw her. And it was no coincidence, she thought then and later, that a pain ripped through her abdomen at exactly the moment his eyes met hers.

Her twins were born the next morning, two months too soon, and died that night.

Bobbie wanted her to leave him. Betty knew—the small part of her that could still think rationally, that wasn't muddled with grief and rage and yearning—she *should* leave him. But Bill was broken. The death of the babies, both boys, had compounded his guilt to such an extent that Betty began to worry about his sanity. He didn't leave her side for a week, sleeping on the floor in the hospital next to her bed. The nurses would kick him out when visiting hours ended, but somehow, some way, he would sneak in again, and there he would be in the morning, curled on the floor with his head resting on Betty's overnight bag.

He brought her flowers. He brought her a ring with a tiny blue sapphire, representing fidelity. He swore to her that it was one time and that it had gone no further than a few kisses. The woman was a secretary at Boeing, and she'd flirted and flirted with him, and he'd been weak, pathetic really, and he had no idea why. Except that he was terrified by the responsibility of having kids, of being moored to his desk job and Seattle and a life of unbroken sameness stretching ahead of him endlessly like railroad tracks across the prairie. But now even that wasn't as terrifying as the thought of losing her. He loved her.

She spent the first week in a haze of narcotics and sleep. Bobbie floated in and out, as did Mother, and Grammy. Bill was the one constant.

"You can come home with me," Bobbie whispered to her several times.

Betty shook her head. How could she make a decision like that, especially now? She was broken and Bill was broken and they were broken. She wanted to stay in the hospital forever, with the efficient nurses and the smell of rubbing alcohol and the crisp sheets. She wanted to float away on little blue pills and have other people bring her food and help her bathe and pet her—*baby her. Baby* her.

It was something about that thought, as well as the fullness of her aching milk-laden breasts and her empty belly and empty arms, that finally induced Betty's grief. She lay on her back and the tears rolled down from the corners of her eyes into her ears. She cried for the babies, for Bill, for herself, for all of it. Bill was asleep on the floor but woke up when he heard her sobs. He came over and knelt next to the bed and wrapped his arms around her and buried his face against her side.

"I'm so sorry," he said, over and over. "So sorry. It's because of me you lost the babies. The shock—I know I did it to you, and I can't forgive myself for that. Just give me a chance to make it up to you, please, Betty." And then, for the first time since she'd known him, he cried.

Reflexively, she put out a hand to stroke his head, and at her touch he looked up at her with those eyes. She looked back at him, at the shame and the hope in his face, and felt something inside her soften. Her nod was barely perceptible, but it was enough. His face melted with gratitude, and he climbed onto the bed next to her and spooned her until they both fell asleep.

Six months later, she moved with him to Sounder.

It was a compromise, as Bobbie had suggested, meant to mark the beginning of their new life together, their new commitment to each other. Betty wouldn't go to Alaska—it was too far from Seattle and her family, who were more important to her than ever now that she faced the possibility of a life without children of her own. But Sounder would offer the adventure Bill craved, a place in some ways even more remote and wild than Anchorage. They'd have a farm; they would work together. And, Betty thought, although she didn't say it even to Bobbie, the temptations would be fewer.

For six months they read books on farming and gardening and leafed through government pamphlets on raising chickens. Bill wanted to keep goats, too, for the milk. They saved every penny they could. Bill knew someone who knew someone who lived on Orcas Island and occasionally went over to Sounder, and this buddy kept his eyes and ears open for them and called one day to say he'd heard of a sweet little farm on the west side of Sounder that had gone up for sale.

They put down a deposit sight unseen—hard to get more adventurous than that, in Betty's opinion. The farm abutted a sheltered bay, and included a white cottage, a barn, and eighty acres of fields and woods. They gave notice to their landlord, sold their furniture, and packed up two duffel bags with their clothes and shoes and the blue and white quilt that had been a wedding gift from Grammy. Bobbie saw them off at the pier downtown. They were catching a ride on a fishing boat to Friday Harbor, and then they'd take the Sounder mail boat from there.

Bobbie took Betty's face in both her hands. "You have yourself a good adventure," she said. "I love you. Don't work too hard, and don't take any crap." This last with a nod toward Bill, who was loading their bags onto the boat. "I know this is what you want, so I'm behind you." She leaned in closer to whisper in Betty's ear. "And if, *if*, for any reason, you need to leave him and come home, you are always welcome to live with me."

As Bill came up to say it was time to go, Bobbie turned to him. "Take care of my sister," she said. "*Good* care."

Bill met her eyes and nodded and placed a protective arm around Betty's shoulders. "I will," he said.

Betty was prepared for the stab of loneliness that hit her as the Seattle skyline disappeared from view, and the fear. But it wasn't until she turned to look at her husband, who stood next to her with his hands on the railing, that she realized how angry she was, and that she had no idea what she would do with all that rage.

She stayed angry for most of the next six months. And the damnedest thing was that she didn't *want* to be so angry. She and Bill had talked and talked about this move. She had agreed to it. She had even in a sense *chosen* it; the San Juan Islands had been her idea, after an evening spent studying a map and knowing she could never go to Alaska and knowing, too, that Bill had to get away. She wasn't going to have children—she was convinced of that even if the doctor wasn't—and she didn't want to stay in Seattle and be the doting aunt to her sisters' children, or the housewife with the impeccable living room and perfect garden. She might as well find something to do, and do it with Bill.

She read the books on farming and the pamphlets on chickens and decided that burying herself in physical labor might be the answer. Sounder it was, she said to Bill, and meant it. He was excited at her excitement, humble and grateful that she'd forgiven him, that she was willing to make this move.

But once they arrived, she could feel the anger spread in her like an infection, seeping out from her core into her limbs, her face, her eyes. Her throat choked with it; her tongue was thick with the words she wanted to say and didn't.

Sounder wasn't the problem. She liked the farm and the island and the people more than she could have imagined. Neighbors pitched in to help them plow and plant and build the chicken house, and they were constantly getting invited to "bees" of some kind or another—a cleanup bee at the schoolhouse to wash windows and paint walls, a cider bee at the Cummings' to pick and press apples, a work bee at another couple's farm to rip out hardhack and scotch broom and wild gooseberry.

The cottage was fine, too, and suited Betty much better than the neat little overly decorated house her sister had in Seattle. Sure, the bathroom was a hundred yards away behind a towering cedar, and the floor sloped so badly that if you dropped a marble it would roll all the way from the front door to the back, and the curtains didn't match the couch. But the big cast-iron stove warmed the whole living area, and the old green rockers on the porch were the most comfortable chairs she'd ever known, and the quiet all around them penetrated to a deep place within her and calmed her.

Bill was attentive and thoughtful and careful with her, but on guard. She tried not to let her anger show—he had apologized and apologized, after all, and what was the point of holding on to it or talking it to death? But she knew it was evident in the set of her lips and the tone of her voice and the tenseness in her body when he touched her, in the staccato sound of her knife on the cutting board and the way her eyes slipped away from his gaze. They didn't talk about it, but it rose up between them like steam from a locomotive, growing thicker and thicker.

Bill, to her surprise, didn't respond to her anger with a frustrated fury of his own, or with the kind of hangdog shame that would have sickened her, would have made her feel as though she'd been the one to do something wrong. Instead he got up in the mornings in the gray light of early day, got the fire going in the stove, made a pot of coffee, then went out to the chicken house to collect eggs, feed and water the chickens, shovel out droppings, and milk the goats, all before breakfast. By the time he came in, she often had bacon cooking, and griddlecakes they would eat with honey from Alice MacDonald's bees. Then they'd head out together to begin the weeding or mulching or harvesting in the fields they'd managed to get planted in the spring after they moved in.

Within a month Betty could see that they wouldn't come close to breaking even in their first year, with all the money they'd put into buying the farm and building the chicken house, not to mention paying for and feeding the chickens. They'd had the help of other islanders in the planting, or they'd have had even more expense. "We'll give it two years," Bill had said when they decided to move to Sounder, and Betty doubted they'd break even by then. But she surprised herself with her lack of worry over their finances, or the future. Her husband had cheated on her; she'd buried two babies—what was the worst that could happen?

And then, after five or six months, her anger began to fade. Bill didn't say or do anything different; she had no sudden flash of insight, or word of wisdom from a friend. But more days than not she woke up next to Bill and lay there for a few minutes listening to his breathing and the vast silence of Sounder, and felt content. She was physically stronger than she'd ever been before in her life from all the time spent planting and digging and chopping wood and scrubbing and lifting, and she liked the way her body moved and looked. She didn't have to pretend an interest in fashion or decorating or entertaining, as she'd often felt she had to do at home. Bill had worked harder than she'd ever known him to work before, and she thought she could feel a change in him, something solid and true and permanent.

In the mornings she would press herself against Bill's warm back in the bed, marveling at how far they had come and all they had been through in the four years since they'd gotten married. She could begin to see a useful life for herself here, she thought, even without children of her own. And it was, at long last, a life she relished.

Chapter 10

Susannah 2011

Susannah was desperate for a cup of coffee. At the crack of dawn she had slipped on her wool clogs, ventured outside, and made her way through the frost-covered grass to squat by a tree at the back of the house, where she had promptly peed on her clogs. When she came in, after running through the cold grass in her bare feet, the fire in the stove had gone out, so she'd had to stack it with wood and get it lit. Now her clogs, which she had slid under the stove to dry out, were giving off a distinct aroma, and the water in the teakettle still hadn't boiled. She turned the handle on the hand-cranked coffee mill and sighed.

"I don't want to go to school," Quinn said. He slid into a chair at the round oak dining table and stared at the glass of orange juice she set there for him.

"It's natural to be a little nervous," she said.

"What if I throw up?" he said.

"You can run outside," she said. "Jim said the school has outhouses, one for boys, one for girls." She picked up a thick blue dish towel and wrapped it around the handle of the teakettle, which had finally started to whistle. "But you're not going to throw up."

"Really?" Quinn said. "The school doesn't have indoor bathrooms?"

"Nope," Susannah said. She poured the hot water into the French press and put the kettle back on the stove.

Quinn contemplated this. "So I can just walk outside when I want?"

"Well, I assume you need to let Jim know you're going, but with only fifteen kids I would guess it's not a big deal."

Quinn looked more cheerful. "So you can go outside if you feel like throwing up. *And* there's no bus and no bus stop. I think I might like it here."

"You didn't like riding the bus?" she said.

Quinn picked up his glass, took a sip of juice, and put it back down. "Not much."

Something in his tone caught her attention. "Why not?"

To her surprise, Quinn turned a bright, furious red and said, "I just didn't. I don't want to talk about it."

Katie walked in and sat down on the living room sofa, dressed in jeans and a skin-tight tank top.

"You're kidding that the school bathrooms are outside, right?" she said.

Susannah shook her head. "No. And that shirt is too tight and too low cut to wear to school. Go change. Do you want scrambled eggs?"

"Outdoor bathrooms? Oh, my God." Katie threw her head back on the couch and closed her eyes. "I will never forgive you for this," she said, her face turned toward the ceiling. "You have no idea what you're doing in bringing us here."

And Susannah—sleepless, coffeeless, shoeless—felt a familiar jolt of shame. *Look what you've done*, the little voice in her head said. *You always make mistakes.*

Sometimes, with a start, she recognized in Katie's words the echoes of the harsh, critical voice her father had used whenever he was loaded up with a few drinks. For a while it had lain silent: During all those early years when her children were small she knew, in the way she loved them and the way they blossomed, that she was doing something right. But over this last year, Katie—with her words, her looks of contempt, her disdain for everything Susannah said and did and thought—had brought that voice roaring back, and Susannah didn't know how to still it now.

Someone tapped at the window. "They're here," Quinn said, standing up so fast that he bumped into the table and almost knocked over his juice. "I see Baker."

Quinn and Katie grabbed their coats and backpacks and were out the door before Susannah had a chance to make Katie change her shirt, or even eat breakfast. With a sigh, she pressed the plunger down on the French press and poured herself a cup of coffee. She sat down at the table and wrapped her hands around the mug, grateful for its warmth. She was alone for the first time in the quiet, quiet house. This is what she had chosen; this is what she wanted.

And now that she had it, she wasn't sure she wanted it after all.

"But how did you get this up here?"

Susannah stood in a grassy patch at the top of Crane's Point. Before her, set up on a short scaffolding of lumber and steel tubing, was a twenty-seven-foot boat. The hull was white with a blue stripe running along the top. A wide wheelhouse, covered with a navy blue canvas roof, stood in the center. The name *Gota* was painted across the back in gold letters outlined in black. This was the shape on top of the cliff that Susannah had noticed as they'd come into the bay yesterday.

Barefoot scowled. He stood shoeless on the rocky ground, khakis rolled up above his ankles, immune to the cold wind that whipped at Susannah's hair and reddened her cheeks.

"What the hell does that matter?" he said. "It's here, and it needs work."

Susannah had driven Betty's truck up the mountain to pick up Barefoot, who didn't own a car. They were going down to the dock, and then to Friday Harbor on Barefoot's other boat, the one anchored in the bay. She had parked at the end of the long gravel road and walked up a slight rise to find the incongruous sight of Barefoot standing on the deck of the *Gota*.

"What exactly are you doing to it?"

"Refinishing the wood in the cabin, building a new table and some shelves, fixing the plumbing for the sink and the head—" Barefoot paused and looked at her. "Why? You know something about boats?"

"God, no," Susannah said. "I haven't been on a boat in more than thirty years."

"Right," Barefoot said. He tilted his head back and stared at her from under thick, wiry brows. "You're a strange woman," he said. "Can't quite figure you out." He shook his head. "Oh, well. I need to get my wallet. Come on down to the house."

Barefoot's small, white frame farmhouse sat downhill, to the left of the cliff top. Susannah stepped onto the gray painted porch, where Toby lay sleeping, and followed Barefoot into the house. She stood in stunned silence for a moment. The room that faced her was rectangular, with a row of windows along the front, white walls, and a stone fireplace. Ordinary enough. But a beautiful Indian miniature painting in deep jewel tones glowed above the mantel; a sterling silver tea service reflected the light from the windows; two perfect Chippendale chairs framed the fireplace. Other exquisite objects—a set of Minton porcelain, a carved stone head of the Buddha, a string of jade beads—sat on the tabletops. Beneath her feet lay a silk rug with a pattern of richly detailed leaves and flowers on a ruby red background. Instinctively, she slipped off her shoes.

"You have such beautiful things," she said.

"I used to travel a lot. Picked things up here and there."

"Here and there?" She eyed another painting on the wall.

"Asia, mostly, and Africa. Part of the job."

Before dinner last night Jim had told her a little bit about Barefoot's past. He had worked as a scientist for the U.S. Department of Agriculture during a career that had spanned more than sixty years. He had tramped through India, Tibet, Assam, Nepal, and Iran in search of plants for the USDA and for museums in the United States and Europe. Along the way he had collected and cataloged some of the most exotic species ever seen, in places with names like Kulu Valley, Yusufabad, and Zahedan.

"Jim told me you spent a lot of time in the Middle East."

"Persia—Iran. And farther east—Tibet, Nepal, India."

He disappeared into the bedroom to get his coat, and Susannah took the opportunity to peer into the kitchen. Bundles of drying herbs hung from the ceiling, tied neatly with twine. Another beautiful rug—this one in shades of turquoise and orange and red—covered the worn wood of the floor. A verse was painted in flawless black cursive above the back door that led out to the greenhouse:

> *Since my house burned down / I now own a better view / of the rising moon.*
>
> —Mizuta Masahide

"Anything else you'd like to see?" Susannah jumped as Barefoot appeared at her elbow.

"I didn't mean to snoop," she said. "But I'm fascinated. I like your house very much." She looked up again at the quote above the door. "Who's Mizuta Masahide?"

"Seventeenth-century Samurai warrior and poet. That was the first thing I did when I moved into this house: paint those words up there."

"Why?"

Barefoot turned his blue eyes on hers. "Because I like to remind myself that we all decide for ourselves whether things are bad or good. It's all how you choose to look at things."

Susannah picked up a small, framed photograph from the counter. It showed a woman in a long dark skirt and flowered tunic sitting barefoot in front of a tent. Strands of black hair escaped from the scarf on her head and fell across the angle of her cheekbone. She was strikingly beautiful.

"Who's this?"

"My mother. Dorelia. That was taken in 1920, when she was nineteen."

"She's lovely."

Barefoot shrugged. He picked up a string bag from the counter and stuffed it in the pocket of his parka. "Enough yammering. We need to get to town."

They drove down to the dock, parked in the gravel by the Laundromat, and rowed the green dinghy out to Barefoot's other boat, the *EmmaJeanne*. Susannah climbed on board and looked around with suspicion. There was a pilothouse, covered at the back with a thick canvas flap. Barefoot held the flap open and she stepped in. At least you were inside here, not sitting out uncovered, where you could fall or get bumped out of the boat. She took a deep breath and sat down.

Barefoot looked at her, at her pale face, her hands clenched together in her lap. "Good God, we haven't even untied yet," he said. "You know, this could be fun."

That's what her father had said, Susannah remembered.

This will be so much fun. That boat, the one her father had rented for their outing, had been big, with two seats in front that swiveled and two more big, padded seats at the back, on either side of the inboard engine. Lake Michigan had been calm when they set out under clear blue skies. She remembered the boat skimming across the surface, the exhilarating sense of speed, her father's brown-black hair blowing back in the wind, the dark sunglasses that made him look even younger, even more handsome.

"Come here," Barefoot said. He stood behind the wheel of the boat and put the key in the ignition. "Stand next to me."

She stepped back. "You want *me* to drive the boat?"

"Yes, I want *you* to drive the boat. What are you, five years old? You can drive a car, you can drive the boat."

He flicked a switch. "That's the battery. You turn that on first. This"—he pointed to a red knob—"is the fuel shutoff. You push it in before you start the engine. Then it's like a car: you turn the key and start the engine." He turned the key and the motor chugged to life. "It's got a two-hundred-and-sixty-five-horsepower diesel engine. The top speed is less than thirty miles an hour. You control it; it doesn't control you. Ever ridden a horse?"

Susannah nodded.

"That horse has a mind of its own. No matter how good a rider you are, that horse can still do things that surprise you. Not this boat. You're in charge. Worst it can do is quit on you. And with a diesel engine like this, it's not likely to do that."

You're in charge. That day her dad had been in charge. He'd been behind the wheel of the boat.

Barefoot stood next to her as she got the feel of the wheel, showed her how to work the throttle. She tried not to think about Janie, about the bright orange life jacket. She took a deep breath.

Barefoot backed the boat away from its mooring, then put it in forward and stepped aside to let Susannah take the wheel. The *EmmaJeanne* moved steadily forward, lifting and falling gently with the waves, the motor a reassuring hum. *This isn't so bad*, she thought. But Barefoot looked at her, at the whiteness of her knuckles gripping the wheel, and said, "Here." He reached a bony hand inside the front of his parka and pulled out a silver flask. He unscrewed the top and handed it to Susannah.

"What is this?"

"My heart medicine. It'll calm you down."

"Heart medicine?"

She opened the flask and sniffed. "What is it?"

"You sure ask a lot of questions." Barefoot took the flask from her, put it to his lips, and took a long swig. He wiped his mouth on the back of his hand and held the flask out to her.

She looked at it. *It's just a few beers*, her father had said. *Nothing I can't handle.*

"Here." Barefoot took the wheel from her while she drank. The whiskey warmed her, and there was a sweetness, too—sugar? Orange juice?

"I hope this doesn't make me seasick," she said.

"I hope it doesn't make you seasick, too," Barefoot said. "And if it does, remember: the first rule of boating is puke over the rail." He stepped aside so she could take the wheel again, and then took another long drink, screwed on the cap, and put it back inside his jacket. They were in open water now, beyond the bay.

"So your sister drowned, eh?" Barefoot said. "She go over the side?"

Susannah nodded, numb. She wasn't about to explain to Barefoot how Janie had fallen overboard. She'd never told anyone except Matt.

"Okay. Then let's review what to do if someone goes over the side."

"Oh, God, no."

Barefoot glared at her. "You don't want to talk about it?"

Susannah kept her eyes on the bow, on the gray waves in front of the boat. "No," she said. "I'm not interested in reliving that particular day."

"Jesus Christ! No one's asking you to spill your guts. I'm telling you what to do if you're on a goddamn boat when someone falls overboard. You live on an island now. You've got two kids. Like it or not, you're going to spend a lot of time in boats in all kinds of weather. If you can't handle that, then once we get to Friday Harbor you should hop on the next ferry and head home. I'll ship your kids after you."

"Okay. You're right." The boat continued to chug steadily forward, and the swells were gentle, even out in the open expanse beyond the bay.

"As I was saying," Barefoot said, "the first thing to do is point and yell." He jumped up and shouted, *"Man overboard!"* and pointed to the side of the boat. The wiry hairs of his eyebrows stuck straight out from his face underneath the edge of his red bandanna. "Man overboard *port side!*"

He looked at her. "You get that? You spot the person and name their location and don't take your eyes off 'em, no matter what."

Susannah nodded. *If only it had been that easy.*

"Then, you swing the stern and propeller away from the person in the water. Then throw anything that floats at 'em—a life jacket, a cushion, even an empty cooler. Maneuver the boat as close as you can, then cut the engine so you don't chop 'em up with the propeller."

Oh, Jesus. She was going to need the entire flask of heart medicine.

"Then get 'em up the ladder. That's all there is to it." Barefoot gave a satisfied nod. "People fall overboard all the time.

Hell, a goddamn puppy fell off the ferry a few years back and they turned the ferry around and lowered a lifeboat and saved the puppy. Local newspapers loved it."

"That's good," Susannah said. "I mean that they saved the puppy."

Barefoot looked at her. "Getting the feel for it? It's not that hard. That snotty daughter of yours could even do it."

"That's what I'm afraid of," Susannah said. "I'm not sure I want her behind the wheel of anything."

Barefoot pointed out the window to Susannah's right. "Look."

She looked at the waves and couldn't see anything. Then, all at once, a huge dorsal fin and glistening black back broke the surface, then another one, and then another.

"Orca," Barefoot said.

She watched them, the fins rising and disappearing in the waves.

"You see 'em all the time," Barefoot said. "Anyway, I could teach your girl to drive the boat."

"Oh, no. No thanks." Susannah wanted to change the subject. "Do you have kids?"

"Nope. For one, I've never been married and never wanted to be. For two, the whole world's going to hell in a handbasket, and I don't know why I'd add to the misery by throwing another human being into the mix. We should euthanize at least twenty percent of the ones who are already here. Total waste of resources."

"You can't mean that."

"Maybe I do; maybe I don't. I could give you a convincing argument either way." Barefoot leaned over and spat onto the floor. "I like plants. And birds. More than most people." He shook his head. "Too much has changed. When I was a kid the ducks would flock so thick on the pond the sky would get dark when they took flight. I could have walked on water across the backs of the salmon in the bay. Now the whole place is shot."

"Quinn's like that," Susannah said. "He loves plants and animals. I think he relates to them better than he does to people."

A sudden swell caught the boat, started to lift it, and in a panic Susannah swung the wheel to the side, so the boat was broadside to the wave. The port side of the boat rose up and up and the floor tilted at an alarming angle. Barefoot slid over, bumping into her, and grabbed the wheel with both hands, fighting to bring it back around. It only took a few seconds, and he had the boat turned right again, bow headed into the wind.

"Governor's Channel," Barefoot said. "The winds and currents can shift fast here. Just have to be ready for it."

Susannah shook her head. Her heart was hammering in her chest. She kept seeing that other boat, that other day—the bright blue sky, the fluffy white clouds, the sudden, heart-stopping impact.

"I'm sorry," she said to Barefoot. "I'm done."

He looked at her with an expression she couldn't quite read—pity? disgust?—and *tsk-tsk*ed with his tongue. "If you say so." He stepped over and took the wheel from her and didn't speak again until they reached Friday Harbor.

She huddled on the seat across from Barefoot, hating her own fears. The trip back that afternoon, through rough seas, did nothing to reassure her. When she stood on the Sounder dock again at last, she drew in a deep breath and decided she would never pilot a boat again.

So much for facing her fears.

Chapter 11

Betty 1955

One sunny Saturday in early November, seven or eight months after they'd moved to Sounder, Betty was walking up the gravel drive to the post office when Annette Fahlstrom stepped out onto the front porch. Annette's husband, Corky, ran the mail boat to and from Sounder. They had two young sons, and Annette helped out often at school. Betty had talked to Annette dozens of times at beach picnics and dances at the post office, and Corky had stopped by to help Bill with this or that on the farm. Betty was still much more comfortable around men than women, and wasn't quite sure how to lay the foundations for one of those intimate, girly friendships that Bobbie always had with all her friends. And Annette was the kind of petite, feminine woman who always made Betty feel tall and ungainly, all big feet and elbows and knees. But she and Annette had had some pleasant conversations, shared a joke or two.

Betty remembered vividly the cool air, the sunlight hitting the tall grass in the field next to the post office, turning it gold. She remembered the flowered cotton dress Annette wore, lavender, with a dark green coat. She remembered feeling Annette's eyes on her as she walked up the steps and feeling a sudden sense of shame, although she had no idea why. And then she saw it—a fleeting, possessive smile that passed across Annette's face, a smug smile—and Betty knew: Annette had slept with Bill. She didn't know *how* she knew it, she just knew it deep in her gut, and she knew, too, in that instant, that she had married the wrong man.

She didn't say anything to Bill, not that night or the next or the next. She watched him, and thought hard about what to do. She was twenty-three years old and hadn't held down a "real" job in five years, since before she'd gotten married. Bobbie was married with a baby of her own, and Mel, who suffered from panic attacks, was living back home with Mother and Grammy, who was a little crazy herself. Jimmy had moved to New York. Where would she go if she left Bill?

Every day that week—as she boiled endless vats of apples for apple ketchup and applesauce, and kneaded dough for the bread, and chopped wood, and dealt with the goddamned chickens—she thought about what to do. Every time Bill left the farm to go pick up the mail, or borrow a tool from a neighbor, or take eggs to sell over to the post office, Betty wondered: *Is that really where he's going? Is he meeting Annette someplace? Where?*

She started to feel sick thinking about it, about Bill running his hands over Annette's tiny waist, her perfect little breasts, kissing her rosebud mouth. One morning she woke up and vomited into the kitchen sink after thinking about it all night long.

"You eat something bad?" Bill said, coming in to the kitchen from outside, where he'd been milking the goats.

"No," Betty said. She wiped her mouth with the back of her hand. She turned to face him.

"I know about you and Annette," she said.

She saw the truth in his face right away—shock, guilt, then

the quick calculation, his eyes darting back and forth, as he tried to figure out what she knew and how she knew it and whether or not he could lie his way out of it.

"It was one time, Betty," he said, his voice low. "It was a mistake."

"You bet it was a mistake, you goddamned son of a bitch," she said. "Because I won't stay here, and you're going to lose your cook, cleaning lady, laundress, egg picker, and goat herder, all at once. The girl in Seattle was one time, too."

He turned full eyes to her. "I'm sorry. You were so angry about moving here—"

"Don't you dare make this my fault," she said. The rage that had simmered in her during all those early months on the island boiled up, threatened to choke her. She fought the urge to vomit again. "I'll leave on the mail boat tomorrow."

And she did. She packed her clothes and wrote out instructions for the hand washing machine and the recalcitrant pump and the other things that had been her domain. Bill drove her to the dock in silence. She didn't look back when the mail boat pulled away, but threw up over the rail as soon as they had rounded Crane's Point.

Bobbie met her at the ferry dock in Anacortes, and brought her home to the little house she shared with Dick and their baby girl. She never once said, "I told you so." Over the next two months, Betty got up every morning and circled ads in the Help Wanted section and then put on Bobbie's smart tweed suit and her black pumps and took the bus downtown to interview. But time and again she was told, "No thanks."

"Not many jobs for women anymore," one man told her. He glanced at her left hand, where she still wore the small gold band Bill had given her. The man didn't say anything, but Betty knew what he was thinking: Why would a woman look for a job if she had a husband? What was wrong with her husband, or with her?

For the first time in her life, food lost all appeal. Bobbie was a terrific cook and made things she knew Betty loved—lasagna and garlic bread and seven-layer chocolate cake. But the smell of the garlic bread turned her stomach, and the cake tasted sour in her mouth. She lost weight, and had to pin the waistband of Bobbie's skirt before she went on interviews.

Bill showed up the third week after she'd left, braving Bobbie's wrath to stand on the front doorstep with his hat in his hands. Bobbie wouldn't even open the door because she couldn't trust herself not to lose all control and pummel him. Betty heard his voice, pleading through the door. He wasn't asking for forgiveness, he said, or even for Betty to come back home to Sounder. He just wanted to say he was sorry, that he'd wait for as long as she needed for her to come back, even if it took years, and that he wanted to do what he could to provide for her in the meantime.

He left two dozen eggs on the porch.

Betty could have cursed herself for being a damn fool, but didn't. Her love for Bill had had very little to do with reason from the beginning, and she saw no point in berating herself for falling in love and then trying to make it work. But the future did worry her now, because she couldn't live with Bobbie forever and knew Bill didn't have two nickels to his name, other than what money he had tied up in the farm. He could bring her two dozen eggs every day and it wouldn't be enough to pay for clothes or shoes or food or rent.

She also felt awful. The strength and vitality she'd developed on Sounder faded with her weight, and she dragged herself out of bed every morning and tried to make it through the

day without lying down on the floor to nap. She went on her
job interviews; she helped Bobbie with the baby and the shopping and cooking. Finally one day Bobbie looked at her and said,
"I'm taking the baby in to see Dr. Kositch tomorrow, and I'm
bringing you, too."

Sure enough, Bobbie's doctor confirmed what Betty had
never even suspected because she had assumed her weariness,
the constant taste of bile in her mouth, and her lack of appetite
were due to the trauma of leaving Bill.

She was pregnant.

She decided right away that she wouldn't tell Bill. She assumed
this pregnancy would end as her others had, with a miscarriage or a premature birth. The doctor put her on full bed rest,
so she stayed on at Bobbie's house. Her mother had sold the
Queen Anne boarding house and moved into a small apartment
with Grammy and Mel, whose panic attacks had turned into
a kind of crippling anxiety. Mel was afraid of thunder, afraid
of heights, afraid of cats and sirens and rain. And Jimmy was
across the country in law school. Bobbie's house was the only
place she could go.

After four months, Bobbie wrote Bill a matter-of-fact letter,
explaining that Betty was expecting a baby in July. They knew
he would send money to support his child, she wrote, but Betty
would not be returning to Sounder. Bobbie did not call him
any of the choice names she used when discussing him in front
of Betty, nor did she threaten to chop off his member with a
kitchen knife, something she had also discussed with Betty.

Bill sent a letter back to Bobbie with a check for fifty dollars and a sealed envelope for Betty. Betty knew he had to have
sold something—his fishing gear and tackle box, maybe—to
come up with that much money. Bobbie came in and put the
envelope on the walnut table next to Betty's bed and said, "I

thought about throwing this away, but you can decide for your-self." Betty didn't throw it away, but she didn't open it, either.

What she did do was think. She had nothing else to do, given that she was in bed every day except for little forays to the bathroom. Bobbie moved the television into her room, but Betty had so little interest that she moved it back out again. Her mother or Grammy stopped by every day to visit or bring food. She talked to them and pretended to read the books they left, and leafed through the glossy magazines Bobbie brought home for her to read. But her brain wouldn't take in the words.

What am I going to do? she thought every day. If the baby died, as she expected, given her past history, she could get back out and find a job, any job, and maybe get a room in a boarding-house. But if the baby lived—she didn't let her mind go there. She didn't want to hope for what she might never have.

She felt the baby's first kick in February; by June she was farther along in her pregnancy than she'd been with the twins, and the baby kicked and squirmed inside her all the time. She started to think that this baby might live. *And then what?* She didn't want to live off her sister's charity forever. Bill had put the farm up for sale, but it seemed clear it wasn't going to sell, so she couldn't get even the little bit of money she might have received from her share.

One day Bobbie brought in a bouquet of early roses from Grammy's garden, in an exquisite shade of pale pink. She filled a blue glass vase with water, put the roses in it, placed it on the dresser across from Betty's bed, and stood back to admire them.

"They're lovely," Betty said.

"Aren't they? Roses are my favorite. Mel loves dahlias, of all things, which should have been our first clue that she wasn't quite right."

Betty smiled. Bobbie always managed to make her smile.

"How are you feeling?" Bobbie said.

"Fine. Bored."

Bobbie sat down on the edge of the bed and put her hand on Betty's and looked at her earnestly.

"Oh, no," Betty said. "I can see we're about to have *a serious talk*." She sat up a little, pulled her hand from underneath Bobbie's, and adjusted her bed jacket around her shoulders. She took a deep breath. "All right. I'm ready."

"You're not a bit funny," Bobbie said. She turned and opened the drawer in the bedside table and pulled out a pack of cigarettes and a silver lighter. She tapped a cigarette out of the pack, put it between her lips, and flicked the lighter. She took a deep drag.

"The baby is due in less than a month," she said. She blew out a long stream of smoke, her head turned to the side, away from Betty. "You know you're welcome to stay here. You and the baby."

Betty shook her head. "I can't do that," she said. "I already feel guilty about being here all this time, in bed, with you taking care of me and taking care of Dick and Macy, too. It's not right."

"You'd do it for me."

Betty picked at the pink chenille circles on the bedspread. "I know. But I'm not. You're doing it for me." She looked up at her sister. "If I can stay for eight weeks or so after the baby is born, I should be able to look for a job then, and find a room in a boardinghouse, one that will take me and the baby."

Bobbie leveled a long look at her. "Really? You think that's going to be easy to do?"

"What, find a room, or find a job?"

"Either one. You're twenty-three years old. You've haven't worked in four or five years. You're separated, and your husband doesn't have two cents to rub together to support you or the baby."

"He sent that fifty dollars." Why did she feel compelled to defend Bill?

Bobbie looked at her again, with pity this time, which was even worse than the "be realistic" look she'd given her a few minutes ago. "Listen, I'm on your side, Betsy. I'd do anything for you; you know that. But you need to think hard about what your life is going to look like in six months."

"What do you think I do all day, every day? I do nothing *but* think about it."

Now it was Bobbie who dropped her head, who began to trace a finger around the circles on the bedspread. "Dick mentioned something I hadn't even though of, but that might be worth considering."

"What?"

Bobbie lifted her head. "One of the guys he works with is married to a social worker. She works in adoption placement."

"Adoption?"

Of course. The thought of giving up the baby hadn't even occurred to her, but of course it would have occurred to everyone else. Bill was a cad; she had no money and Bill had none to give her; she was still young and might marry again—but not if she was tied down with a baby. Another couple could give the baby things she couldn't—two parents who loved each other and were loyal to each other, financial security, a future.

But she *knew* this baby. She knew the baby was a morning person, kicking and wriggling most days before six. She knew the baby didn't like tomatoes, because it hiccuped and wriggled for hours after she ate them. She knew the baby startled easily, especially when the dog barked. The baby was so real to Betty already that some mornings she awoke and was surprised to find herself still pregnant, surprised the little person she knew wasn't already lying beside her.

Bobbie must have seen something in her face, because her

eyes filled with tears. She ground out her cigarette in the ash-tray on the table and leaned forward and wrapped her arms around Betty. "I'm sorry. Forget it; I shouldn't have said any-thing. I know you want this baby. And so do I." Bobbie let her go and wiped a finger under each eye, careful not to smudge her mascara. "We'll figure it out."

But how? What was she going to do? Betty thought about it for a long time after Bobbie left, and was still thinking about it a week later when the roses in the blue vase wilted and began to drop their petals. And that's when she began to form her plan.

Chapter 12

Susannah 2011

One Saturday morning about three weeks after they arrived, Susannah found herself climbing a tree—something she hadn't done since she was twelve, when it had been a heck of a lot easier. Hood had demonstrated how easy it was a few days ago, clambering up the branches in about thirty seconds. Of course, Hood was six inches taller and more than thirty years younger than she was. The trunk and lower branches were covered with moss, which made the footing slippery, and she was a little nervous she might surprise some squirrel that would object to her presence and sink its little squirrel fangs into her hand or arm.

She was climbing this particular tree, a bigleaf maple, because it stood on a slight rise, and if you climbed up seven or eight feet you could actually get a decent cell phone signal. In the past three weeks she had talked to Matt only a handful of times. He'd been impossible to reach, for one thing—always in meetings or, because of the three-hour time difference, asleep or eating a meal. He'd even been gone several evenings, which was strange because he usually hated to go out. When she did reach him, their calls were often interrupted because the wind blew or the rains came and the signal was lost.

She wedged her butt into a V where the main trunk split into two smaller trunks, uncomfortable but secure. She punched in Matt's number, only to have the "searching for service" message appear.

"Shit," she said.

She had an urge to hurl the phone into the forest. She peered down through the fading gold leaves and sighed. She had been here three weeks and she couldn't escape the sense of a giant, looming *something* lurking beneath the surface of their new life here. She just didn't know what it was or when it would strike. The different rhythm was part of her unease. The kids disappeared for hours at a time without checking in with her, something that would have had her calling the police at home, but which was normal on Sounder. There were no pedophiles lurking in the schoolyard, as Jim and Betty pointed out; no drug dealers hiding in the shadows.

"Most people let the kids start to roam on their own when they're four or five," Jim had said. "It's safe. They walk to school, climb trees, navigate through the woods. They get hurt they deal with it. It's great. They learn independence."

But how do I learn independence? In Tilton she did what every mother did and tracked the exact whereabouts of her kids at every moment via phone calls, text messages, and a network of other parents. But here Katie left for school at eight in the morning and didn't return home until dinnertime at seven or later. She didn't carry her cell phone because reception on the island was so spotty. She spent hours with Hood and Baker in the woods and the barn and on the beaches. She was exploring, she said. She was making new friends. This is why Susannah had brought her here, right?

Well, yes and no. On the one hand, Susannah loved living

closer to the natural rhythm of her life—rising with the sun in the morning, working up a sweat chopping wood, falling into the deep sleep that comes from physical exhaustion and fresh air at night. She loved to stand at the kitchen sink in the mornings, gazing out the window at the mist over the meadow. She saw ring-necked pheasants scratching through the tall grass in the field, and heard the sweet, lilting song of winter wrens trilling from the Douglas firs and pines. She marked the coming winter with the fading light, the long shadows of the trees that fell earlier and earlier every day. The food she prepared and ate came mostly from the same ground she walked. It was a completely different life than the one she had known in Tilton, as she had hoped.

But it unsettled her, too. She knew, better than most, the capriciousness of nature and circumstance. The night was vast and black, the water infinite and unyielding. A sudden windstorm, like the one they'd had last week that had felled a two-hundred-foot Doug fir; a sudden ocean swell; a slight miscalculation with a tractor or chain saw—any small thing could turn on them, turn this from a place of refuge and protection to one of isolation and despair. She knew it—and feared it.

"Life was better here before cell phones," a voice beneath her said.

Susannah, lost in her thoughts, was so startled she almost fell out of the tree. She looked down and saw Betty, who stood in the field about ten feet away.

"I saw you walking out here and came out to say hello, but you were up that tree before I could catch up," Betty said. "You're in pretty good shape."

"Thanks," Susannah said. "But you should see Hood climb up here."

"I've seen him," Betty said. "He's quick."

She pulled out her cigarettes and shook one out and lit it.

"I wanted to thank you for bringing over those loaves of bread, and the cookies. And for taking the time to help the boys clear out the barn. Jim showed me all the work you did. That's a big help to us."

"It was nothing. You've been so kind to us," Susannah said.

"Don't let me bother you. Go ahead and make your calls. I'm just going to rest a minute before heading back." Betty sat down on the grass.

"You're not bothering me," Susannah said. She felt faintly stupid sitting in the tree, so she wriggled out of the crevice she'd been sitting in and stood on the thick branch just below her.

"Don't climb down on my account," Betty said. "Stay. You can try your call again in a few minutes."

Susannah took a deep breath, and wrapped one arm around the tree's main trunk. "I'll come down," she said. "I'm not crazy about heights."

"In that case, Barefoot would tell you to stay in that goddamned tree until you got over it," Betty said with a smile.

"He would," Susannah said.

She'd seen Barefoot often since the day of their boat ride. He stopped by Betty's most days—to check on the herb garden, drop off some tonic he'd brewed, or even to chop and cord her wood. Sometimes he'd come over to the white cottage and talk to Quinn, who had taken to life on the island like parched earth to rain. Quinn spent his afternoons roaming the woods and meadows and shorelines after school, sometimes with other kids, often alone, collecting crab shells and rocks and leaves and berries and strips of bark. He spread his collections across the dining table and the floor of the utility room where he slept. He asked Barefoot's help in identifying plants he didn't know, and listened to Barefoot tell stories about the animal life of the island, like the summer twenty years ago when beavers had suddenly appeared in the marsh down by Sitka Bay. They built countless dams and lodges, deepening part of the marsh into a pond that drew snowy white trumpeter swans and small hooded mergansers until nine years later when they disappeared as quickly as they had come.

Susannah looked at the thick branch beneath her feet, and at the ground below her, which was farther away than she'd realized. Now that she thought about it, she didn't remember how Hood had gotten *down* from up here. She lowered herself carefully and sat down, straddling the wide branch as she used to do when she'd climbed trees as a kid.

"Did you reach your husband?" Betty said. She sat on the grass with her knees up, feet flat on the ground. From this distance she looked young, almost girl-like, with her long, lean legs and her graceful neck, wrinkles hidden by a thick turtleneck sweater.

"No," Susannah said. She sighed, and her breath rustled the leaves by her head.

"It's hard having a long-distance marriage," Betty said. "I did it for twelve years." She blew out a long stream of smoke.

"Really?"

"Yup. Sounder is a hard place to make a living. So Bill worked up in Alaska fishing for king crab, and came home summers."

"That must have been tough."

"In some ways. It was hard on Jim, not having his dad around."

From where she sat in the tree, Susannah couldn't see Betty's face.

"And Bill and I—" Betty shook her head. "It was complicated."

Complicated. Maybe that was the word to describe the restless unease that Susannah felt about her own marriage. In the three weeks she'd been here she hadn't really missed Matt, not in the way she expected to, or in the way she thought she should. In many ways this distance between them was a relief. At home she always felt like she *wanted* something from Matt that he wouldn't give her, but if you'd asked her to name what it was she wanted, she wouldn't have been able to say.

She still remembered that time, years ago in Ann Arbor, when he'd come up to visit her at college. They'd gone for a long bike ride and wandered around bookstores and drank ouzo and then, inevitably, ended up in bed. The next morning she was lying there, with the spring rain washing the world in vivid green outside the window, when she had looked at him and thought, "What if I fell in love with Matt Delaney?" The thought startled her so much she had jumped, there in the bed, and woken him up.

She did love him, of course. He was so tied up in all the unspooling years of her life that he was like the golden oak newel post in her mother's house, something you passed by and touched every day but didn't notice. Then, one fall weekend they'd rented a little cottage on Lake Michigan, near their old camp. They were walking on the pebbled beach when a storm came up, the clouds thick and full over the lake. The skies burst and they were pelted with hail, stinging their cheeks and legs and arms as they ran. It was right after that, after they were back in the cabin and sitting by the fire with steaming mugs of coffee, that Matt had said, "Do you ever think about getting married?"

Does he mean do I want to get married ever? *Does he mean married to* him?

"I don't know," she said. "Do you?"

"Only to you," he said, and he turned then to look at her, his eyes on hers. And she had felt something rise in her like the waters of the lake after a storm, swirling and full and warm. So he loved her like that. She was the one. And the fact that he felt that way about her—that it was so clear and direct to him, like the layers of bright angel shale in the canyons he studied—was enough to make her forget any doubts, to want nothing more than to let herself feel that way about him, too.

But here she was eighteen years later and three thousand miles away, plagued with a doubt bigger than she had imagined, or wanted to admit.

"But I'll tell you," Betty said. "Once Bill died I missed him more than I ever thought I could."

Susannah brought her attention back to the present. "Jim told me he died young," she said. "I'm sorry."

"Car accident," Betty said. Her voice was matter-of-fact.

"That's awful. I'm sorry. Here on Sounder?"

"Yes," Betty said. She shrugged. "Accidents happen."

Something in the tone of her voice caught Susannah, tugged at her.

"That's what everyone said when my sister died," Susannah said. " 'Accidents happen.' But it didn't help."

"Right," Betty said. "Because people say, 'Accidents happen,' but what they really *believe* is 'Accidents happen, *but not to me.*' Then when it does happen and it's you—it's hard to know how to live with that. I didn't want anyone's pity, or blame."

"What happened?" Susannah's curiosity overwhelmed her.

"Just one of those things," Betty said. "I tortured myself with a lot of what-ifs for a long time afterward. But you have a choice: you let it eat you up, or you eat it up."

If only it was that easy. Susannah was tempted to tell Betty all about the day with the blue, blue skies and Janie and her orange life jacket. *Maybe she would understand.* Or maybe she'd avoid her, too, as her mother had, as her father had. She couldn't remember that her dad had ever looked at her again—really looked at her—after that day.

"It's funny. I still think about Bill almost every day, even though he's been dead forty-three years."

Susannah looked up at the sun hitting the bright gold leaves above her. "I know. I think about my sister every day. And she was only three; it wasn't like losing someone you've been married to for years and years."

"I don't know," Betty said. "When someone dies you mourn the loss of all that possibility, whether they're three or sixty-three, don't you think?"

"Janie would have turned thirty-six this past summer," Susannah said. Somehow it was easier to talk about, sitting up here in the tree, without having to look at Betty's face. "I keep thinking she'd be married and have kids of her own, and that her kids might have been friends with Katie and Quinn, or might even have looked like them. Janie had brown eyes, too, and wavy brown hair like mine. She was ten years younger, so maybe we wouldn't have been *best* friends, but I bet we would have been close."

Unlike Susannah, Janie was fearless. Why, one time their father, drunk and furious, had made Susannah and Jon stand against the wall while he sat in his big leather chair and screamed at them. Susannah couldn't even remember what they'd done wrong. Out of the blue Janie had toddled over and put her little hand over his mouth and said, 'No yelling! You stop that.' He'd been so surprised that he'd shut right up, and then had started to laugh. Nothing like that had ever happened in their house before. No one—not Jon, not Susannah, not their mother—had ever talked back to their father. But Janie, who was all of two and a half at the time, Janie did.

"I have two sisters," Betty said. "Bobbie, the one who's closest in age to me—she's my best friend. My sister Mel—Mary Ellen—and I never clicked in the same way. You don't know who your sister might have been." She paused for a moment, and then said, "It's hard to know about Bill. He was always restless. Sometimes I think maybe he would have settled down as he got older, maybe been happy to stay here, to have a second chance at being a parent with the grandkids. Who knows?"

"I know what you mean about possibility," Susannah said. Her father's death at fifty-eight had slammed a door forever on things Susannah had longed for—understanding, forgiveness, approval. Poof. Gone. No chance.

"That's what we mourn in every death," Betty said. "Even if it's just the possibility of seeing someone one last time. Anyway, enough philosophizing." She leaned forward to peer up at Susannah. "Can you get down?"

"I think so."

"Well, good, because I'm not sure I can get up. My hip's been bothering me, which I should have thought of before I sat down on the cold ground and let it stiffen up."

Susannah turned, hugged the trunk of the tree, and managed to slide and scramble her way down. She helped Betty up and they began to walk back toward the cottage. Betty looked at her out of the corner of her eye. "You're a worrier, aren't you? Like Jim."

"Like Jim?" Susannah was surprised. Jim seemed so easygoing.

Betty shook her head. "God, yes. Why do you think I decided to raise him here? He thinks too much."

Susannah stuffed her hands in the pockets of her coat against the cold. "It's hard not to worry about teenagers," she said.

"But worrying doesn't change it," Betty said. "That's what I tell Jim every time he's pacing the floor about Hood."

Susannah looked at her. Little alarm bells were already starting to sound off in her brain. *Hood? The boy my daughter spends every waking minute with?*

"Why? What has Hood done?"

Betty looked at her. "Oh, calm down. He's not a *bad* kid. You don't have to worry about Katie. He would never do something like you told us about, like that boy she was involved with at home."

"I'm not saying he would. But of course I'm curious."

"Typical dumb kid stuff. The motorcycle—he saw some video online of motorcycle jumpers and set up a course of his own on Gravel Pit Road. Broke his arm and wrecked the motorcycle. That was last year, when he was thirteen. Another time he convinced Baker to race him in the golf carts and they went up to Crane's Point and almost went over the cliff. Daredevily, boy kinds of things. Or this summer—"

Betty stopped walking. "People view things differently here," she said. "So you have to understand this in the context of this place and the kind of people who live here."

Susannah nodded. She stopped, too, and listened, her eyes on Betty.

"Hood was very good friends with Mary Lou and Ralph Flanagan, who lived up on East Road. Ralph was a navy pilot in World War Two and used to tell Hood all kinds of stories. He got sick last year with cancer and was in a lot of pain. Hood visited him every week for almost six months. After he died, Mary Lou wrote Jim and Fiona a note thanking them for all Hood had done. They thought she meant the visits." Betty paused.

"What's wrong with that?"

"Then Mary Lou stopped by the Laundromat one day and ran into Fiona. She told her Ralph wouldn't have lasted as long as he did without Hood's 'medicine.'"

"Medicine?"

Betty looked at Susannah. "Marijuana. Hood was growing a couple of plants under lights in the barn and taking it over to Ralph to help with the pain."

Susannah tried to still an instant sense of panic over the fact that Katie's new best friend knew how to grow and cultivate pot. Susannah herself had never smoked pot. As the child of an alcoholic, she had no interest in doing anything with the potential to twist her mind and personality the way alcohol had twisted her father. The loss of control implicit in anything more mind altering than a single glass of wine terrified her. Zach's casual fondness for drugs and drink had scared Susannah almost as much as his disgusting bet on Katie's virginity.

Betty sighed. "Sounder has a long and complicated history with marijuana. For the most part, people have a live-and-let-live approach. But four or five years ago a couple moved here and bought a few dozen acres of land deep in the middle of the island. We all knew they were raising crops; we just had no idea *what*. Someone tipped off the sheriff, I guess, because the DEA raided the island one morning. It was crazy."

"Seriously? The DEA raided Sounder?" Susannah couldn't imagine poky, remote little Sounder being invaded by an army of government agents.

"Twenty-four DEA agents and police officers, with rifles and flak jackets and camouflage," Betty said, confirming Susannah's impossible vision. "They swarmed all over the island. They found six hundred marijuana plants on Bob and Alison's farm. They even put Barefoot in handcuffs for three hours because they found two marijuana plants in his greenhouse."

Barefoot —Quinn's new best friend—grows pot, too?

"The DEA agents scouted the island for a week before the raid. Agents with assault weapons roaming the woods where my grandkids were playing. It's the only time I've been afraid here—afterward, when I thought about what could have happened with all those men and guns and the boys right there."

Betty pushed a wiry strand of hair behind her ear with her hand. "Barefoot grows a small amount of pot for medicinal purposes only," she said. "Normally *he'd* have taken care of Ralph. But Ralph hated Barefoot—they had a bitter fight forty years ago about Kent State—so he wouldn't go to Barefoot for help when he got sick. I think that's why Hood stepped in. He researched varieties of medical marijuana, and grew it out in the barn, where we grow hydroponic lettuce. Jim and I didn't even notice; the boys tend to those lettuces, and neither one of us gives them a second glance. We're guessing he got the seeds from Barefoot's greenhouse.

"Listen," Betty continued. "I know how scary the situation with Katie was for you, with that boy at home and the drinking. But this is different; you understand that?"

"I understand," Susannah said. "Although I'm glad you told me." She felt again the giant, looming iceberg in her chest—the danger underneath the surface of things. "I trust you and Jim, and Hood."

Only later did she realize what she *hadn't* said: *I trust Katie.*

Chapter 13

Betty 1956

The baby was born in Ballard General. Betty named him James Llewellyn because she liked the name James and didn't mind the accompanying nicknames, and because Richard Llewellyn was her favorite author.

She refused all anesthesia and pain medication. If she was finally going to give birth to a live baby, then by God she was going to experience every moment of it. And after all those months in bed feeling like someone half dead, someone who moved and breathed but didn't *feel* anything, giving birth was like an open-handed slap across the face, bringing her back suddenly to the world of feeling and loving and hating and caring. With each contraction she screamed out all her anger at Bill, pounded her fists in fury at her own naïveté, cried for all she'd lost.

The baby was born after ten hours of hard labor. Betty looked at his scrunched-up little man face, his tiny fists, and felt a wave of euphoria and fierceness like nothing she'd ever experienced before. *To hell with Bill*, she thought. *I don't know how to be married.* She picked up the baby and held him close. *But this I can do.*

Bill arrived two days later. Bobbie had already told the nurses that he wasn't to be allowed in to see Betty or the baby.

"He looks terrible," Bobbie told her. "He's thin, and he hasn't had a haircut, for God's sake."

"I used to cut his hair," Betty said. "And he probably came straight from the farm when your telegram arrived. We should let him see the baby. It's his son."

"He should have thought of that before he started chasing every skirt that walked by." Bobbie held up a big box wrapped in blue paper. "I told him he couldn't come in, but he did bring a present for the baby."

Betty tore off the wrapping and opened the box and found a baseball glove, a scorecard, and a pen. Bill had scrawled one word across the scorecard, *PLEASE.* Betty remembered that day at the baseball game when he'd told her she was a hell of a woman and kissed her and torn her scorecard into little pieces. She thought about the week after she'd lost the twins when he'd slept on the floor next to her bed in the hospital. She thought about her early mornings on Sounder, lying in bed next to him and feeling content. She thought about Annette Fahlstrom, and the woman in the yellow dress.

"I want to see Bill," she told Bobbie. "I want to show him the baby."

Bobbie shook her head and started to say something, but Betty put out a hand and gripped Bobbie's arm. "It's okay," she said. "I know what I'm doing. It's not going to happen again."

Bobbie looked at her. "You're crazier than Mel. Of course it's going to happen again. He's a cheater, Bets."

But I'm not going to care again, Betty thought.

She didn't put on lipstick or fuss with her hair before he

visited. When he walked into her hospital room she felt a stab not of longing but of familiarity, the same sense she'd had as a child every time she walked through the front door of her family's house on Queen Anne Hill. He was thinner than when she'd seen him in November, but tanned and lean. He wore a blue chambray work shirt and khakis and had combed back his dark hair with water so it lay flat, but it was so long that it curled under from behind his ears. Betty didn't want to look at him too long.

"I named him James," she said, pulling back the blue blanket so Bill could see the baby's face. "But we'll probably call him Jimmy."

Bill didn't speak for a few minutes. She felt his eyes on her for a long time but wouldn't look up at him. When he saw that she wasn't going to make eye contact, he stepped closer to the bed and peered at the baby in her arms.

"My God, Betty." Bill's voice was full of wonder, then concern. "He's so small. Is that normal?"

Betty smiled. "Yes. He weighed eight and a half pounds when he was born. Bigger than normal."

"And he's all right? He's going to be okay?"

Losing the twins had scarred Bill, too. Betty laid the baby in her lap, his tiny head against her knees, and unwrapped the blanket around him so Bill could see his sturdy legs and arms, his perfect fingers and toes. "Yes, this little guy is fine."

Bill studied his son. "His eyes are gray."

"They'll change. They could be brown, like mine, or green."

"Do you think he looks like me?"

I hope not, Betty thought, *because it will break my heart every day.* "I don't know. I think it's too soon to tell. Bobbie says that Macy, her daughter, looked exactly like Dick for six months, and then started to look like her."

Bill raised his eyes to hers. "Betty—"

She lifted her hand. "Shhh. Don't say it. There's really nothing you can say that changes what is." She wrapped the baby up again and stroked his head, and he started to nod off, there in her lap.

"But this, but having the baby, it changes everything," Bill said.

Betty looked at him. "Honey, I wish that was true, but I know it isn't."

Bill had a weakness for other women; she understood it and understood it was never going to change. And she had a weakness for Bill; that was probably never going to change, either. It was something they shared, these weaknesses of theirs. But she had this baby now and needed to do what she could to raise him well.

"I've been thinking a lot," Betty said. "I don't want to have to go to work and leave the baby all day. Bobbie says she'll take care of him, but she and Dick already have Macy to look after, and they want another child, and that's not fair." She was dying for a cigarette, but the nurse had taken hers away. "Do you have a smoke?"

Bill took a pack out of the front pocket of his shirt and shook one out for her and lit it. She took a deep drag, and it calmed her.

"I can't get a job that's going to pay me enough to have my own apartment," she continued, "and pay for the things the baby and I will need."

"Jesus Christ! You think I'm not going to help take care of my son?"

"Calm down. I'm not insulting you. I'm being realistic. We own a farm that is not even breaking even, am I right?"

"Not yet, but—"

"All right."

"But I was thinking I'd move back to Seattle," Bill said. "Sell the farm and see if I could go back to work for Boeing."

"No one is going to buy that farm, and we've got all our money tied up in it. And what makes you think you're going to be any happier working for Boeing now than you were a year ago? What makes you think you can get your job back, for that matter?"

Bill was silent.

Betty took another drag from her cigarette and turned her head to the side to blow out the smoke, away from the baby. "I've got an idea," she said.

What if their marriage were simply a business arrangement? Betty would return to Sounder with the baby. And since the farm was not making any money and was unlikely ever to make any money, Bill could leave to work in Alaska or wherever the hell he wanted to go, and send money back. They would sell off as many acres as they could, so Betty could manage the farm while he was away with the help of one hired man. She could grow enough to supply herself and Jimmy with food for most of the year, and see if they could at least break even through selling eggs and the goat's milk. The money Bill made would get them out of debt and give them enough of an income to afford to buy things for Jimmy, or save for him to go to college someday. Bill could tomcat all he wanted while he was away; when he was home he was to avoid other women so as not to embarrass Betty or their son.

"You'll get to be with Jimmy when you're home on Sounder, and be part of his life."

Bill rubbed his hands through his hair. "You're crazy. I don't want that. It's true I may have to leave the island to work; I can't make enough money with the farm, and I don't see how that's going to change. You know the Fahlstroms sold their farm and moved to Oregon. Corky's working as a carpenter now. And the Burnses moved to Seattle; Joe's teaching school. Sounder is a hard place to make a living."

"I know," Betty said. "But it's a good place to raise a child. So go make your living where you can."

Bill shook his head. "I don't want to be off for months at a time and leave you and the baby—"

"Other families on Sounder do it," Betty said. "Paul Duning works on the fishing boats up in Alaska. Don MacKenzie works for that steamship company. His wife told me he was gone ten months one year."

Bill sat down on the chair next to her bed. "We are in debt," he said. "If I can't sell the farm I have to figure out some other way to make money."

"This is the way," Betty said.

A long silence filled the room. Finally Bill looked down at the beige tiled floor and said in a low voice, "I've learned my lesson. I am sorrier than you'll ever know. I'm not going to have other women."

"Maybe not," Betty said. "But I don't want to pretend or hope that you won't."

Bill flinched. He sat for a long time, quiet, gazing out the window. Finally he turned to her. "But that's not a normal marriage."

"It doesn't have to be normal," Betty said. "It just has to look normal, for Jimmy."

Bill leaned forward in the chair, with his arms resting on his knees and his hat in his hands. He turned his hat over and over, studying it as though the answers to all his past and future lay hidden inside it somewhere.

"I'd like to have you and the baby come home to Sounder," he said at last. "It's more than I expected."

"It's more than you deserve," Betty said. She had to steel

herself not to reach out and push back the lock of hair that fell across his forehead as he leaned forward there, not to put her hand on his arm. "But it will be good for Jimmy, and for me. Sounder's an easier place for me to live."

He looked up at her. "You are a hell of a woman, Betty," he said. "I wish—"

"Don't," Betty said. The baby stirred in her lap and she bent to him, grateful for the distraction.

"That's all," she said. "So we're agreed. You'll find work as quickly as you can, and I'll move out to Sounder at the end of the summer with the baby."

Bill stood up. "Okay. If that's what you want."

Betty kept her eyes on the child in her lap. "It's what I want," she said. "And one more thing: The doctor said I shouldn't get pregnant again. I was lucky to have Jimmy, but he thinks it's too risky for me to have another child. Since our marriage is now a business arrangement, I want to be sure you understand what is and is not included in that arrangement."

Bill stood for a long time next to the bed, gazing at her. "I understand," he said finally, and turned around and left.

Betty moved back to Sounder in September. Bobbie, who had spent the summer trying to argue her out of it, refused even to drive her downtown to catch the bus to Anacortes.

"I love you, Betty," she said. "And I love that baby of yours. And I won't lift a single finger to help you get back to that man."

Betty had looked at her with full eyes and nodded. She couldn't explain why she was doing what she was doing; she just knew in her gut that Sounder was the right place to raise her son and a good place for her to be. She knew, too, that she'd never be able to get Bill out of her blood and that this arrangement of theirs was something she had to try. Maybe she'd divorce him someday. But not yet.

Bill left in October for a job on a fishing boat in Alaska that would take him away through March. The money was good—more than they'd imagined. If he could make a similar amount every winter they'd be able to get out of debt within three years. Nick Condon, the man they hired to work the farm, was thorough and tireless. Most importantly, friends she'd only begun to get to know during her first year on Sounder turned immediately into family when she returned with the baby and a clear commitment to stay. Claire MacKenzie, Don's wife, had two toddlers and a husband who was gone nine months a year. To Betty's surprise, Claire became the kind of close girlfriend she'd never had, a surrogate sister who helped her through Jim's first ear infections and croup and confided in her about her own marital troubles. Her openness and lively curiosity emboldened Betty to talk, hesitantly at first, about the babies she'd lost, and Bill.

Ellen and George MacPherson, who lived on the next farm over, were always ready to help with farming questions or even hands-on labor. Lem Jacobsen, a young botanist who lived on Sounder when he wasn't traveling the world, took a shine to Jimmy during a party at the MacPhersons, and then came over the next weekend and built a raised bed outside Betty's kitchen door and planted a small garden of medicinal herbs—comfrey for healing cuts and scrapes, lobelia for cough, chamomile for toothaches and earaches.

She took the baby home to Seattle that first Christmas. Bobbie and Dick and Macy and Mother and Grammy and Mel were all there. Even Bobbie had to admit that Betty and Jim were thriving. Betty was strong from the physical work of the farm and life on Sounder. Pregnancy and breast-feeding had rounded her hips and filled out her breasts and face, so she wasn't all cheekbones and hip bones and elbows as she'd been before. Jim was the fattest little baby anyone had ever seen, even though he was still getting almost nothing but breast milk. Betty loved to grip one of his plump thighs with her hands and shake it, reveling in his sturdiness.

Her connection to the baby was so all-encompassing that she didn't even miss Bill, not at first. She was busy from the time Jim's first cry woke her in the morning until she lowered her grateful body into the bed at night. Jim slept next to her in the double bed—after all, who could afford to buy a crib on the mainland, carry it by bus and ferry and haul it up the long ramp on the dock, and truck it home? Claire's oldest boy had slept in a dresser drawer for his first year, she told Betty, but the younger one had fussed so much she'd brought him in bed with her, and there he'd stayed for ten months, until Don came home and built a small bed for him with a rail on one side.

After six months, though, Betty began to miss Bill. She missed having someone to talk to in the dark, lying in bed late at night. She missed his strong back and arms when she carried heavy loads of wood from the shed to the porch, or bent to plant row after row of early lettuces (God knows he was a cad but never one to shirk hard physical work). She missed the way he'd clamp one hand on her thigh when they drove somewhere in the truck. She missed the way he'd throw back his head and laugh at her tart retort to something he'd said.

When he returned home, at the end of March, she sent Nick to pick him up at the dock. She dressed in the same dungarees and warm flannel shirt she wore most days, and brushed back her hair, which had grown long and curly, into a ponytail. She put on bright red lipstick, but then she did that even to go to the post office, just for the hell of it, just because it was something she loved to do, even though few women on Sounder bothered with makeup.

When she heard the scrape of the tires on the gravel road her heart began to beat faster. But she steeled herself not to go to the door to greet him, busied her trembling hands with scrubbing the grit off the cast-iron skillet in the kitchen sink. Jim was asleep on a pile of blankets on the floor in the living room, where she could see him. She'd made up the twin bed in the back room for Bill.

She heard the front door open and close behind her. She straightened up and waited, still facing the window above the sink, her hands in the dishwater. She turned her head to the side, so he could hear her.

"The baby's sleeping there, on the floor in the corner, if you want to see him."

She bent again to the skillet. She heard his footsteps as he crossed the room behind her, the creak of the old floorboards as he bent down next to Jimmy. Then she heard the floor creak again as he stood, his footsteps as he came up to her and stood behind her without touching her. She paused in her work and stood still, one hand holding the skillet and the other holding the dishrag. He leaned forward, so his lips were next to her ear.

"He's incredible, Betty," he said, his voice low. He paused. "And so are you."

She could feel the warmth of his body behind her even though he wasn't touching her, could feel his breath warm against her ear. She wanted his lips on her neck, his arms around her, his hips pressed into her.

"Oh, hell," she said, dropping the dishrag in the sink. She let go of the skillet, too, and turned around to face him. She put a damp hand on either side of his head and pulled him toward her and kissed him. He kissed her back urgently, parted her lips with his tongue, and grabbed her hips with both hands to pull her to him. They made love until the baby woke up an hour later, and then all night long after he went to sleep that night.

Chapter 14

Susannah 2011

"I have a favor to ask of you," Jim said.

Susannah looked up from the pizza dough she was kneading. Jim opened the back door of the white cottage. He wore his teacher clothes—a shirt and tie under a warm sweater, a waterproof parka, and thick corduroys with the right pant leg tucked inside his sock. His commute involved a trek on a mountain bike through the woods, which explained the pant leg. He held his backpack in one hand.

"Sure," Susannah said.

"Next week is Pizza and Poetry Day. I've mentioned it before, right?" He pulled a thick book out of the backpack and placed it on the counter.

Susannah nodded.

"Great. I want to have some posters this year—portraits of famous poets, with a few lines from their best-known poems. I heard about your artistic ability, and I wanted to see if you'd consider doing the posters for me."

Susannah wiped her floury hands on her apron and looked at him with surprise. "I'm a window designer."

"I know. But I heard you're also a terrific artist."

Susannah shrugged. "I used to paint quite a bit." She thought again about the brilliant colors of the landscapes she'd painted during those heady early years of her marriage. She thought about the mural she had painted on the walls of Katie's room when she was a baby, filled with cartwheeling flowers, dancing trees, swirling waters, and a flamboyant sun. She had painted tiny faces in the flowers, friendly animals in the curling leaves.

"It's been years since I painted," she said. "Once Katie was born I never seemed to have the time, and then when Quinn came along . . ." Her voice trailed off. "Anyway, Quinn shouldn't have told you—"

"It wasn't Quinn," Jim said. "It was Katie."

"Katie?"

"She was quite complimentary, too. Said you painted her room when she was a baby, and that you used to illustrate stories for her when she was little, about a family of fairies."

"I did," Susannah said. "I haven't thought of those in years."

"Would you mind trying your hand at the posters? Just some simple pen-and-ink drawings. Give it an hour or two, and if it's too much work, forget it."

"I'll try. It's been a long time."

"That's okay." Jim nodded toward the book. "Surprise me. Draw a few poets—you can choose any poet in the book. I marked some favorites with sticky notes, but it's up to you." He reached into his backpack and pulled out a paper bag. "I brought you some art supplies from school, too."

She smiled. "All right, I'll give it a try."

"Thanks. Could you do it by Monday?"

"Sure." It was the first time in years she'd agreed to something without consulting her calendar first, she realized. Come to think of it, she didn't even *have* a calendar here.

"Great." He slung his backpack over his shoulder. "So I'm

getting to know your Katie better and better. She's an interesting kid. Terrific writer."

"Really? You think so?"

"Yes. Did she show you the essay she wrote last week, on Steinbeck's *Travels with Charley*? It was incredible."

"No. She didn't even tell me about it."

"I figured. Kids don't like to be known at this age, at least not by their parents. Ask her to show it to you sometime."

"I will. Thanks for letting me know about it."

He paused, one hand on the counter. "There's one more thing. Generally, I keep what I hear at school to myself. If the kids trust me enough to talk to me, I don't want to betray that trust."

Susannah's heart thumped, a frantic rabbit leap in her chest.

"Don't look like that," Jim said. "It's not something terrible. You told me about some of the problems she had at home, like writing that newspaper story about that girl."

Susannah sighed. "Yes."

"The girl she wrote about? She sounds like a mean kid. Katie said she asked out some shy boy, seduced him into kissing her, and had a friend secretly videotape the whole thing. Then she posted the video online and turned it into a big joke. The boy was devastated; Katie says he left school."

"You're kidding." Katie had refused to discuss the whole newspaper episode.

"That same girl bullied other kids, according to Quinn," Jim said. "I asked him about it. Katie's newspaper story seems like just retribution to me. Seems she can't stand it when something is not fair."

Like Matt. Susannah suddenly had a vision of plump, moon-faced, ten-year-old Davey Godwin, with his black-rimmed glasses and striped T-shirts. Matt—lean and competitive and the best athlete at camp—had always picked Davey first for every team he captained—kickball, baseball, Capture the Flag. He would coach Davey on the fine points of running the bases, or fixing his swing so he didn't hit so many pop-ups. Davey idolized him. "Why do you always pick him first?" Susannah had asked. After all, Matt could have waited and picked him second or third or next-to-last. "It's not fair," Matt had said with a shrug. "Everyone deserves to be first sometimes."

"I had no idea," Susannah said. "She never told us."

Jim shrugged. "She was pretty fierce about protecting Quinn the first few days of school, too. He was nervous, worried about the germ thing and fitting in."

"She's pretty mean to him at home."

"As I said, she lets you see what she wants you to see."

Susannah absorbed all this. "Thank you for telling me," she said. "Matt will be happy to hear this."

"How is Matt?"

"Oh, fine. Busy." To be honest, Susannah wasn't sure how Matt was doing. He was still hard to reach on the phone, and when they did talk he sounded tired, or annoyed. Lately she had the sense that everything she said irritated Matt, but she didn't know why, or what to do about it. When she'd ask him if anything was wrong, he'd say, "I don't know what you're talking about," and then there would be a long, uncomfortable silence.

"Good. I've gotta run," Jim said. "The posters by Monday is okay?"

"Yes, Monday," she said, getting back to her pizza dough. And for some reason, when the door closed behind him, she felt lonelier on Sounder than she ever had before.

On Monday Susannah stopped by the school with her posters. She'd spent several days working on them, reading poem after poem in the books Jim had given her, doing sketches, experimenting with moving her sketchpad around to take advantage of the natural light. It had been years since she'd attempted anything artistic, and she was plagued with doubt. At last, after crumpling up drawing after drawing and stuffing them in the woodstove, she'd decided to try something different.

School was over when Susannah arrived. As was usual now, she had little idea where her kids were. Katie was probably with Hood and Baker somewhere; the three of them were inseparable. Quinn was likely headed over to Barefoot's house. Barefoot was teaching him how to identify and catalog plants, an endeavor Quinn loved. And if he wasn't with Barefoot, he was with Evelyne Waters, his new best friend. Ten-year-old Evelyne lived on the other side of the island, where her parents farmed lavender. They sold lavender jelly and lavender sachets and lavender-scented soaps. Susannah wondered if the sweet, soothing scent of lavender that clung to Evelyne—to her hair and clothes and even her skin—was part of her appeal. She was Quinn's personal aromatherapy.

Susannah saw Jim perched on a wooden ladder by the big windows along the west side of the building, with a rag in one hand and a spray bottle in the other. "Hey," she said. "You're the window washer, too?"

Jim put the rag down on the top step and climbed down. "Yes, that would be me. You did the posters? I can't wait to see them."

Susannah felt shy. "I'm not much of a portraitist," she said. "Is that the right word? I'm good at landscapes and still lifes, but people aren't my area of expertise. So they're not exactly *portraits* of the poets."

"I bet you underestimate yourself." He gazed at her with those green eyes—a look that went right through her, as though he saw all the self-doubt that had gone into her work. "Come inside," he said. "We'll spread them out on the table and take a look."

He slipped off his shoes, sturdy clogs with rubber soles, and stepped into the white frame building. She did the same. No one wore shoes inside the school, to protect the old pine floors. It added to the quiet, too; so different from the noisy classrooms at home. She took the rubber band off the roll of posters and spread them out on the big oak table, sliding books over to weigh down the corners and keep them from curling up.

They were colorful; she had to give herself credit for that. Frustrated by her attempts to draw realistic portraits, she'd resorted instead to collage, illustrating one image from a single poem for each poet, using scraps of newsprint, paint and pencil, bits of fabric and feather. She had chosen Robert Frost's "Design," and made a "dimpled spider, fat and white" out of tufts of sheep's wool and bits of twine, sitting on a bright blue flower against a pale pink-orange sky. On another poster she'd created a purple raisin out of scraps of fabric, baking under the brilliant rays of a shiny sun made from gold foil, to illustrate Langston Hughes's "Dream Deferred."

Jim leaned over the posters and then looked up at her in surprise.

"This is not what I expected."

"I know. You wanted something more traditional—drawings. I thought—"

"Oh, no. These are perfect. I love them. They're just kind of"—he gave her a speculative look—"I don't know, *bold*, surprising. As I said, not what I expected."

"Should I be flattered or insulted?"

"Flattered, Susannah. Bold is good. Unexpected is good." He pointed to the third one. "What's this?"

"Oh, God, I know." Susannah laughed. "It's a slug. I thought the kids would like it. I picked poems by the poets you suggested, but I wanted to throw something different into the mix. That's for Sam Green's poem 'Scripsit.' Do you know it?" She fumbled with the messenger bag and found the sheets on which she'd written out the poem. "It's about a slug whose trail makes a perfect cursive *o*."

"Believe it or not, I know that poem. Sam Green is a favorite of mine." He sat on the edge of the desk opposite her and cocked his head to one side. "You're altogether way too intriguing for a runaway suburban mom."

When had Matt last found her intriguing? Or bold, or unexpected? Her parched self looked at Jim Pavalak and wanted to gulp down his vision of her in a long, refreshing swallow.

"Don't be insulted," Jim said. "I'm teasing about the runaway suburban mom stuff. You're a good artist. I had no idea. These will be great."

"Thank you."

She felt warm and happy and attractive—yes, attractive!—and guilty, all at once.

Her attraction to Matt had been such an elemental part of her life for so long that she was shocked to feel herself even a little bit attracted to Jim. From the time she was fifteen, Matt had elicited something raw and hungry in her. She remembered one summer after college when she was living in Seattle and hadn't seen Matt in more than a year. He'd surprised her and walked into the store where she was working, and when she looked up from the counter and saw his blue, blue eyes, his lopsided smile with the dimple in the right cheek, and the way his faded jeans settled on his firm hips, she had been ready to strip down and take him right there, in the middle of Nordstrom's.

But over these past few years, with the kids' crazy schedules and the fights about Katie, their sex life had slowed. Often at home she'd be making the bed or driving to pick up the kids and suddenly remember a moment of intimacy—she and Matt tangled together, her body warm and throbbing. Her skin would tingle and she'd anticipate the coming evening, envision turning to Matt in the dark, exploring him with her hands and lips. But Quinn would need help with a science project, and the cat would throw up on the good rug, and Katie would announce she needed to cram for a math exam, and Susannah wouldn't have time to look at Matt, let alone seduce him. God, there were moments, though, when she longed for some good head-banging-against-the-headboard sex—raw and uncomplicated by resentment over who forgot to load the dishwasher.

But of course that longing had nothing to do with Jim.

"My mom wants to come for Thanksgiving," Susannah said to Matt. She cradled the phone between her ear and shoulder while rooting through the cupboards for flour.

"That's fine," Matt said. "Is there somewhere for her to sleep?"

"She can sleep at Betty's. All the beds here will be full." She found the flour and set it down on the counter. "It's just—it's the first time you and I and the kids will be all together again. It might be nice to be alone, just the four of us."

"So do you *not* want your mother to come?"

"I can't exactly say no, can I? Jon is going to Texas to be with Ann's family. Mom hasn't seen the kids since March. I'd feel too guilty if I said no."

Matt sighed. "Is there anything you *don't* feel guilty about?"

"I just find it hard to be around her." Susannah started to measure out the flour and sugar for the applesauce cake she was making to bring to Pizza and Poetry Day.

"It's just four or five days, Sooz."

"I know. But she sets my teeth on edge."

"Come on. She's not that bad. She's had a hard life."

"I can't help it." Susannah cracked an egg on the edge of the bowl. "Every time she's around I look at her, and I look at our kids, and I think, *How could you?*"

How could anyone send her children out on a boat with a

man who got drunk every day? Mixed with her rage at herself, at the cruel way fate had played out that day, was rage that her mother had set it all in motion with her quiet acquiescence. To this day Susannah had never confronted her mother, never said, "Why did you let him take us out on the boat?" Her mother had lost a child; it was punishment enough.

"Susannah." Matt's voice cut through her thoughts. "Have your mom for Thanksgiving. It'll be fine."

She tried to picture her mother—with her well-coiffed hair, her ironed blouses and creased slacks and cashmere cardigans, her matching necklaces and earrings—stepping along the muddy path in front of the white cottage, stuffing splintery logs into the woodstove, wearing the same clothes day after day. But Quinn would be thrilled to have her; Matt and Betty and Jim would be here as buffers.

"Okay," Susannah said into the phone. "Okay. I'll invite my mother."

"All right," Matt said. "I've got to go."

"But we've only been talking a few minutes. I miss you, Mattie."

"Okay. I still have to go."

"Is something wrong?"

"What do you mean?"

"We just don't talk much. I mean, it's been hard to reach you on the phone, and when we do talk you always seem kind of distant. What's going on?"

"I don't know what you're talking about," Matt said.

"I do miss you," Susannah said.

"Well, maybe you should have thought of that before you moved three thousand miles away."

His statement hung in the air between them.

Susannah stopped stirring the batter. "I thought we agreed this was what was best for the kids, for our family."

"*You* agreed, Susannah. To be honest, I can't believe you're out there with our kids, who are *my* kids, too, and I'm here alone grinding out the paychecks so you can live out your little escape fantasy."

She was caught off guard by the anger in his voice. "We should talk about this, then. I want—"

"Forget it. It is what it is, and you're out there now, and we'll make the best of it. At least, I hope we'll make the best of it. But don't expect me to like it. I've got to go."

"You *hope* we'll make the best of it? What's that supposed to mean?"

"Look at what happened before our wedding."

"Matt! That was nothing like this."

They were married the year they both turned twenty-nine. Susannah moved to Chicago to move in with Matt two months before the wedding. With all the years of knowing each other, they had never lived together before, day in and day out. Susannah was more scared than she could admit. Her father was on his third wife; her mother had retreated into a shell of civility and distance; and she herself felt a yearning for love and attention that felt almost bottomless, that threatened to devour her.

One morning, with another long, empty day ahead of her, and Matt off at school, she panicked. Matt was so steady, so sure—but who was she? She'd given up her job to move to Chicago and didn't know if she'd be able to find another one. Her parents' marriage had been rocky at best, until Janie's death had crushed it. She didn't know how to be a good wife or mother, and Matt wanted kids. What if she failed him, failed their unborn children? She left the apartment, went to the bus station, and took a bus north to Ann Arbor, where she'd gone to college. She spent a week in a little bed-and-breakfast, wandering in and out of bookstores and reading—all the survivor stories she relished about people who'd survived wars and plane crashes and famines and drug addiction and kidnappings and shipwrecks, things far more devastating than what she had endured. She left a cliché-filled note for Matt about needing some time and space, but what she really needed was the conviction that she was really and truly worthy of him. She didn't find it in Ann Arbor, but she married him anyway.

"Mattie," she said. "That was different."

"You ran away," he said. "It sure feels the same." And with a click, he hung up.

The next morning Hood and Baker stopped by to get the kids on the way to school. Hood was wearing a green T-shirt that read "I'm Going to Thoreau Up."

"Lovely," Susannah said.

Hood grinned at her and winked. "Thoreau *was* a poet."

That afternoon the fresh applesauce cake she'd made was warm in her hands on the walk to school. Gold and red leaves from the bigleaf maples carpeted the ground, and a few late apples, pitted with holes by the woodpeckers, still hung in the top branches of the trees. The apples had been so plentiful this year that Susannah had looked up as many recipes as she could find, and made apple butter, apple ketchup, apple pie, apple crisp, and *tons* of applesauce. Her cake would not be the only apple-related treat at the party today.

Susannah slipped off her shoes and walked to the food table to lay down her cake. All the chairs were pulled into a circle for the event, and desks and tables, now laden with pizza, salads, cupcakes, and other homemade dishes, were pushed against a back wall. The six posters Susannah had made hung across the blackboard at the front of the room.

With fifteen students, their parents, and Jim, there were more people than chairs, so Susannah stood in the back next to Betty. She scanned the room. She knew everyone by now and even had most of the names straight. She saw Evelyne Waters with her parents. Quinn sat next to Declan O'Meara, the youngest of the O'Meara clan of five children. Barefoot stood in a corner, head covered in a blue bandanna, and an unlit pipe clenched between his teeth. Susannah wondered if he used it to smoke anything other than tobacco. An excited buzz spread around the room as Jim stood at the front of the room to welcome everyone.

"Thanks for being here," he said. "This is my first Pizza and Poetry Day as a Sounder *teacher*, and I'm excited. I want to acknowledge, too, our other first-timers, the Delaney family—Katie and Quinn—who have been a wonderful addition to our classroom, and their talented mother, Susannah, who created the posters you see up here." Jim smiled at her. He went on to thank the other parents who had helped out.

"As we all know, there's no such thing as a bad poem on Pizza and Poetry Day," Jim said. "We laud all efforts, and we all appreciate the difficulty of writing a good poem." He introduced Declan, who stood to applause and read his poem quickly, finishing with a bow. Jim continued around the circle. When it was Quinn's turn, Susannah was thrilled at the way he stood and spoke out, the corners of his blue eyes turned up in a smile, heartened by the laughs of the crowd at the funny bits in his poem. After Quinn came Evelyne, then Katie.

Susannah leaned forward to hear. Katie had pulled her long brown hair out of its usual ponytail, and she shook her head a little, so it covered the sides of her face.

"The title is 'Captain Blue,'" she said. She continued:

> *"Ah, happy, happy bud! That may provide*
> *Forgetfulness, and ease, an end to pain.*
> *On whose sweet wisps of smoke doth freely ride*
> *Serenity, peace, joy, a dream long lain*

Fallow, now ripe and happily brought forth
To stand grinning in that most happy land
Of warmth and pleasures yet to be enjoyed
Wherein each breath evokes long gusts of mirth
And appetite so strong that none can stand
To resist. Ah! Happy bud! How we toyed!"

She sat down, her face flushed.

Susannah leaned over to Betty. "Is it just me? I have no idea what that was about."

Betty's eyes met hers. "I may be almost eighty," she said, "but I believe your irrepressible daughter has just recited a well-researched ode to marijuana."

Chapter 15

Betty 1961

Betty's life with Bill went on like that, year after year. Bill left in early fall to work the king crab fishing season in Alaska, and returned six or seven or ten months later. In the summer he came home and helped with the farm, and spent as much time as he could with Jimmy.

Betty never asked about other women, and Bill never volunteered any information. But she knew. She knew in the way he'd mention a movie he'd seen, or a new restaurant in Seattle. "When were you in Seattle?" she'd ask, and he'd say he had spent a few days there at the beginning or end of crab season, but wouldn't look her in the eye when he talked about it. She knew by the trinkets she'd find in his pockets or on the dresser—a silver cigarette lighter, a Hawaiian puka shell necklace. She knew even in the way he touched her, differently sometimes than the last time he'd been home.

But this was what she'd signed up for, the arrangement *she'd* proposed. Bill honored their agreement by not seeing other women when he was on Sounder; she trusted him there. He loved her, in his own way. He loved their son. He wrote Jimmy almost every week from Alaska, starting the year Jimmy turned three. When he was home in the summer, he taught Jim how to play poker, how to mooch for salmon, how to skip a stone across the smooth surface of Jake's Lake.

Of course she had dark nights of the soul, nights when she'd wander the cottage after Jimmy was asleep, filled with a longing she couldn't name. It wasn't just sexual desire, although she had plenty of that, nor was it plain old loneliness, which she also had plenty of. It was a yearning to be yearned for, and it was unquenchable.

At least it was unquenchable as long as she stayed married to Bill.

Jim was a handful. At eighteen months he figured out how to open the back door by putting both hands on top of the cast-iron thumb latch and pressing down hard. The first time he did it, Betty didn't realize he was missing for almost ten minutes. She saw the open door and made a frantic search along the shore by the bay until she heard the uproar from the chicken coop and found him there, crowing at the chickens.

At three, he found the handgun Bill kept in a box at the back of the closet in their bedroom and picked it up and fired it through the mattress. She heard the shot from the kitchen and screamed Jim's name and he hid under the bed. She walked into the bedroom to see the smoking gun on the floor and no sign of her little boy, and was too terrified to look around or under the bed because of what she might find. She sat on the floor and gave in to her grief, and her sobs brought him out of hiding.

At four, he nearly drowned when Claire's son Stephen, who was six, found a gull egg on the beach and threw it as far out into the water as he could, where it promptly sank. Jim rushed into the waves to save the unborn baby gull. Betty, sitting on the sand next to Claire, looked up in time to see his brown head disappear under a wave. She leaped up, sprinted into the water, and saw his bright yellow T-shirt through the swirling water—thank God, thank God, thank God, she had snatched that off the clothesline that morning and put it on him—and reached down and pulled him up, coughing and spitting and crying about the lost egg.

She feared the water more than any other island danger. It would be so easy for a wave to catch Jim as he played on the beach, for a rock to tumble as he walked the path at the edge of the bay, for his foot to slip on a slick dock. She was determined he would be a strong swimmer. The summer he turned five she decided to ask Lem Jacobsen, who had swum competitively in college, to teach her son how to swim.

Lem was thirty-one, strong-willed and eccentric, known around Sounder for his encyclopedic knowledge of herbs, his mercurial moods, and his raw strength. He kept to himself much of the time in the farmhouse he owned up on Crane's Point. When he wasn't traveling for his work, he was busy in his kitchen making up teas and poultices from the herbs in his garden, or roaming the island engaged in feats of strength training.

Betty saw him often in the field by the post office, flat on the ground with arms spread wide, doing dozens of what he called "crucifix push-ups," or on the school playground, doing pull-ups on the steel bar along the top of the swing set, or running with a pack on his back along Sounder's dirt roads. The first time Betty saw him running, wearing only long khaki shorts and his pack (not even shoes!), she assumed he was in a hurry to get home and slowed her truck to a crawl and pulled up beside him and offered him a ride. He glared at her with those bright blue eyes and said, "Why would I ride when I have two strong legs to run?" and sprinted off ahead of her down the road.

Betty didn't know Lem well. She knew what she had heard.

She'd heard he had worked hard to help build the new school a few years ago—felling trees to clear the field, digging out stumps, lifting and placing rocks for the wall that protected the field from the road. She'd heard he brewed a special tea for Marie Doucette, who was dying of cancer, and took it over to her every evening after dinner to ease her pain. She'd also heard he hadn't spoken to George Hamlin for six years because of some casual remark George had made that had so angered him he'd written him off as a fool.

"Do you think Lem Jacobsen would teach Jim to swim?" she asked Claire. They were out in the meadow by the white cottage, pinning the freshly washed laundry to the clothesline while the kids played nearby.

"The kids call him 'Barefoot' now," Claire said. "No one ever sees him in shoes." She pushed her dark hair back behind her ear. Claire was small, with a heart-shaped face and glossy brown hair and brown eyes. It had been hard for Betty to get past her good looks and trust her as a friend. She had become too wary of women who might draw Bill's attention.

"Whatever you call him, he's a great swimmer. Do you think he'd have the patience to teach Jim?"

"Barefoot's not known for his patience," Claire said. "He might do it, though. He likes kids, although I doubt he'll ever have any of his own."

"Why not? He can't be much older than I am," Betty said.

"He's not. But he's not the marrying kind."

"What does that mean?" Betty said.

"I don't know. He travels all the time. He was in Iran for six months this year, and in the Ukraine last year. He's never so much as looked twice at any woman on the island, although I guess there aren't many single women." Claire looked at Betty with a sly smile. "And God knows Barefoot's easy on the eyes. Have you seen him doing those pull-ups on the swing set?"

Betty reached up to pin the corner of a large white flat sheet to the line. The wind blew up under the sheet, lifting it and then dropping it back against her.

"Of course I've seen him. I can't say I've *noticed* him the way you have."

"There was a rumor a few years ago that he had a wife in Tibet—he goes there for two or three months every year. But then someone else said he was divorced. My personal opinion is that he's like Heathcliff—you know, desperately in love with a woman he can't have, so he's forsworn all others."

Betty rolled her eyes. "I don't care if he's got six wives or a dead lover or fourteen unclaimed children. I need to make sure Jim learns to swim."

"So ask him."

"I will." She grinned at Claire. "Should I tell him how much you admire his physique?"

Claire had the grace to blush. "No, thank you. I *am* married, after all."

"I know," Betty said. "Glad you remembered."

And she didn't tell Claire, but the next time she walked by the post office and saw Barefoot doing push-ups in the field (wearing only shorts, no shirt or shoes), she had to look away because it gave her such longing for a man to hold her.

The crab fishing was rich that season, and the captain asked Bill to stay on until mid-August; he agreed because the money was so good. Betty was spending her first summer alone on Sounder and wasn't happy about it. Was the extra two months' salary worth the hurt to Jim, who lived for the time when his father was home? And didn't Bill yearn for *her*, enough to say to hell with the money? She chastised herself for being a romantic fool.

Barefoot didn't hesitate when she asked him to teach Jim to swim.

"I like Jim," he said. "I'll do it."

The moment he agreed she was suddenly filled with doubt. Jim at five possessed little of Bill's natural grace and athletic ability. He had long legs and arms like Betty, and often stumbled over his own feet. And no matter how many times Bill showed him how to grip a baseball across the seams, step with his left foot, and push off with his right to throw, Jim couldn't do it. He stepped with the wrong foot, or he pushed off so hard he'd spin around and tumble into the dirt.

Jim was also what Betty thought of as a "thin person"— which had nothing to do with the way he was built. People on Sounder often talked about the island as a "thin place," a place where the veil between the ordinary and the sacred was thinner than in other places, a place where you could touch God more readily if you were a believer (which Betty wasn't). She did, however, believe there were "thin people," like Jim, for whom the boundary between feeling and experience was whisper thin, who worried and loved and despaired and rejoiced with an intensity Betty found alarming. She worried that Barefoot would have little tolerance for Jim's exaggerated sensitivity.

The day of the first lesson, Betty drove her son along the leafy roads to the central part of the island and parked by the side of the road. They walked on a dirt path for almost twenty minutes to Jake's Lake (named after one of the early Sounder pioneers), where Barefoot waited for them. She had no idea how he got there; the lake was a good two miles from his house on Crane's Point. *He probably ran barefoot through the woods with twenty pounds of rocks on his back,* Betty thought with a smile. Claire seemed to regard him as some kind of physical demigod.

Jim was excited, but nervous. He peppered her with questions about Barefoot as they walked through the woods, and his eagerness broke her heart. Her son missed his father, and sometimes her anger at Bill throbbed in her like a live thing.

She watched Barefoot size Jim up as they approached him on the rocky shore of the little lake, narrowing his eyes to focus on Jim's gait, his long limbs, his face.

"I bet you're not very good at baseball or football," Barefoot said to Jim as they walked up to him.

Jim's face fell. *You son of a bitch*, Betty thought. She was ready to turn around and march back through the woods when Barefoot said, "That's because you were made to be a swimmer. I can see it."

Jim gave Barefoot a wary look.

"Look at your wingspan," Barefoot said, reaching for one of Jim's hands and stretching his arm out to the side. "The thrust in swimming comes from arm propulsion, not the kick. Bet you see your friends kicking for all they're worth when they swim and getting nowhere. You're going to outswim everyone you know in a few weeks."

"Really?"

"Yes," Barefoot said, his eyes on Jim's. "I don't say anything that isn't true."

Barefoot started out by demonstrating for Jim what a real swim stroke looked like. Betty sat on a rock near the water, watching. Barefoot moved naturally in the water like a fish or a seal, rolling almost on his side with each stroke and then gliding. He was beautiful.

He spent the first day teaching Jim to roll in the water. "Forget your arms and legs for now," Barefoot said. "Your rhythm and movement should come from your core, from here"—he tapped Jim's stomach. Jim was an eager pupil, imitating Barefoot's moves and practicing drills over and over—gliding on his side with one arm outstretched, rolling to the other side, gliding again. After an hour Barefoot said, "Good work. If you do this well all week, I'll give you something in reward at the end of the week."

That Friday, Barefoot gave Jim a small glass bead—a "head bead," Barefoot called it—with an intricate bearded face painted on the front and a tiny crown on top. He told Jim he had six of them, all different, and he'd give him one a week if Jim did well with his swimming.

Betty asked Barefoot about the bead, and he shrugged. "I bought a handful of them in Israel several years ago," he said. "They're old: fourth or fifth century B.C., I believe."

"My God! You can't give them to Jim. He's six years old! He might lose them, or break them."

"I trust him. I told him these are precious. Earning one means something, and he has to work hard to earn one each week." Barefoot's gaze was direct. "If he loses or breaks one, he won't have the chance to earn another one."

"But once you're done teaching him to swim—"

"Once I'm done teaching him to swim the beads are his to do with as he pleases."

Betty shook her head. "I can't accept them."

"They're not yours to accept or refuse," Barefoot said. "They belong to your son."

"But—"

"You argue too much," Barefoot said. He leaned over and picked up his blue bandanna from the beach beside her. She couldn't help but notice the thick muscles of his back and shoulders, the firm ridges of his abdomen, the smooth strength of his chest. Damn Claire for putting such ideas into her head in the first place. He folded the bandanna diagonally in half, placed it on top of his head, and tied it in the back.

"See you tomorrow," he said, and was gone down the path before she could say another word.

Jim treasured the beads, and stored them in a box he lined with wool that Claire gave him from her sheep. Betty could see his confidence grow as he became more and more proficient in the water, as he added another unique head bead to the box each week. Barefoot didn't say much, so every compliment that came from his lips was hard earned and genuine, and Jim knew it. By early August, when the last lesson was finished, her son looked taller to Betty.

She invited Barefoot to dinner as a thank-you. She invited Claire and Don and their boys, too, but that afternoon Stephen fell and broke his arm, and Claire and Don had to take him over to Friday Harbor to get it set. Betty offered to take Graham, their younger son, for the night. She debated with herself for a moment about the propriety of dining alone with Barefoot and the two little boys, but then if she really cared about what was proper, she wouldn't be living on Sounder and married to a serial philanderer.

Betty didn't much like to cook, but the fruit and vegetables were fresh, and she killed a chicken, cut it up, marinated it in cider vinegar, lime juice, and brown sugar, and grilled it until it was crisp and tender. Barefoot brought a bottle of homemade dandelion wine. Jim and Graham played some game in the meadow that involved running like mad from one end to the other carrying various "treasures"—a pail of water, an egg on a spoon. They tried to run carrying a protesting chicken, but Betty stopped them. By dusk, which came now at nine, they were run out, and she put them to bed in Jim's room and went to wash up.

Barefoot came in and saw her standing at the sink and made a disgusted clicking sound with his tongue.

"What?" she said, turning to face him.

"You can't enjoy a fine meal and then just sit?" he said.

"Those same dishes will still be there in the morning, but the rising moon won't be."

"There'll be two hungry boys here in the morning, too," she said. "And chickens to feed and goats to milk."

Barefoot shrugged. "You have a point."

An idiotic one, but a point, Betty thought. She dropped the dishrag and walked outside.

Barefoot followed, and they stood on the porch for a minute, watching the sky fade from pale blue to deep blue, the first faint twinkling of stars. She felt an odd loneliness. Jim's swimming lessons were over; Barefoot was leaving in two weeks for a six-month trip to the Middle East. Bill would be home for only four weeks before leaving again. She shivered.

"I'm cold," she said. "I'm going inside."

Barefoot came in with her. "It was a fine meal," he said. "Thank you. I can do the washing up."

"You're welcome," she said. "Don't worry about the dishes. It's not much." She held out her hand. "I can't thank you enough for the swimming lessons. But more, for all you did for Jim's confidence. You've been very good to him."

"I was as good to him as he deserved," Barefoot said.

He didn't take her outstretched hand, and she dropped it to her side. Barefoot's eyes burned into her.

"God, you're a sexy woman," Barefoot said. "I'd like to bed you now."

She was startled and embarrassed by his directness, and by her body's clear response to his words.

"What makes you think I'd go to bed with you?" Betty said.

"What makes you think you'd have a choice?" Barefoot said.

She wasn't afraid of him. Barefoot was many things but not cruel, and she knew he would never touch her without her consent. But his raw desire for her, and his boldness, excited her.

Bill was in Alaska; Bill had cheated on her more times than she could count. Why shouldn't she have that, too, someone to hold her and satisfy her and still some of her loneliness?

"If you were my wife," Barefoot said. "I sure as hell wouldn't leave you alone for nine months a year."

"I'm not your wife," Betty said.

Barefoot placed his hands on her hips and pulled her toward him. Betty leaned back away from him and looked straight into his eyes.

"I'm not a cheater," she said. "I won't do this."

Barefoot smiled at her. "I'm not a cheater, either," he said. "I'm also not a monogamist. Which is why, unlike your husband, I chose not to get married."

"You son of a bitch!" Betty said, pulling away. "You don't know anything about my husband. How dare you judge him?"

She was angry now, and could feel it rise in her, thick and hot. She glared at Barefoot, and he smiled at her, bemused, as though enjoying her rage and confusion. Something in her snapped, and she reached out and slapped him across the face.

The blow caught him straight on the side of his face. His hands shot up and he grabbed both her wrists.

She stood looking at him, at the red mark of her hand on his cheek, breathing hard. She wanted to slap him again; she wanted to grab his fierce head between her hands and kiss him, hard, and pull his body inside hers. She was so torn between anger and desire that she couldn't think clearly.

Barefoot waited a few minutes, his hands around her wrists, until her breathing slowed and her body relaxed.

"I'm sorry if I insulted Bill," Barefoot said at last. "I was out of line. I've long admired you, Elizabeth, and hate to see how hard you work with so little reward. You've got a fine son, and I'm sure that's reward in itself, but to my mind you deserve more."

He let go of her and stepped back, out of range in case she came at him again.

"I won't suggest such intimacies again," he said.

"I'm sorry I slapped you," she said.

Barefoot made a mock bow. "Forgiven," he said.

He bent over and picked up his bandanna, which had fallen to the floor. He stuffed it in his pocket, and then turned to her.

"I've enjoyed the swimming lessons," he said. "Jim's a fine boy."

Barefoot didn't touch her again that summer, or mention the incident again. But again and again she could feel his hands on her wrists, see the intensity in his blue eyes, hear the low, throaty growl of his voice saying, "You deserve more."

She didn't sleep well that summer. And even once Bill came home, Barefoot and his goddamned blue bandanna still haunted her dreams.

Chapter 16

Susannah 2011

Jim poured three fingers of scotch into each of the glasses on the kitchen table and handed one to Susannah.

"Let's sit on the porch," he said.

Susannah took the drink and followed Jim out onto the small back porch of the white cottage and sat down in one of the faded green rockers. It was almost six, and dark already. She could see the sky deepening from blue to indigo to black above the silhouettes of the fir trees, and a few early stars. She took a deep breath. She still had to talk to Katie, who was in her room, about her poem, but Jim had convinced her to calm down and have a drink first.

"Let me put your mind at ease," Jim said, settling into the chair across from hers. "I do not think Katie is smoking pot. She wrote that poem to unnerve you."

"You don't know that," Susannah said. "And what about Hood? Your mother told me he was growing pot last summer."

"Susannah, Hood is not growing pot or smoking pot. That thing with Ralph Flanagan was a one-time deal."

"But how can you be sure?" Susannah said.

"I can't," Jim said. "But I trust my kid. He tells me he's not doing it, I believe him. And honestly, Hood doesn't have that much free time. He and Baker have work to do on the farm every day, in addition to homework. Hard to imagine he's doing all that and getting stoned."

"I know a lot of people don't think pot is a big deal," Susannah said. "But it's like alcohol: My dad always thought he had his drinking under control. He had *no* idea. I worry that Katie could have inherited some tendency for abusing alcohol or drugs."

Jim leveled a steady look at her. "As far as *I* can tell—as her teacher in a very small school, and as your neighbor, *and* as the father of her closest friends here—Katie is not abusing anything or anyone, except you. That poem was Katie's 'screw you,' her way of letting you know that even though you brought her here, you still can't control her."

Susannah sighed. "I know." She took a slow sip of her drink. She never drank scotch, and it made her cough. She swallowed hard and cleared her throat. "But there has to be some consequence, even if it was just a poem. It wasn't an appropriate thing to read to a roomful of children."

"I agree."

"I plan to ground her, but it's hard to have her here in the cottage with too much time on her hands. Maybe she needs her own job."

"That's a good idea."

"But where could I put her to work? Do you need more help on the farm?"

Jim shrugged. "Not really, especially not at this time of year. Ask Barefoot. He's got his greenhouse and his herb farm, and that boat he's renovating."

"Barefoot?" Her voice was skeptical.

"Barefoot is a botanist. He grows a variety of herbs for medicinal purposes in his greenhouse. Yes, the DEA found two pot plants during the raid a few years ago. He may still be growing it, *as medicine*. But he would never, under any circumstances, give it to a child." Jim's green eyes were serious. "I have known Barefoot Jacobsen my entire life."

"All right," Susannah said. But the knot of worry in her chest wouldn't go away.

Jim was quiet a moment, then leaned forward in his chair to look her in the face. "Listen, you're not immune from problems here. Kids may not have the same opportunities to get into trouble that they do in Virginia, but still, I know two girls in Friday Harbor who got pregnant at sixteen. Kids drink and get in boats. A boy over on Orcas got drunk and fell overboard and drowned last year."

"That's terrible." Susannah didn't want to think about the boy's family or whoever might have been with him on the boat, watching for his head to break the surface, waiting for the normal, the familiar, before realizing nothing would ever be normal again. "Bad things happen everywhere, I know."

They sat in silence for a while, watching the sky. "What are you so afraid of?" Jim said at last. His voice was gentle. "I mean with Katie and Quinn."

Susannah closed her eyes. She could smell the smoke wafting from the chimney, the loamy scent of the woods. She was comfortable with Jim. He clearly liked her, and understood her kids weren't perfect and didn't judge her. He and Fiona were working out some kinks in their own marriage, just as she was with Matt—something he'd alluded to but not discussed. She trusted him.

"My sister died because of me," she said at last, in a low voice. "It was my fault."

"Do you want to talk about it?"

"No. But that's why I have to do everything I can to protect my kids. I'm afraid something awful will happen again, on my watch."

Jim let out a long breath, and his breath turned to fog in the cold evening air. "You said you came here because you had to make a change," he said. "Maybe this is the thing you need to change."

Susannah's laugh was bitter. "I can't bring Janie back."

"No," Jim said. "But maybe you can let her go." He paused a minute. "What I mean is—and I say this as your friend, not as a criticism—even *if* your sister's death was 'your fault,' as you put it, it doesn't mean you deserve to be ill-treated by your daughter, or by anyone."

Susannah was quiet. And she was still quiet, thinking, long after they'd said their good-byes and Jim had gone home.

Later that night, after dinner, Susannah stood next to Katie at the sink, drying dishes while Katie washed them. Quinn had walked over to the Pavalaks' to find Baker, who was helping him with math.

"I'm not smoking pot, Mom," Katie said, her eyes on the sink. "I never have, okay? I was bored, and we had this assignment, and I thought it would be cool to take a really formal, old-fashioned thing like an ode but make it about something totally informal and present-day, like smoking pot."

"Your poem was full of some pretty vivid details for someone who's never tried marijuana," Susannah said. She put down the plate she was holding and turned to face her daughter. "I don't know what half of it was about. Captain Blue?"

"It's a variety of pot. I read about it in the *New Yorker.* Online."

"Thrilled as I am with your Internet research skills, I still can't believe you'd read a poem about the joys of marijuana to a roomful of *children*, including your little brother. You're grounded for a week. And I talked to Jim. He's suspending you for two days."

"I'm suspended?" Katie dropped the dishrag in the soapy sink and turned to look at her mother.

"The public school system has a low tolerance for behaviors that 'disrupt the educational process,' as he put it."

Katie was incredulous. "I'm suspended because *I wrote a poem?*"

"The kids are going to ask what your poem was about. I'm sure several of them figured it out. They'll tell the littler kids. Like it or not, as an eighth grader and one of the oldest students at a very small school, you're a role model."

Katie turned back to face the sink. "Okay," she said. Katie picked up a sponge and began to scrub the cast-iron skillet, with her head tilted forward so her hair fell and hid her face. At one point, Susannah leaned in toward her just a little and started to say something, but Katie shook her head. When she finished washing the skillet, she handed it to Susannah to dry. She didn't look at her. Finally she said, "I'm sorry, okay?"

"Okay," Susannah said. "Thank you. I appreciate that." She put down the skillet. "Katie, I want you to be happy. I brought you here to keep you safe, not to punish you."

"I know."

Katie looked uncomfortable.

"Listen, I'm proud of what a great writer you are. Jim was telling me about some essay you wrote, about Steinbeck. I'd love to see it."

"Oh, God. I don't want to show it to you."

"Really?"

"Maybe some other time."

"All right. You know what else?" Susannah looked at her daughter. "Thanks for telling Jim about my art. It was a lot of fun for me to do those posters."

Katie shrugged. She draped the dishrag over one of the towel bars on the side of the wood stove to dry. "I'm going to my room to do homework, I guess, since I'm *grounded* and can't go to Hood's."

She paused, her hand on the door to the utility room. "The posters turned out pretty good," she said. "You should do more art."

"Thank you," Susannah said. She was pleased by Katie's praise. "I thought—"

But Katie opened the door and closed it behind her before Susannah could finish her sentence.

Early the next morning Susannah drove over the rutted roads up to Crane's Point. She found Barefoot in the greenhouse, cutting flower heads from chamomile plants. Toby, who lay on the floor by his master's feet, stood up and wagged his tail in a furious rhythm when she walked in.

"Morning," Barefoot said, although he didn't pause in his work. Susannah watched him a few minutes in silence.

"What do you do with the chamomile?"

"Lots of things."

"Like?"

"Brew it into a tea for colic and indigestion, and nerves. Grind it into a paste for burns and rashes. Brew it in the bath for hemorrhoids."

He put his clippers down on the wooden table and looked at her.

"You drove up here at seven-thirty in the morning to talk about chamomile?"

"No," Susannah said. "Listen, Katie needs something to do. I was wondering if maybe she could help you restore the boat up here, work for you on a regular basis."

Barefoot's eyebrows rose.

"Not for money," Susannah said quickly. "I'd consider it a favor. You could teach her how to do the work you need to finish up the boat; it would occupy her time and she'd learn some new skills. And it might help you get the boat done faster."

"Hmm." Barefoot picked up the clippers and began again to clip the chamomile's little white flowers, dropping them into a stainless steel bowl on the table. His hands were steady and sure, in spite of fingers swollen with arthritis.

"Why would she want to do it?" he said.

"She won't," Susannah said. "But it will be good for her. In the end, I think she will want to do it. She likes learning new things; she likes being good at things."

"She's got some attitude," he said.

"She's not a bad kid," Susannah said. "She's just"—she searched for the word—"curious, and adventure-craving, if that makes sense. She needs to be doing something all the time or she's bored, and that's when she gets into trouble." *Oh, my God. I sound like a mother in Tilton.* Those parents with the crazy round-the-clock sports and activity schedules were just like her, trying to keep their kids busy, productive, safe. "Work will be good for her. Katie's had a very privileged life so far, and I'd like to open her mind a little. She has such a sense of entitlement."

"Born on third base and thinks she hit a triple," Barefoot said.

"*Exactly.*"

"All right. Bring her by this afternoon around four. But just on the boat; I don't want her near my plants."

I don't want her near your plants. "I have to ask," Susannah said. "I heard about the DEA raid."

Barefoot stared at her from under wiry eyebrows. "Yes?"

"I understand you were growing marijuana. Katie's been

suspended because of that poem she wrote, the ode to marijuana. And I wondered—"

Barefoot scowled and pointed his clippers at her face. "Get
out!"

"What?" Susannah stepped back.

"Get the hell off my property. You think I'd waste good can-
nabis on your goddamn brat of a daughter?"

"I—I'm sorry."

"What I grow and what I do with it is my own damn business," Barefoot said. "And I don't give anything I grow to *anyone*, unless I know what they're using it for. And I don't give
herbs to children."

"I apologize," Susannah said.

Barefoot was silent. He turned from her and began to clip
the chamomile again.

"Would you still consider letting her work for you? She
could come right away. She's not at school today."

Barefoot didn't look up. "Have her here after lunch, say at
one. I'll get her started. She can do the refinishing work inside
the cabin, stripping and sanding, some woodworking. I'll show
her how to use the tools. She can come a couple days a week
after school, too."

"One o'clock," Susannah said. "Thank you."

"Don't thank me yet. I might fire her by one fifteen."

When Susannah told Katie she was going to spend the afternoon working for Barefoot, her face registered complete aston-
ishment.

"Barefoot is crazy," Katie said. "Hood and Baker told me he
blew off some guy's hand with a shotgun because the guy was
trying to rob him."

"Jim has known Barefoot forever and trusts him around *his*

kids. *If* that story is true, which I doubt, I'm sure there's more to it than that."

"Yeah, well that's the kind of thing you might want to find out *first*."

"I'll take my chances," Susannah said.

Katie sat up in bed. "Mom, you are so overreacting to this poem. You know, marijuana is legal in, like, twenty states. Maybe you should try it sometime."

"Very funny. Get up and get dressed."

"Seriously?"

"Yes, seriously. We'll see how working for Barefoot goes. Also, you're going to have to stick closer to home for a while. No more wandering all over the island or disappearing with Hood."

"What?" Angry tears sprang to Katie's eyes. "You can't do that!"

The iceberg was out there, looming. "Yes, I can," Susannah said. "Get dressed."

After lunch, she drove Katie up to Barefoot's in the truck, barely slowing down to drop her off. As she made her way home along the dirt roads, she noticed, as always, the piles of junk on some of the properties she passed, the rusted shells of old cars and stoves, mounds of broken pottery, rotting wooden crates—the detritus of human lives, more visible here because it couldn't be easily discarded, carted away. There was a similar pile near Betty's house, and as Susannah pulled the truck up to the end of the dirt drive, she stopped and hopped out and knocked on Betty's door.

"I have a question about the junk pile," Susannah said, as Betty opened the door.

"Oh, Jesus," Betty said. She put a hand on one hip. "Don't tell me you're going to try to 'civilize' us by asking me to hide the junk behind a decorative fence or something crazy like that. Junk is part of life here."

"I know," Susannah said. "I wanted to know if I could *use* it, if you'd mind if I went through it and took a few things."

Betty looked incredulous. "Would I mind if you took the junk? Honey, you can hang it from the trees for all I care. I've been throwing things on that heap since I moved here fifty-six years ago, and the folks who lived here before me had a junk pile there, too." She looked at Susannah over the rims of her glasses. "What are you going to do with it?"

"I'm not quite sure." Susannah rooted through the pockets of her coat for her gloves. The collages she'd made for Pizza and Poetry Day had unleashed something in her. She wanted to *create*, to focus on something other than her kids, herself, her marriage, her failures.

"I don't know. Make something." She paused. "I miss my job. I loved doing windows. Once, I painted a bunch of old wooden picture frames gold and hung them all over the window, with a single shoe in each one. They really did look like works of art." She stood still for a moment, remembering. Another time she had painted a landscape on a backdrop—a deep blue lake with little waves edged in gold, surrounded by mountains in bright shades of yellow and orange, their slopes covered in green and black trees. For the whole painting she used brushstrokes that resembled the stitchery in Nordic knitting, then filled the window with white sweaters and mittens that stood out like spots of light against the richly colored background.

"That sounds like a lot more fun than any work I ever had," Betty said.

"It *was* fun," Susannah said. "But I quit when Katie was born." At the time, quitting had seemed like the only thing to do.

Her own mother was a vague background figure in Susannah's

memories of childhood—often distracted, or in bed with a headache or backache or sinus infection, or standing in helpless silence when her father was drunk. Susannah was determined she would never be *that* mother, the mother with the fearful, lonely children. Her children would always feel loved, protected, secure. So she nursed them each for a year, made baby food from scratch, took them to toddler gymnastics classes and art classes. She volunteered in their classrooms, played endless imaginary games, told stories, sewed costumes, threw memorable birthday parties. She even gave them handmade Christmas gifts every year, along with all the other toys and games.

Even when the kids had entered elementary school and then middle school, Susannah was still involved—maybe a little *too* involved, she thought now. She volunteered to oversee the book fair, organize the International Dinner, shelve books in the school library. But with each commitment, with every meeting and event, she had found herself bored, even resentful. She was sick of baking brownies for the baseball team and xeroxing flyers for the book fair and cleaning up after the team pizza party. Her life was an endless round of obligations. She couldn't remember the last time she had done something for no other reason than that *she* felt like it—she, herself, Susannah.

She eyed the junk pile again with eagerness. "Can I look through it now?"

"Sure. Let me get my coat. I'll help you. Or at least, advise you."

Susannah pulled on her gloves and began to sort through the pile. It was, indeed, junk—pots and pans with holes burned through the bottom, rusting bedsprings, broken dishes and teacups, a discarded rototiller, a wooden chair with only two legs.

Betty returned in her thick green coat, hands in her pockets. "When does Matt arrive?"

Matt. Susannah had called him five times in the last twenty-four hours but hadn't reached him, nor had he called her back.

"The day before Thanksgiving."

"What did he think about Katie's poem?" Betty sat down on one of the wooden steps in front of her house.

"I don't know. I haven't talked to him since early yesterday morning." Susannah stopped picking through the junk and stood for a moment, leaning on a purple wooden shutter. "I think he's having a harder time than I thought he would with us being out here. But it must seem silly to you. You didn't even have cell phones or e-mail when your husband was away."

"We wrote letters."

Susannah remembered Matt's angry voice on the phone. "Maybe that was better."

Betty eyed her. "We didn't really communicate much when Bill was away."

Susannah sighed. "Matt's not much of a communicator even when we're together."

Betty crossed both arms over her chest and hugged herself against the cold. "A lot of men aren't. I was lucky to have a man in my life who was good at understanding me, who was a good listener, and comfortable with talking about all kinds of things."

Susannah shook her head. "You married well, then."

Betty looked at Susannah and raised one eyebrow.

"I didn't say that man was my husband."

Chapter 17

Betty 1962

Nineteen sixty-two was a hard year. Even now, almost fifty years later, much of it was a blur to Betty. Bill left for a nine-month work stint in September. In October, Jim, who was six, caught his foot in a hole while running in the meadow and broke his leg. The cast he wore (after the trip to the hospital, which involved a bone-jolting drive in the truck to the landing strip on Sounder, where her friend Wiley Loughran waited with his plane to fly them to Bellingham) stretched all the way from his foot to his hip bone. Once they were back home, Betty had to carry him everywhere, from the truck to the house, from room to room inside, from the bed to the couch. Jim was tall for his age and weighed almost fifty pounds. It was hard physical work.

In November, Claire and Don and the boys moved to San Francisco, and Betty missed her keenly. Claire's light heart and loyalty had eased much of her loneliness on Sounder, and her boys had been Jim's closest playmates. Then, in December, she got a telegram from Bobbie that their mother and Grammy had been in a car accident. By the time Betty found someone who would take Jim for a few days, and traveled by boat and ferry and seaplane to Seattle, Grammy was dead.

She stayed for the funeral and to help figure out what to do with Mother, who faced at least another two months of physical therapy and walking with a cane, and Mel, whose anxiety in the wake of the accident was so crippling that she couldn't leave the house. They finally agreed that Mother would move in with Bobbie for a few months, and Mel would come to Sounder with Betty until March 1.

Betty didn't sleep for the next two months, or at least it felt that way. Jim awoke at least once every night needing to go to the bathroom, and even though she'd put a bucket in his room so he could pee at night, he needed her help getting into an upright position with his clunky cast. Mel didn't sleep much and often wandered the little cottage at night, pacing in circles around the dining room table, pausing to warm her hands by the woodstove, then pacing again. Betty drove Jim to and from school every day and carried him up and down the wooden steps to the schoolhouse, then went home to take care of the goats and chickens and cook and do laundry until her hands were callused and raw. Mel helped with small things— she loved to fold laundry, and was good at peeling carrots and potatoes—but in many ways having Mel there was like having another child to care for.

Late one afternoon in February, with the shadows of the pines long across the meadow, Betty got in the truck and drove up to Barefoot's house to get some cowslip and betony for Mel, and a special tea for Jim to strengthen his bones.

She found Barefoot standing in the kitchen, contemplating five piles of dried leaves arranged in a line on the counter. He wore khakis and a white V-neck T-shirt, and no shoes. He wasn't wearing his bandanna, either, and his thick dark hair curled around the back of his neck. He picked up the first pile and rubbed the leaves between his two hands over a bowl until they were crumbled into tiny bits.

"Hello."

Barefoot glanced up at her, then back at the bowl. "I'm making the tea for Jim."

"What's in it?"

"Oat straw, horsetail, nettles, red clover, and comfrey. Put plenty of honey in it, and he'll drink it right down."

"His leg is healing well. I hope he can swim a lot this summer. The doctor said swimming would be good for him."

"It will be." Barefoot finished crumbling the leaves. He turned to look at her, and his blue eyes traveled from her face down her body to her boots and back up again. She felt exposed by his stare, and turned her head.

"You look like you could use a tonic yourself," Barefoot said. "How much weight have you lost?"

"I don't know. We don't have a scale."

"Are you sleeping?"

She shook her head. "Not well. I wake up a lot. If Jim needs to go to the bathroom during the night, he needs me. And Mel doesn't sleep well, so she wanders the house sometimes. You know how the floors creak."

Barefoot picked up a little metal scoop from the counter and began to spoon the tea leaves from the bowl into a small brown paper sack.

"When is that husband of yours coming home?"

Betty leaned against the doorframe. "April fifteenth." She didn't want to talk about Bill. She had sent him a telegram when Jim broke his leg, and then written him a letter about Mel. He'd written her back, full of concern about Jim, but hadn't offered to come home early, or expressed any concern at all about her, about how lonely and exhausted she might be, caring for Jim and Mel at the same time.

"I wish I had a cigarette," she said.

"You shouldn't smoke. I've never let tobacco touch my lungs."

She looked around the kitchen. She liked Barefoot's kitchen, with the paned windows that let in the golden afternoon sun, the white porcelain sink, the simple wood counters and white cupboards, the beautiful orange and turquoise rug on the floor. She looked up at the quote painted in black above the back door, the one that led out to the greenhouse:

> *Since my house burned down / I now own a better*
> *view / of the rising moon.*
> —Mizuta Masahide

"Why do you have that quote up there?"

"I like it."

"Why?"

He turned to face her again. "Because it reminds me that the only thing that gives an experience any weight is the way you look at it."

She was bone tired suddenly. She even had that thought, *I am bone tired*, but felt as if she really understood it for the first time. All at once her very bones seemed like too much weight for her exhausted muscles and tendons and skin to hold, as though she might collapse like a house of cards, tumbling down into nothingness.

"Sit down," Barefoot said. He came over and grabbed her elbow, led her to the long red velvet couch in the living room, and pushed her down onto it. "I'm going to make you tea and some food. Are your people all right for now?"

She looked up at him. "Yes. Jim's at a friend's house, and Mel is sleeping. That's why I came over. I had a minute."

"Elizabeth," he said, "you are killing yourself slowly with too much work and too much worry. Good God, why not drink laudanum and be done with it?"

"I don't have a choice," she said. "What do you want me to do, tell Jim I won't carry him to the bathroom or up the steps to school? Or tell my poor crazy sister she has to go live in an asylum?" She felt all at once as if she wanted to cry, which she had not done even once over these last five long months. But she'd be damned if she'd cry in front of Barefoot.

"Tell that asshole husband of yours to come home."

Betty stood up. "Please," she said. "I'm too tired to argue with you."

He came to her then and put his arms around her. She rested her head against his chest, just for moment. *I shouldn't be doing this*, she thought. But then his gentleness undid her. He pulled back from her and kissed her eyelids, then the tip of her nose, then her ear, and her throat. He kissed her collarbone, and her jaw. He didn't touch her, except with his lips. She felt her body swell and flush under his touch.

She shook her head.

He stepped back and opened his blue eyes wide and stared straight into hers. "What do you want?" he said.

"I want to go home," she said.

He nodded slowly. "All right."

He walked across the living room of the farmhouse and opened the front door. "Want me to drive you?"

She shook her head again. "No," she said. She didn't move. He came back to where she stood. "I'm so tired," she said.

And then he scooped her up in his arms, as though she were a small child and not the tall, ungainly woman she had always felt herself to be, and carried her up the narrow staircase to his bedroom and laid her down on his bed. He pulled a comforter over her that smelled faintly of cedar, and before she could protest too much, she fell into a deep, dreamless sleep.

When she awoke it was dark. She sat up in a panic, thinking about Mel and Jimmy, and flung the covers off. Barefoot opened the bedroom door, carrying a kerosene lantern in one hand. "Don't get up," he said. "I drove over and asked Alice MacDonald if she could spend the night with your two. She used to be a nurse. They'll be fine."

"I can't spend the night here."

"I'll sleep on the couch. Wait here. I brought you dinner."

He disappeared and returned with a tray. A beautiful gold-rimmed porcelain plate held freshly grilled salmon, and there was also homemade bread, a salad of greens and herbs, and a glass of dark purple wine. She scooted back against the headboard and he placed the tray in her lap. She couldn't remember the last time she had eaten food she hadn't grown or killed or shopped for or prepared herself. She was ravenous. Barefoot sat across from her in a plain, straight-backed wooden chair, and watched her eat. When she was done, he picked up the tray and took it downstairs, returning with a pot of warm herbal tea and a thick slice of chocolate cake. She ate that, too.

"Why are you doing this?" she said at last, as she leaned back, satiated, sipping her tea.

"I want to take care of you," he said.

She laughed. For all of her thirty-one years she had been strong, independent, competent, and a caretaker. She'd taken care of her younger brother and sisters, she'd taken care of Bill, and now she'd cared for Jim and Mel. She hadn't worked in an office in more than a decade, but she handled everything at home, from managing their finances to repairing the pump to inoculating the goats.

"I don't need to be taken care of," she said. "I take care of everyone else. That's what I do."

"Well, I don't want to be taken care of," Barefoot said. "Maybe it's your turn."

And it was then that something in her broke, all the practicality and self-control that had allowed her to maintain her marriage to Bill and raise Jim and run the farm alone. She put down her teacup on the table next to the bed and looked at Barefoot.

"No one has taken care of me in a long time," she said.

He shrugged.

And then, without even thinking, she slid over to the edge of the bed and leaned forward and rested her forehead against his and closed her eyes.

"Thank you," she said.

And this time she was the one who touched him with her lips, gently at first and then more urgently, until he pushed her down on to the bed. At first his lips and hands and body felt strange—Bill was the only man she'd ever even kissed—but Barefoot's touch was so tender and his concern for her so clear and direct that she relaxed and felt her body respond as it hadn't in years. He talked to her as he moved inside her, staring directly into her eyes, telling her how beautiful she was, until his words and the rhythm of their bodies moving together exploded inside her.

So Betty, who wasn't a cheater, became one. And Barefoot, who wasn't a monogamist, became one.

Chapter 18

Susannah 2011

Susannah was drunk. At least she *felt* drunk, although she hadn't had more than a glass or two of Barefoot's blackberry wine. Maybe the homemade wine had a bigger kick than she'd expected. She needed to eat. She hadn't eaten anything since lunch, except for a cupcake. And she was *starving* now. But just as she was contemplating whether or not to stand up and find a piece of bread, Jim carried over a huge platter and set it down on the table, on top of a thick dishtowel. He stood back.

"Voilà," he said. "My paella."

"Yes!" Baker said. He pumped a fist in the air.

The old pine walls of the Laundromat glowed with the soft light from the fireplace and the woodburning stove. Jim had offered to cook dinner for the Delaneys as a way to thank Susannah for the posters. Betty had suggested the Laundromat, with its big room and long table, as the perfect venue for a party.

"What's in it?" Quinn asked. He eyed the platter with suspicion.

"Chicken," Jim said. "Shrimp. Squid. Clams. Mussels. Bacon. Many herbs, thanks to Barefoot." Barefoot was here, too.

He'd helped Jim and the kids plant an indoor garden at the school in the fall.

"Smell that," Betty said, closing her eyes and inhaling the steam from the platter. "Incredible."

Susannah felt a little sick at the thought of eating squid. It was the chewing that was so hard with squid, because it gave you so much time to *think* about what you were chewing. Something about the idea of chewing squid struck her as funny, and she giggled.

"Something funny about paella?" Jim said with a smile.

Susannah shook her head. "No, no. It looks amazing." She looked at the paella, thinking about all those mussels and clams and shrimps, not to mention the squid.

"Is SpongeBob SquarePants in there, too?" she said.

All at once she found this so funny that she couldn't stop laughing. She laughed so hard it brought tears to her eyes, and she collapsed into Betty, who sat next to her. "I'm sorry," Susannah said, wiping her eyes. "I don't know what's wrong with me. Too much wine."

"Oh, my God," Katie said.

Susannah straightened up and took a sip of water. "I can't wait to try it," she said. She spooned a large helping onto her plate and avoided looking at it, so she didn't start laughing again.

"So how's work going?" Jim said, as he passed the wooden salad bowl to Katie.

"Fine, I guess, if you don't mind working for someone who is *crazy*," Katie said, with an impish smile across the table at Barefoot. "Did you know Barefoot had a pet boar when he lived in Iran? It weighed five hundred pounds."

Susannah paused, her fork in midair, awaiting an outburst from Barefoot, but he smiled. *He likes her*, Susannah thought.

"That's cool," Quinn said.

"It's a *pig*," Katie said.

"The most intelligent of all creatures," Barefoot said.

Susannah looked at her paella. "So I'm about to eat smart bacon?" she said, and then, helpless, she started to laugh again.

Barefoot turned to her. "What is so funny now?" he said.

"I don't know," she said. "Nothing."

Susannah closed her eyes and slipped a forkful of the paella into her mouth. The buttery flavor of clam hit her tongue, followed by a rich hit of garlic, and the delightful saltiness of bacon. It was the best thing she'd ever tasted.

For the first time since she'd arrived on Sounder, she felt totally relaxed. She took another sip of wine and leaned back in her chair, nodding and smiling but not really paying attention. It felt good to not pay attention for once, to let her guard down. She stared at Jim's face across the table as he debated something about Søren Kierkegaard with Barefoot. Jim had a lively, interesting face, she thought. She was intrigued by his ears, which stood out at a slight angle, making him look boyish in spite of the lines in his forehead, the creases around his eyes.

"So, how's your art?" Jim said. It took Susannah a moment to realize he was talking to her.

"What do you mean?"

"Mom told me you amassed quite a collection of junk from the junk pile."

She didn't want to talk about her "art," if you could even call it that. "It's not really art," she said. "Just a kind of project I've been fooling around with."

In the days since she'd picked over Betty's junk, Susannah had set up a studio in a corner of the barn. With Betty's blessing, she had cleared out the old gardening tools and fishing tackle and piled all her found junk in one corner, filled with light from a small, south-facing window. She had sorted the junk into piles of broken pottery and glass and metal pieces and bits of rubber from tires and hot water bottles. She was happy to be working with her hands again, away from the confines of the small house. She had to pace back and forth in the cold and jump up and down once in a while to stay warm, but she relished even that, running in tiny circles or doing silly dances there in the barn, with no one to see her but the goats.

She had borrowed a drill and soldering gun from Barefoot and bought wood glue and paint and other supplies in Friday Harbor. She had been nervous about using the soldering gun, but Barefoot had given her a careful demonstration.

"Good God, woman," he had said. "Is there anything you're not afraid of? You should have stayed in your tidy house in the suburbs and knit doilies!"

"I'm trying, aren't I?" Susannah had said, and Barefoot had given her a smile of acknowledgment and said, "Yes, you are."

Since there were no store windows to decorate on Sounder, she'd decided to make garden spikes, little sculptures to add a bit of whimsy and color to the many gardens on the island. But her first few attempts had been laughable—copper tubing with bedsprings soldered on like crazy petals, looking more like junk than what she'd started with. She had stuck the small spikes in the dirt outside the barn and stood back, hands on hips, to contemplate them. These little sculptures were small and safe, like her whole life. She wanted to create something big and bold and dramatic, something completely unlike her, unlike her life in Tilton.

"Are you going to tell us about your project, then?" Jim said.

"I'm making a scrap metal scarecrow," Susannah said.

Barefoot's wiry eyebrows rose.

"Good idea," Jim said. "The crows are always in our corn."

"The only problem is I don't know if my scarecrow is scary enough," Susannah said. She giggled. "Actually, it's more of a friendlycrow. I don't think you could call it a *scare*crow."

Katie gave her a nervous glance.

"So technically it would be a *reassure*crow," Jim said.

"Yes!" Susannah said. "Exactly. But I don't know who it's reassuring—the farmer or the crows." She mulled this over in her mind. Was the scarecrow reassuring the farmer? Or was the scarecrow reassuring the crows? It seemed very complicated.

"*Mom.*"

Susannah looked up at the insistent tone of Quinn's voice.

"Mom, I've been talking to you for like ten minutes," he said. "I'm going to walk down to the beach with Toby, okay?"

Susannah nodded. "Yes, just don't go on the dock in the dark."

Toby barked at the mention of his name, and Quinn went to the door, with the dog at his heels.

"Don't you want to wait for dessert?" Betty said. "I thought I heard someone mention cupcakes."

"I don't like chocolate," Quinn said. "And Katie made chocolate cupcakes, of course. Someone else can have mine." He disappeared out the door.

Barefoot caught Susannah's eye. "Toby'll keep an eye on him, don't worry," he said. "Smartest dog I've ever had."

"I'll get the cupcakes." Katie jumped up from the table and brought the cupcakes out now, arrayed on a bright orange plate. She had given one to Susannah to sample as they drove over to the Laundromat in the truck. But just as Katie approached the table, she tripped over the braided rug and tumbled, dropping the plate and scattering cupcakes across the floor.

"God! I'm sorry," Katie said. "What a mess. We can't eat these now." She started to pick up the cupcakes and pile them back on the plate.

"Where did you get those?" Barefoot stood up.

Katie looked up at him, her voice oddly shaky. "I made them. This morning, while my mom was here doing the laundry."

Barefoot leaned over and picked up one of the cupcakes from

the floor. "These look a lot like the cupcakes I made yesterday, the ones you saw on my counter that I told you not to touch."

"They're not," Katie said. "I made them."

Barefoot stuck a finger in the icing and licked it. He opened his eyes wide and then reached over and grabbed Katie by the shoulder.

"Those are my cupcakes, you lying little fool! Unless you expect me to believe that you somehow spontaneously came up with an identical recipe for chocolate-lavender frosting with thyme. What the hell is going on? You knew those were not for you. Those cupcakes were for someone else!"

Katie stared at him. The entire table stared at him. Barefoot muttered to himself as he picked up the cupcakes, piling them in a crumbled, messy heap on the plate. Then he stood up and hurled it all into the fireplace. The plate smashed against the back wall of the fireplace, and the sugary icing made a hissing sound as the cupcakes hit the flames.

"Jesus Christ, Barefoot!" Betty said.

"Those were not to be shared," he said. He glared at Katie. "And you knew it. You're fired!"

"What's the problem?" Jim said.

"I don't know," Barefoot said, his eyes still on Katie. "But it stinks like rotten seal. I've got a friend on Orcas who's got multiple sclerosis—Walter Katz, you probably know him. Marijuana works very well in controlling some of his symptoms. I bring him cupcakes every week. Katie knows it; she saw 'em in my house, and I told her to leave 'em alone, that they were medicinal. I've told her not to touch *any* of my stuff."

"Pot cupcakes?" Jim said.

"Oh, my God," Susannah said.

Barefoot looked at her. "Did you eat one?"

"Yes." Katie had offered her one before dinner. It was so

good she'd sneaked another one while Katie was helping Betty set the table. Susannah looked at her daughter. "Kate?"

Katie turned her head toward the wall. "You were so crazy about my poem, and so *judgmental* about smoking pot, I thought—" She pulled her lips together. "I dropped the plate on purpose, so no one else would eat them."

"That explains why the paella was so funny," Jim said.

I'd be really mad, Susannah thought, *if I weren't so stoned.*

"You've definitely gone too far," Jim said.

Barefoot turned to Susannah. "You'll be fine. But *no one* should ever be given any kind of medicine without his or her knowledge or consent."

"Actually, I ate two," Susannah said. She found this funny, and covered her mouth with her hand to hide her smile.

"*Two?*" Barefoot said. "Well, you'll still be fine, but you may feel a little fuzzy tomorrow. Goddamn it, Katie!"

Susannah had never liked the sensation of losing control— she never drank too much, or smoked pot, or tried any other kind of drug. But now, she had to admit, she felt very pleasantly relaxed and removed. The thought that she should be angry— or even scared—floated into her head and floated right out. She watched the thought pass like a wisp of cloud across a blue sky.

Barefoot continued to yell at Katie, and Katie started to cry. Jim was trying to sweep the broken shards of plate out of the fireplace without catching the broom on fire. Betty was picking up the smashed bits of cupcake from the floor. The whole situation was funny, really. Susannah pulled her lips together and tried not to laugh, because Katie's behavior was truly appalling. She tried to think about something else, so she wouldn't laugh, but the only thing that came into her head was the image of SpongeBob SquarePants dancing in the paella. She laughed. And once she started, she couldn't stop. Finally, she gave in and sat back in her chair and let the laughter roll out of her, like water burbling up from a kettle.

"Oh. My. God," Katie said.

"I'll drive you guys home," Jim said.

She heard Quinn shout from outside. "Mom! Mom!"

Susannah wiped her eyes, and tried to still her laughter.

"Yes!" she said.

"Mom! Come here!"

Susannah got up and walked out onto the porch. Quinn stood in the road in front of the Laundromat, yelling for her. She could barely make out the white stripe on his jacket in the darkness. Toby stood next to him, barking over and over again at something farther down the road that Susannah couldn't see. Quinn ran toward the dock and disappeared.

"Quinn?" Susannah walked to the edge of the porch and leaned over the railing, peering through the evening shadows. "Quinn?"

A familiar figure strode up the road, with a duffel bag in one hand and one arm around Quinn's shoulders.

"Oh, my God," Susannah said.

Matt looked up at her and smiled his familiar, lopsided smile.

"Surprise," he said.

Chapter 19

Betty 1963

Of course she felt guilty. No matter what Bill had done or continued to do, she was his wife and she had taken vows and she had made promises she meant, and had meant to keep.

But she was tired. It wasn't just physical exhaustion, although some days the fatigue settled into her bones so deeply she could almost feel herself heavier, slower, with the weight of it. She also felt a spiritual exhaustion. Once she and Barefoot became lovers, Betty understood how thoroughly loneliness had permeated her life, like water seeping into a foundation, pooling in the deepest recesses of her soul. She had been starving and not even known it.

At first, it was hard to separate her feelings for Barefoot from the overwhelming power of her physical desire for him. She had enjoyed her sex life with Bill, but Bill was the only man she'd ever known. In the early days of their marriage, Bill had been an eager lover, and she, young and inexperienced, was simply happy if he was happy. His caresses excited her, but she was reluctant to let him see her excitement, afraid it wasn't "lady-like" and also somewhat scared by the power of her own sensuality. And she didn't know how to tell him that if he touched her just a little differently she might enjoy it more. She longed for a closeness with him that she approached but never fully realized. Bill didn't like to talk during lovemaking. And he always closed his eyes and turned his face away from hers, as though slightly embarrassed by his own urgency.

The first time Barefoot made love to her she was lying on her back in the bed and he entered her slowly, looking into her eyes the whole time. When she turned her head to the side, overwhelmed by the intensity of his gaze, he put one hand behind her neck and turned her face back to his. "Elizabeth," he said, and the word was something precious and tender on his tongue, a whisper, a prayer. The contrast between the persona of him—lean and rock hard, every muscle carved into definition by his hours of pull-ups and running, independent and fierce, brilliant, harsh—and the reality of his tenderness with her was almost too much to bear. The first few times they made love, she wept every time, overcome with gratitude for his nurturing and relief that she could be her own self with him. He learned her body slowly and talked to her, asking if she liked to be touched here or there, gently like this or more roughly. She learned her *own* body through his touch. He told her over and over again how he loved her body, loved her long neck and firm thighs and even the curve of the little belly she'd had ever since her pregnancies. He wanted to make love to her in daylight, or by the glow of the fire, or with the lamps lit, so he could see her, revel in her.

Her happiness overwhelmed her and even, for the most part, overwhelmed her guilt. Bill had made his own choices, after all. But the guilt she couldn't escape was her guilt over what she saw as a betrayal of her son. Barefoot never touched her in Jim's presence, not even so much as placing a hand on her arm. She never spent a night with Barefoot, never made love with him in her home, even if Jim was at school, or at a friend's. But she wrestled with her demons, and Barefoot knew it.

"You're torturing yourself needlessly," he said one morning, as they sat on his porch sipping coffee. Jim was at school, and she had driven up to Barefoot's farmhouse as soon as she finished her chores, as she did many days now. Deep pink peonies bloomed against the side of the house in the late May sunshine, and the fat buds on the apple trees were starting to unfold. Bill was due home in four weeks. It would be the first time she'd seen him since starting her affair.

"It's not Bill," she said. She leaned back in her rocking chair and put her bare feet up on the porch railing. They had made love for more than an hour, and then she had gotten out of bed and put on one of Barefoot's button-down flannel shirts, and nothing else. This was the other thing he had taught her. He was so completely at ease in his own body that he often walked around the house naked, and he admired her body so openly that her confidence grew. Instead of getting dressed as soon as they finished making love, now she would often sit up naked in bed while he brought her tea, or slip on one of his shirts against the cold and sit out on the porch.

"At least, Bill isn't the biggest part of it. Bill and I never talked about whether or not I'd be faithful to him while he's away. I think he just assumed I would. And as you know, he broke our marital vows a few years after we were married, and God knows how many times since." She closed her eyes and saw again the woman in the yellow dress, laughing as she leaned against the railing of the ferry, Bill's hands on her tiny waist. But the sting of that moment was gone. "Of course I feel *some* guilt about Bill—but what bothers me is Jimmy. I'm the moral center of his universe. I don't want to do something that would shake up his world."

"I don't want that, either." Barefoot stood opposite her, leaning against the railing, one hand caressing her foot. "You're a good mother and a good role model who has taught that boy everything that matters. You've shown him how to live by how you live, and what you value."

"But if he found out *I*—"

Barefoot held up a hand to shush her. "Sssh. He's not going to find out. Does he know his father is unfaithful?"

"No, of course not. At least, I don't think so. I've never spoken badly about Bill to Jimmy, or in front of Jimmy."

"I know. But your boy isn't stupid, and he's sensitive. He may not know about Bill intellectually, but I'm sure he intuits it. He knows his father spends too much time away, more than he needs to."

She sat up. "But do you think that means he'll sense that I'm not faithful to his father? That I'm—"

"Elizabeth." He let go of her foot and leaned forward, putting both hands on her knees and staring into her eyes. "You are confusing guilt and shame," he said. "I understand why you feel some guilt about your relationship with me. It steps outside the boundaries of what is conventional and expected in our culture. It's okay to feel guilty over something you *do*. But this *shame*—this feeling badly about *who you are*—it's unnecessary, and it's wrong."

He stood up, and picked up his coffee mug from where it rested on the worn board of the porch railing. He took a long sip of coffee.

"Jim is a little boy. But as he grows up he's going to think more and question more why his father is away so much, and understand just how much you have sacrificed and how hard you have worked to make a good, secure life for him. At some point, he may even be able to understand why you might have found the kind of love and respect you deserve outside of your marriage."

She shook her head. "No," she said. "I don't want him to know about this. He idolizes his father."

"He's seven years old," Barefoot said. "In nine or ten years, he will see the world differently." He leaned back against the porch railing again. "This is very new. We don't know what might happen and where this might lead us as the years unfold. I can tell you now, though, it does not feel trivial to me."

She looked up at him. "Nor to me."

Silence filled the space between them for a while, but a comfortable silence. Finally Barefoot spoke. "I leave June fifteenth for India," he said.

She felt her heart lurch. "For how long?"

"Four months."

She took a deep breath. "That's a long time."

"Not long, actually. I'll be gone during the summer when your husband is home. It will be easier for you."

"Yes." She wrapped both hands around the warmth of her ceramic mug. "What will you be doing there?"

"Researching melons and collecting seeds in India. There's concern about the blight that hit the California melon crop a few years back, and they want to see if I can find some disease-resistant varieties, maybe some wild species we haven't grown here before. I'll be hunting for some herbs in Tibet and Nepal, too."

"Claire told me once that you had a wife in Tibet."

Barefoot arched one eyebrow at her. "Is that so?" He smiled. "I don't, although I loved a woman there once. The Buddhists have a different view of marriage."

"How so?"

He shrugged. "The Buddhists look at marriage as a social arrangement, not a 'sacrament,' as we would have it here. Most Buddhist texts are silent on the subject of monogamy, although the third precept warns against engaging in 'sexual misconduct.' And to my mind, sex between two people who love each other is not misconduct."

"I'm not a Buddhist," Betty said.

"Meaning what?" Barefoot said. "You think this"—he gestured toward her, and then toward himself—"is a sin?"

"No. I don't know."

"*I* know," Barefoot said. "I believe love—real love, not lust and infatuation, but romantic love that includes deep, caring, generous, kind, and often selfless commitment—is the preeminent and transcendent moral value. It trumps the marital vow. We fulfill our deepest human potential in the context of loving relationships. That can't be wrong."

"It doesn't *feel* wrong."

"Trust that, Elizabeth."

She looked up at him. "Why do you always call me 'Elizabeth'? No one calls me that, not even my mother."

" 'Betty' is a maid." He looked into her eyes. " 'Elizabeth' is a queen."

She flushed, embarrassed, and looked down into her coffee mug, then back up at him. "Oh, please. That's a little corny, isn't it?"

He shrugged. "Decide for yourself which name you prefer, and that's what I'll call you."

She felt the fullness of his love for her, of who she was with him.

"Call me Elizabeth," she said.

When Barefoot left in June they agreed not to write or talk until his return in September. She spent the late spring and early summer shearing the sheep, planting and sowing lettuces and watercress, and thinking hard about her marriage and herself. She came to realize that the problem with Bill was that he wanted something different from what he *thought* he wanted, but didn't know himself well enough to understand that. He had thought he wanted a woman who was strong and independent, someone feisty and different, but in actuality he wanted a woman who would do what *he* wanted 96 percent of the time. Living on Sounder might have been an unorthodox choice, but everything else about their marriage was as traditional as could be. She'd given up her job for Bill, moved to Sounder for Bill, spent months and months alone for Bill, and chosen to ignore— hell, *bless*—his infidelities.

And as she looked hard into the mirror of her marriage, she didn't much like what she saw of herself, either. She had given up a job she loved because Bill hadn't wanted her to work outside the home. She'd listened and encouraged him about Alaska, a place she had no desire to visit, let alone live in. She'd moved with him to Sounder even though she hadn't wanted to leave Seattle and her family. She'd taken up farming—*farming, for God's sake.* If you had told her at eighteen, the year before she got married, that she'd be getting up at four thirty every morning to take care of chickens and muck out goat stalls while wearing dirty dungarees, and then pore over seed catalogs at night, she'd have laughed at the sheer lunacy of it all. For better or for worse, she had made herself over in Bill's image of what he wanted her to be. Now, *that* felt like a sin.

Barefoot had unlocked parts of her she hadn't remembered were there. Over these past months he had asked her about authors she liked, and so she had dug out some of the novels she loved from the bottom of a duffel bag in her closet—in eight years on Sounder, she hadn't unpacked them—and she and Barefoot read aloud to each other: *How Green Was My Valley* and *Memoirs of Hadrian* and her favorite, *East of Eden*. They talked and argued about the books, and he introduced her to new books—*Siddhartha* and *The Story of the Stone* and *The Arabian Nights*.

He never stopped admiring her body, and she took a re-
newed pride in her sinewy strength. As a child and teenager
she'd been adventurous and physical—the only one of the four
kids in her family who learned to snow ski and water-ski, the
fastest in every foot race. He encouraged her to try push-ups
and chin-ups and lauded her increased strength. He challenged
her to a push-up contest—he'd do two for every one she did—
and laughed when she won. He cooked for her—fresh scallops
sautéed in white wine and butter; lamb chops marinated in soy,
ginger, garlic, and mint; bouillabaisse with local fish and shell-
fish in coconut milk. He would leave the food on her porch in
a big cast-iron skillet with a lid, so she could set it on the stove
to warm up before Jim got home from school.

She listened to his stories, debated religion and philoso-
phy with him, rubbed his sore muscles with sesame oil, and
didn't question his absences when she didn't see him for a few
days. Sometimes she would drive up to the white farmhouse
on Crane's Point and find it empty, the fireplace cold, and then
she would drive home and go back to her chores and her child.
Sooner or later Barefoot would appear on her back porch—
sometimes within an hour or two, sometimes two or three days
later. She understood that he was a wild, independent creature,
and had no desire to tame him. His absences gave her a chance
to pull herself together again, recover a little from the intoxica-
tion of her time with him.

And then Barefoot was gone, and Bill was home. Bill was
almost forty now, with weathered lines around his eyes and
across his forehead from his years of work on the boats, but his
eyes were the same rich green, his smile the same seductive
smile. He brought gifts, of course—genuine Indian arrowheads
for Jimmy, and a necklace of crimson beads for Betty. He mar-
veled at all she had done on the farm and with the house in

his absence, at how much Jim had grown. He helped her with the chores, but several times she caught him referring to his summer on Sounder as "my vacation." *That's great*, she thought. *When's* my *vacation*?

She worried that when they made love he would notice some difference in her, in the way she moved, or touched him, or responded to his touches. But he was the same as always, eager for sex, considerate enough to try to make sure she came before he did, and then sleepy or indifferent afterward. She found it more difficult than she had expected to respond to him sexually. She was used to Barefoot's hand behind her head, Barefoot's solid weight on top of her, Barefoot's smooth chest and back beneath her hands. Bill—her husband—felt like a stranger to her now. He was taller and leaner than Barefoot, with a thick thatch of hair across his chest. She missed the way Barefoot talked to her during lovemaking, missed being able to talk herself. She tried once or twice to tell Bill, in a gentle voice, that she wanted him to touch her a certain way, or that she wanted to move in a different rhythm, or even that she liked something he was doing, but he seemed embarrassed by her words and didn't respond.

But Jim was happy. They went to the big annual July Fourth barbecue on Shell Beach, and boated over to Friday Harbor the next day to see the parade of ships all decorated with lights, and the fireworks. They went on a family camping trip to Patos Island and from there to the little islands of Sucia and Matia. They fished for tiger rockfish and Chinook salmon and, late in August, for Cohos. Bill built a tree house for Jim in the old Garry oak by the meadow.

Seeing Bill with their son and Jim's eager love for his father tore at her. She wondered if she could turn her marriage into a real marriage if Bill ever came home to stay for more than a month or two, be herself with him and let him get to know her as she was now, forged as she was into someone much more solid and authentic than the girl he had married. She owed that to Jim, she felt, and decided she would say as much to Barefoot when he returned.

She tried to talk to Bill about spending more time at home.

"Do you know how competitive it is to get onto a king crab boat?" he said. "If I said I couldn't work a full season, there are ten guys standing in line who'd be happy to take my job. We need the money too much. I can't do it."

"We don't need it as much as we did. The farm's breaking even now, every season."

Bill looked at her, his head tilted to one side. "You want me at home?"

She thought of Barefoot, of all their late mornings and early afternoons together, of Barefoot's blue eyes locked on hers when they made love, of the tenderness in his voice when he said her name.

She didn't answer his question. "Look at what it's meant to Jim to have you here this summer."

"I can't quit now, for this coming season," Bill said. "It's too late. But I'll talk to the captain this winter, and talk to some of the other guys and see if they know of any boats that might need someone just for a couple months. How's that?"

It was typical Bill. An answer that wasn't an answer. All at once she thought, *So be it.*

Bill left September 1. Then one day in mid-September she stopped in at the post office to pick up mail, and Frances mentioned that Barefoot Jacobsen was back from Tibet.

"Really?" Betty said. She felt her heart thump against her rib cage, and tried to make her voice casual, easy. "When did he get back?"

"Day before yesterday. He came in yesterday for the mail."

"Did he have a good trip?"

"As good as ever, I guess," Frances said. "I've heard he has a wife there."

Betty smiled. "Yes, I've heard that, too."

"He's an odd one," Frances said.

Betty nodded. She gathered her mail and made some excuse about Jim and needing to get home and left the post office, not willing to talk about Barefoot anymore in case her face or her voice or her very body betray her excitement and longing.

She went home and made dinner for Jim and thought about their summer together with Bill, as a family. She thought about the twelve years she'd spent married to Bill, who had done little but pursue his own needs. She thought about Barefoot. Maybe he'd changed. Maybe his four months of travel in exotic lands had reminded him why he had never married, reinforced for him the joys of freedom.

He came to her house the next morning, after Jim had left for school. He walked over, so she didn't hear him come up the dirt road, didn't hear his footsteps cross the meadow to the drying shed, where she was laying out onions and garlic for the winter.

"Elizabeth."

She turned and saw him standing there, and his blue eyes pierced her heart. She walked over to him and held his precious head between her hands, looked at his tanned and wind-burned face, gazed into his eyes, and felt so much love for him she couldn't speak. He wrapped his arms around her and buried his face in her neck, inhaling the scent of her. She looked up at the sky above his head and felt a moment of complete and pure happiness. *If this is a sin*, she thought, *then I'll happily go to hell*.

"Welcome home," she said.

Chapter 20

Susannah 2011

The day after Thanksgiving, Susannah was the first one up, piling more wood in the stove to warm up the living room, grinding the beans for coffee, heating water. Matt and the kids were still asleep. They'd picked her mother up in Friday Harbor on Wednesday and then had Thanksgiving dinner with the Pavalaks there at the white cottage last night. With all the cooking and baking and washing up, Susannah hadn't had a moment alone with her mother, which was just fine. She hadn't had a moment alone with Matt, either, which was not so fine.

She stepped outside on the porch to feed the barn cats. The sky was a pale pink above the eastern horizon, darkening to deep blue overhead. A few late stars lingered in the sky. The morning was cool and calm, and the evening mist lingered in droplets of water pooled on the glossy leaves of the salal and clinging to the tall stalks of the grasses in the meadow. She could smell the sweet smoke from the fire in the kitchen stove, and hear the low, husky warbling of snow buntings.

Katie had apologized over and over again for giving her the

cupcake. She'd written letters to both Barefoot and Susannah. "*I like it here, Mom,*" she had written. "*Coming here was a good idea. I want to be here with you. Please don't send me home.*"

She took a deep breath. A movement caught her eye and she saw a figure on the path—Lila, hair neatly combed, a camel-colored trench coat draped across her shoulders. Susannah's stomach clenched.

"Morning, Mom," she said, as her mother approached. "Did you sleep all right?"

"Yes," Lila said. "It's so *quiet* here. And so dark." She wore red lipstick and small pearl earrings and a matching necklace. The collar of her white blouse was turned just so over the neck of her sweater. All the things you *could* control, neatly in place. She came up and stood next to Susannah. "It's very peaceful. I can see why you wanted this. You were always so *busy* in Tilton. On the go all the time."

"Yes," Susannah said.

"It's also cold," Lila said, rubbing her hands together. "There's a lot to be said for central heating."

"Come on inside. I've got the stove lit and I'll make tea."

Susannah led Lila inside and made a pot of strong black tea. After gazing out the windows at the meadow and the fir trees, and running a hand over the worn corduroy of the couch, Lila sat down at the table and wrapped her hands around her mug.

Susannah looked at her mother—her sharp profile, so unlike Susannah's rounder features; her fine, white hair, so unlike Susannah's thick, dark hair; her pale blue eyes, so unlike Susannah's brown ones. Even at seventy-three, her mother was a striking-looking woman, fine boned and pretty. Susannah could see not a trace of herself in her mother, or vice versa. Physically, she was her father through and through. And temperamentally she was her mother, all nerves and caution.

"I had fun talking to Katie last night," Lila said. "She was telling me she's working on that boat up on some cliff. She's learned how to use all kinds of tools."

"Right," Susannah said. She broke three eggs into the big white ceramic bowl for pancakes. "She's learning woodworking skills, and some responsibility. Barefoot Jacobsen, the man she's working for, is a longtime islander—and a very accomplished botanist. Katie got into some trouble at school, and I wanted to keep her occupied. Working on Barefoot's boat has been great for her." Susannah wasn't about to go into the story of Katie's poem, or the cupcakes, with her mother.

"But he sounds very eccentric, from what Katie says—maybe violent. She told me he shot a man in the hand once. And she's up there alone with him."

"He's eccentric but perfectly sane," Susannah said. "And he's not violent. That's an old story that happened fifty years ago in the Middle East. Another time and another country. He's been teaching Quinn how to identify all kinds of plants."

Lila raised both eyebrows. "Quinn is spending time up there, too? You're not worried about this man's influence over your children?"

"No," Susannah said. "It's not like that."

"Well, they're your kids," Lila said, stirring milk into her tea.

"What's that supposed to mean?"

"Nothing. You know what's best for them, I'm sure."

Susannah beat the eggs together with more vigor than she intended.

"Katie's changed a lot since I saw her," Lila said. "She's so tall, and looks so grown-up. And she's so"—Lila searched for the word—"*outspoken*. How old is she now? Thirteen?"

"Fourteen. She turned fourteen in September."

"Ah, right. I'm trying to remember what you were like at fourteen."

I turned fourteen two months after Janie died, Susannah thought. *You were a zombie.* "I was quiet," Susannah said. She picked up the saucepan in which she'd melted butter and poured the golden liquid into the bowl with the eggs. "It wasn't a great year."

Lila closed her eyes. "No," she said. "It wasn't a great year." She opened her eyes and looked up at Susannah. "I wish—" She stopped. "It doesn't matter. It is what it is. Still, we've never talked about it."

"Mom, don't." Susannah began to whisk the eggs and butter and milk together. "Losing Janie was a tragedy. I don't blame you for having such a hard time afterward." *Although I'll never understand why you let us go in the first place.* "As you said, it is what it is. We don't need to talk about it."

Susannah remembered a day ten months after the accident. Their father had moved out, and Lila had found a job as a secretary at the local high school. She was getting up and getting dressed and going to work every day, cooking dinner, acting almost like a normal mom. Aunt Tessa urged Susannah to do something for Mother's Day. Susannah had her reservations. She couldn't articulate them, even to herself, but it didn't take a genius to figure out that Mother's Day had the potential to crush Lila's fragile return to normalcy as carelessly and permanently as a foot coming down on a tiny green shoot.

"She's going to be sad on Mother's Day," Susannah said to Tessa. "She's going to be reminded about Janie."

"You think she ever forgets?" Tessa said. "She also needs to remember she has two living children who love her, and that she's a good mother to them. Do something."

So Susannah, ever the dutiful child, walked Jon over to the drugstore and picked out two cards and a small box of candy. She worried about it. Were the cards too cheery? Too solemn? Should she *make* a card instead? It had been so long since Lila had any genuine relish for food that Susannah couldn't even remember if she liked candy.

Then, at the checkout counter, her eyes lit on a tiny red bird made of folded paper.

"What's that?" she asked the clerk.

"An origami crane," the clerk said. "We sell the kit, over there."

Susannah picked up a box with small squares of bright paper. "Folding a thousand paper cranes is an expression of hope and goodwill," she read on the box. "This beautiful symbol is a perfect gift for special celebrations. The kit contains everything needed to create and display a thousand colorful cranes."

Susannah put the candy back and bought the kit. At home she read the instructions and, after several failed attempts, folded a sheet of pink paper (Lila's favorite color) into something resembling a bird. She made another one in purple and told Jon he could give it to their mother. She didn't have time to make a thousand, which sounded pretty daunting, not to mention dull. But if they gave these two to Lila with the cards and told her about all the luck and goodwill they represented, maybe that would be a good Mother's Day present.

Before dinner that night, Susannah put the cards and the cranes on the table next to Lila's plate.

"What's this?" Lila said. She picked up the pink crane. "This is so pretty." She smiled at Susannah, a warm smile that reached her eyes.

Susannah remembered the hope that flooded into her, a rush of warmth and relief.

"It's Mother's Day," Susannah said. "Happy—," she started to say, then bit it back. That wasn't the right word, not yet. "We wanted to do something for you."

Pain settled into Lila's eyes, darkness coming home to roost. "Oh," she said. "Mother's Day. I forgot. It's good of you kids to remember." She picked up the pink crane and put it down on the outstretched palm of her left hand and studied it, twisting her wrist so she could view it from every angle.

"Did you make this?" she said.

Susannah told her about the thousand paper cranes, that she planned to make ten a day so she could make a thousand by Christmas, and they could hang them in strings for luck like in the picture on the box.

Lila stared at the crane for a long time, while Susannah and Jon stared at Lila. Susannah remembered the sense that her mother was fighting with herself, waging some great internal struggle that, finally, she lost, because her eyes filled with tears and she pushed her chair back from the table and walked into her room and closed the door, leaving the cards unopened on the table, and Jon's purple crane sitting there alone.

Aunt Tessa came over not long after, and told Susannah she'd done the right thing, it was just going to take time. Then Tessa spent a long time in their mother's room with the door closed, while Susannah and Jon tried to ignore the murmuring voices, the sobs. The next day Susannah found the pink crane crumpled into a ball at the bottom of the wastebasket next to her mother's bed.

Susannah didn't like remembering.

"Here." She handed her mother another, smaller bowl, with the dry ingredients inside. "Whisk those together, will you? I've got to find the griddle, and I'm going to wake Matt up. The kids want to take you on a tour of the island. It'll be fun for you to see everything."

"Or I could stay here and help you with whatever you need for dinner. Matt could spend some time alone with the kids. It would give us a chance to talk."

"I don't need help. I've got it under control," Susannah said.

She did not want to spend an afternoon in the cottage with her mother, peeling potatoes and fending off her mother's attempts to talk to her about things that had been left unsaid for thirty-odd years, things Susannah could not and would not discuss. Too late for all that now.

"You go with Matt and the kids. Maybe I'll come, too."

Lila sat back in her chair. All at once she looked older to Susannah, the lines on her face deeply etched, the shadows dark under her eyes. Her eyes searched Susannah's face, but Susannah turned away, to look for the cast-iron griddle.

"Fine," Lila said. "I'll go."

They spent the afternoon showing Lila everything—the barn, Jim's cabin, Shell Beach, the Laundromat. They even drove up to Crane's Point to show her Barefoot's house and the boat. They finished their tour with a stop at the school.

Katie had wanted to go fishing with Hood, but Susannah refused. She didn't want the two of them spending too much time alone together. And this was a family outing: Katie needed to come. She came, but she was a like a tethered wild thing as they visited each place, pacing and rolling her eyes and running nervous fingers through her hair.

Finally, as Quinn started to point out and name the varieties of grasses that grew alongside the road by the school, Katie had had enough.

"Oh, my God," Katie said. "Listen to yourself! You sound like some hundred-year-old biology professor. You can't possibly imagine anyone gives a crap about the name of the *grass*. Seriously. This is why no one liked you in Tilton."

Quinn turned an angry face to her. "Shut up!"

"That's enough, Katie," Susannah said. "Leave him alone."

"Oh, right," Katie said. "Get mad at *me*. Do you have any

idea what was happening to him at home? Or what *I* had to do to protect him?"

"Shut up! I don't need anyone protecting me," Quinn said. He glared at Katie.

"What do you mean?"

"He was like the outcast of the entire sixth grade," Katie said. "At the bus stop these two girls used to hug him and rub against him until he blushed and then everyone would laugh, and then the guys would push him around and call him names. I finally told them off, and then *I* got in trouble."

"Stop it!" Quinn's face was bright red.

"You got in trouble?" Susannah said.

"Yes!" Katie was angry now, the words spilling out. "My bus was late one day, so I was still at the bus stop when Quinn came. And those assholes—sorry, Mom, those *mean people*—were teasing him and I finally told them off. I missed my bus. So I walked to school. Then I ran into Hillary, and she asked me to skip school with her. I was so mad I said, 'Sure.' Then I got in huge trouble. All because of Quinn." She spat his name.

Hillary. The girl who had been arrested twice for selling drugs.

"I *hate* having to protect him," Katie said. "And I hate it you're so clueless."

Quinn took one final, furious look at Katie and then ran, across the school field and the dirt road, disappearing on the path into the woods on the other side.

"Quinn!" Matt called after him. "Quinn!"

"It's fine," Susannah said. "Let him be alone. That path leads home."

"That's why I smashed Otis's stupid wife," Katie said. "I was trying to talk to him about behaving like a *normal* person on the first day of school here, and he wouldn't listen. It pissed me off."

"I knew things were bad at home," Susannah said. "I didn't realize—"

"You have no idea about anything," Katie said. "You worry about totally stupid things like Barefoot growing marijuana or what I'm doing with Hood. Maybe you should be worried about what a completely neurotic person you are. I can't *stand* being stuck with you. Dad can't even stand you; that's why he didn't care that you moved here."

Susannah looked at Matt. He stood with both hands in his pockets, looking uncomfortable.

"We need to end this conversation," he said. He turned to Lila. "Sorry you've had to listen to all this, Lila. Come on, let's get in the truck and go home."

"*Matt,*" Susannah said. She jogged a few steps to catch up to him as he walked toward the truck. "You have to say something to her, shut her down for being so rude."

"Susannah." He stopped and turned to face her. "I have not seen my kids in six weeks. I've been here ten days and spent most of it lecturing Katie for everything she's done wrong. I'm leaving in a few days and I won't see her again for another month. I'm not going to nag her every time she acts like a typical teenager and picks on her brother or sasses you. Quinn needs to learn to give it back to her, to stick up for himself, and you need to learn that, too, frankly."

"What?" Susannah was overcome with a blind anger. "*No,* I don't," she said. "You're just so emotionally uptight you don't understand what it's like to get your feelings hurt."

"Are you kidding?" Matt's voice was incredulous.

"Nothing gets to you; nothing touches you. It doesn't bother you if Quinn's getting bullied or Katie is cruel or if we decide to leave—"

"Oh, for Christ's sake!"

"You think I would have come here if—just once—you had wrapped your arms around me and said, 'Don't go'?"

But of course he hadn't done that; no one, *no one*, could love her that much.

"And if I'd done that, then you would have been mad at me for holding you back," he said. "I can't win. How do you think I feel, being the one left behind? This isn't the first time you've run away."

"Oh, come on. I left for a few days when we weren't even married yet."

"And will you go again the next time things get difficult?"

Lila and Katie caught up, and Lila put a hand on Susannah's shoulder.

"Susie?" she said. "What's the matter?"

Susannah whirled to face her. "As though *you* care," she said. "It's ironic, isn't it, that I married someone just like you, someone who doesn't think I'm worth protecting?"

Susannah ran then, past the truck and into the woods, and on the path toward home. She ran until her lungs were burning and she couldn't run anymore and slowed to a walk. She stopped for a minute and leaned forward, hands on her knees, taking in deep breaths of the clean air. A thrush, with its burnt orange throat, hopped along the ground just beyond the path. Moss grew thick and green in the decaying stump of a fallen cedar, bright against the grays and browns of the bark. She stood up. Looking at it all calmed her in some strange way. She was surrounded by decay—the rotting stump, the moldy leaves, the loamy soil—yet it all fed new life.

Katie's brusque attitude over the last year had opened old wounds. Somehow Katie and her father had become jumbled together, their harsh criticisms a reminder of all her failings. Lila had never stood up for her; Matt wouldn't stand up for her.

Until Katie's adolescence, Susannah had never doubted Matt was on her side, even when she had found it hard to be on her own side. She thought of their wedding day, when he'd faced down her father in front of the entire church. She had planned to have *both* her parents walk her down the aisle, to recognize her mother while not excluding her father. But her father—still an alcoholic, with an alcoholic's quick temper and hypersensitivity to any perceived slight—had been irate at what he saw as an insult depriving him of his right to give away his only daughter.

"After all," he said, "I'll never walk Janie down the aisle."

He'd showed up drunk on the day of the wedding, not slur-his-words-and-stumbling drunk, but drunk enough to have a razor-sharp edge of anger slice beneath his smile. At the back of the church before the music began, he had elbowed Lila out of the way and said, "I'm walking my daughter down the aisle *alone.*"

Her mother had glanced at Susannah, looked at her ex-husband, and stepped back. *She doesn't want to make a scene at my wedding*, Susannah had thought. *I don't want to make a scene at my wedding. And he knows it, he knows us both that well. The bastard.*

"Dad, we agreed—" she had started to say, but her mother shook her head and mouthed: "Don't." The music began; the bridesmaids started to march; the guests turned expectantly in their seats. Susannah's father took her arm and led her to the doorway.

And then Matt, standing in the front of the church with his brothers and Jon, had seen Susannah and her father there alone, with her mother behind them. He had folded his lips into a firm line, waited a beat for the bridesmaids to line up at the front of the church, and then walked straight down the aisle, to the surprised gasps of the crowd.

"You're beautiful," he had whispered to Susannah. Then to her father, "Mr. McGilvra, you look fine. Great day, isn't it?" His words were pleasant, but his voice had an undercurrent of anger so fierce that Susannah drew back. He stepped around them to Susannah's mother, pulled her forward, and placed her firmly on Susannah's other side.

"We all love Susannah," he said. "Let's walk with her together." And he had given them a shove, nodded to the minister, who signaled the organist, and they had walked down the aisle, the four of them, with Susannah's parents on either side of her and Matt behind them, nodding and smiling at the guests.

He had been her champion. Which is why she had felt even more betrayed over this last year when he failed to champion her with Katie.

When Susannah emerged from the woods at the side of the meadow, she headed to the barn. She slid back the heavy wooden door and stepped inside. The pale afternoon light streamed in through the window.

She walked over to stand in front of her work in progress. Her scarecrow was a three-foot-tall angel made of scrap metal and wood and glass. She'd started by painting a face on a piece of tin, a girl with bright pink lips and golden brown hair and penetrating brown eyes. Something about the eyes had looked soulful to Susannah, so she had designed a halo out of a bicycle rim, with spokes still attached, and covered it with pieces of pale blue and green sea glass and bright copper wire. She cut giant tin wings out of scrap metal. The arms were thin plumbing pipes, and the body was a long, colorful, patchwork dress made from old tin cans, the kind that had the colors and words printed right on the tin, and not on paper labels. Susannah had cut them and flattened them and drilled holes in them and stitched them together with copper wire.

She'd been working on it for three weeks now. But all at

once, she saw the angel sculpture differently. It was whimsical, sure. Maybe even bold or intriguing, as Jim might say. But what she saw now, for the first time, was that the angel with the big smile and brown eyes and wavy hair was Janie, the ghost that haunted her life.

Chapter 21

Betty 2011

Betty lowered herself into the armchair in front of Barefoot's fireplace. The white chair was comfortable—plush and soft but not so deep you'd sink down into it and be stuck forever. Barefoot brought over the Tibetan traveling medicine chest he used as an end table and placed it next to her chair, then went to the kitchen and returned with a glass of wine for her and a beer for himself. He put his beer down on the mantel and bent to put another log on the fire. The wood crackled and the flames flared and streamed upward, casting a coppery glow on the still-fine angles of Barefoot's cheekbones, the lines of his jaw. He was a beautiful man, even with the crow's feet and furrows and now-white hair. She never tired of looking at his face.

He picked up his beer and sat down in the armchair opposite hers.

"So has Katie been here this week?" she said.

"Nope. Although she did slide a letter of apology under my door a few days ago."

Betty took a long sip of her wine. "It's a grape variety," she said, looking at him over her glass.

He shook his head. "Rose hips. You like it?"

She nodded. "It's very good." She took another sip. "What will you say to Katie?"

"I'll tell her I can't trust her and don't want her to work for me."

Betty put her glass down on the chest. She knew not to ask for a coaster; Barefoot believed that things—even precious things—should be *used*, not revered.

"She's not a bad kid."

"I know she's not a bad kid," he said. "She's worked her ass off on the boat and done a good job. She's smart, too." He stood up to poke the fire again. "And that mother of hers *could* use a little antianxiety medicine once in a while. Don't know that she'd be willing to try marijuana again, but I could make her a good calming tea."

Betty smiled. "I like Susannah. She's got a good heart; God, she'd cut off a finger to help you if you needed it. But she is a worrier. She's like Jim; she cares about things too much and thinks about things too much." Betty ran her hand over the smooth white fabric on the arm of her chair. "Sometimes I worry she cares about Jim too much. I'm glad her husband's here now."

"Where the hell is Fiona?"

"She'll be back in time for Christmas."

Barefoot raised both eyebrows. "I'll believe that when I see it. She's a fine woman, but she shouldn't leave Jim and those boys alone for so long."

"Susannah's doing the same thing."

"And they're both wrong."

"It's what Bill did."

Barefoot shook his head. "Ah, ah, ah, woman, I'm not going

to fall into that trap. I have not said a word against your husband since the day your son finished his swimming lessons, and I'm not going to start now."

Betty smiled, and nodded in acknowledgment. "I've had my reservations about Fiona, as you know, but I believe she loves Jim and those boys. I think she was just feeling claustrophobic. She's a dozen years younger than Jim, you know, and married him when she was twenty. She's put in plenty of years working and living here. I don't begrudge her this sabbatical, if you will, at least not anymore."

Betty glanced at the window, at the dusk filling the panes, the endless sky above the cliff top. "She e-mails him every day. Jim's showed me a few of the notes. I get the impression she's figured out enough to know she likes and needs to do some kind of work, but that Sounder is home and she's in love with her husband."

"For your son's sake, I hope that's true."

"You've always been a cynic."

"I've always been a realist, Elizabeth."

"So have I," she said.

"Very true."

He had asked her to marry him once, two or three years after Bill's death. She had been planting beets one cool April evening when he had walked up the drive, carrying a basket of fresh herbs and greens from his greenhouse. He never came without bringing her something. One day it had been two glossy black feathers he found on the cliff top ("a Brandt's cormorant," he told her), another day it was a warm felt cap he'd picked up while traveling in Turkey.

He had watched her until she finished planting the row. She straightened up and turned to him.

"I would marry you, Elizabeth," he had said.

She remembered the tenderness in his blue eyes, the gravity in his voice.

"I know you would," she said. "But you don't have to. I don't need that."

Now a knock on the door surprised both of them. Barefoot—ever alert from his years in wild, remote places—picked up the wrought-iron poker and went to the door, the poker gripped firmly in one hand. He opened the door to reveal Katie standing on the porch, her cheeks red with cold. He scowled.

"Can I come in?" Katie said. "Please?"

Barefoot stared at her for a moment, then nodded. "Don't get too comfortable, though."

Katie stepped inside and stood on the richly colored prayer rug by the door, uncertain whether or not to take a step farther. Barefoot closed the door behind her.

"You walk over?"

Katie nodded.

"That's a long, cold walk. Your parents know you're here?"

Katie nodded again.

"And?"

"I wrote you a letter. Did you get it?"

Barefoot nodded. "I did."

"I want to keep working with you," Katie said. "I'm really sorry."

"My herbs are drugs. I can't have someone around here I can't trust."

"I know. I was really wrong. I'll never do anything like that again, I promise." She looked at him straight on. "Please."

Barefoot turned around and walked back to his chair and sat down. He began to tick her transgressions off with his fingers. "One, you stole from me," he said. "Two, you used a medicinal herb I had prepared and gave it to someone without my authorization. Three, you gave a medicinal herb to someone without her knowledge or consent. Four, you destroyed a damn good batch of cupcakes when you dropped 'em on the floor to cover your tracks. And five, well, five the whole thing pisses me off."

"I know." Katie stood on the prayer rug, still in her coat and gloves. Her nose was dripping from the cold outside and she lifted her arm and wiped it on her sleeve. "I know I messed up. But I really like working on the boat and learning how to use all the tools. I think it's amazing you know so much about herbs and what to do with them. And it's really cool you lived in Persia and all those places. I like hanging out here. I even like your stuff." She gestured toward the carved stone horse's head on the mantel, the jewel-toned Indian painting of a Sikh noble and his mistress above the fireplace, the coppery-red Persian rug on the floor.

"I don't care what you like," Barefoot said.

Betty gave him a look. He didn't have to be *quite* so harsh.

"What have you done to make it right with your mother?" Barefoot said.

Katie sighed. "I apologized. I wrote her a letter, too."

"Words are easy," Barefoot said.

"Well, my mom is not an easy person to deal with," Katie said.

"You haven't made it easy for her, have you?" Barefoot said. "I understand you almost drank yourself to death before she brought you out here."

"I can't believe she told you about that," Katie said.

"Is it true?"

"Well, yes, but—"

"Then she only told the truth."

"Oh, my God," Katie said. She pulled the knit cap off her head with an angry hand. "If you knew what my mother was like in Tilton, you wouldn't blame me."

"Blame you for what? Drinking yourself into a stupor, or giving your mother pot cupcakes?"

"Anything!" Katie said. Angry tears filled her eyes.

Betty wanted to go to Katie and wrap her arms around her and say, "It's okay. Someday you won't have this much *feeling* about everything." But instead she turned to Barefoot and said, "Go make this girl a cup of hot chocolate and let her warm up by the fire. Please."

"It's okay," Katie said. "I don't have to stay. I just wanted to be sure you got my letter."

"Take your coat off," Barefoot said. He stood and walked into the kitchen. Katie looked at Betty with some uncertainty, then took off her coat and hung it on the hook by the front door. She came over and sat down on the floor by the fireplace, near Toby, who was asleep on the rug in front of the fire. She put a hand on his head and rested it there.

"His bark is worse than his bite," Betty said. "And I mean Barefoot, not the dog."

Katie smiled then, a genuine smile that opened up her whole face.

Betty shifted her hips and settled back more comfortably into her chair. "Your mom is a worrier. I know that can be hard to live with."

"Oh, my God," Katie said. She was more relaxed now, maybe because Barefoot was out of the room; maybe because Barefoot had relented enough to let her in the door; maybe because she was sitting in front of a warm fire, petting Toby.

"You have no idea. She worries about *everything*. If I get a fever she thinks I have leukemia. If I'm home half an hour late, she thinks I've been hit by a car."

"She has a vivid imagination," Betty said.

Katie rolled her eyes. "Right. But it makes me feel"—she searched for the right word—"I don't know, it makes me feel *more unsafe*. Like everything is dangerous, or might be dangerous. I hate that."

Betty nodded. "I can see that."

Katie was silent for a few minutes, one hand absent-mindedly stroking Toby's ear. "It's like Zach, this guy I was dating that my mom hated? He wasn't afraid of anything; he never worried about things. So I didn't feel worried when I was hanging out with him."

"You don't like the fact that you worry just like your mother does," Barefoot said. He came out of the kitchen with a steaming mug in one hand and a plate of cookies in the other. He brought the mug to Katie and put the plate down on the medicine chest, next to Betty's wineglass. "Oatmeal chocolate chip," he said. "Straight, no marijuana." He scowled at Katie but his anger had lost its edge.

"I am not like my mom," Katie said.

"You are," Barefoot said. He sat down in his chair. "Whether you want to admit it or not. I'll tell you, it's only when I learned to accept that I was a lot like my mother that I began to be happier. I suspect you'll find that to be true yourself. Our mothers are the most influential in making us who we are. As long as you regard your mother with distaste, it's not possible to view yourself charitably, with the kindness and self-acceptance so essential to personal happiness. I suggest you practice standing in your mom's shoes and seeing the world, including yourself, from her perspective. If you do, you might begin to be happier and leave behind the miseries and discomforts that plague all of us in adolescence."

Barefoot finished his speech. Katie's eyes were still on him. Betty couldn't help but smile. Everything he'd said was so quintessentially Barefoot. She was aware now that they were both in their eighties that their time together was not as limitless as it had once seemed to be. He was very precious to her.

"Honestly," Katie said, "no offense or anything, but if I really thought I was just like my mother I wouldn't be able to stand myself."

Barefoot shrugged. "Well, that's a hard way to go through life. Your choice."

A long silence fell then, punctuated only by the steady sound of Toby's snoring and the occasional crackle of the fire. Finally Barefoot leaned forward in his chair.

"I'm going to put you on probation," he said to Katie. "You can come back to work on the boat tomorrow, but you will not be allowed in my house or the greenhouse until you've demonstrated that I can trust you again. What that means is that you show up to work on time, do everything that's expected, clean up and put your tools away, and don't give me any crap. *If* you can do that for a month, I might let you back inside. Understood?"

Katie nodded. "Thank you."

She stood up and put her mug down on the mantel. "I should go. Mom will think I've been crushed by a falling tree in the forest."

Betty smiled. "You have a flashlight?"

"Yes." She went to the door and got her coat, put it on, and pulled her cap out of the pocket. She paused, one hand on the doorknob. "Thanks again," she said.

Barefoot walked over to the door and opened it for her. "Don't mess up," he said.

Betty watched the door close behind Katie. She fished her cigarettes out of her shirt pocket, shook one out, and lit it. She blew out a long, satisfying stream of smoke.

Barefoot came back and stood in front of the fire, facing her. "You've got to quit smoking, Elizabeth."

She raised her eyes to his. "Hasn't killed me yet. Besides, I figure it gives me a shot at dying before you do."

He shook his head. "You want to go first?"

She took another long drag, and turned her head away from him to gaze at the Kashan silk tapestry on the wall. A path of white stones wound through blooming trees and lush gardens of red and yellow flowers, and graceful birds swooped down from a blue sky. She never tired of looking at it.

"It's hard to imagine my life without you in it," she said.

"I know," he said. "Because sometimes I imagine mine without you. Impoverished."

"What?" She turned her head to look at him again.

"Impoverished." His blue eyes held hers, pierced her soul. "My life would be impoverished without you."

"Yes," she said. "As would mine without you."

And she raised her glass to the man who wasn't her husband but whom she loved more than any man she'd ever known— here and now and in whatever world, if any, was yet to come.

Chapter 22

Susannah 1978

Susannah's father was cheerful that morning, whistling some old Beatles song in the funny way he had, sucking the air in through his teeth to make the notes instead of blowing it out. Her mom packed a cooler full of sandwiches and blueberries and fudge and Vernor's Ginger Ale. Lila was going shopping in Harbor Springs with her sister, their Aunt Tessa, while Dad took them out in the boat. Susannah was excited about the outing, but noticed that her mother seemed distracted. Her blue cardigan was on inside out. She told them to be careful, but then almost forgot to put Janie's little life jacket in the bag. *You all have to wear your life jackets all the time. I know you're a good swimmer, Jonny, but your dad has to watch out for all three of you, so you have to keep it on. No horsing around. You have to be seated and holding on when the boat is moving.* And Lila avoided looking at their father until they were almost out the door.

"Are you sure this isn't too much, Hank?" Lila said. "Two kids and a toddler on a boat is a lot. Maybe I should come."

He shot her a serious, angry look that confused Susannah.

"You should stay. I can handle it. Susannah can keep an eye

on the baby, and Jon will help with the boat, right?" Jon, eleven then, nodded with importance.

At the last minute, while their mother was off looking for Janie's sun hat, their father slipped a six-pack of beer inside the cooler, and a small silver flask. "Can't expect me to be out in the sun all day and have nothing to quench my thirst," he said, with a wink at Susannah. She felt a clench of fear but didn't want to jeopardize this special outing. *Mistake number one.*

Her mother ran after them once they'd gotten into the car, and started to say something, but then stopped. "Watch the sky; the weather can come up quickly" was all she said. *As though the weather were the only danger.* She opened the rear door and kissed Janie and Jon, and then leaned through the open window in front to kiss Susannah. "Be careful, Hank," she said. And Susannah knew then that her mother didn't quite trust him. But her father put a hand on Susannah's knee and squeezed it—reminding her of the secret they shared, like they were friends, companions—and she couldn't say anything about the beer, couldn't do something to cause a fight.

"Take care, Lila," he said. "Hope it goes well." Their mother lowered her eyes, unbent from the window, and stood up, smoothing the front of her dress with her hands. Their father looked at her standing there, her hands on her stomach, but he didn't say anything. He pulled his mouth tight into a thin line and turned the key in the ignition.

"We're off," he said. "See you later." And they set out for the marina, for the big yellow boat with the dark blue racing stripe and their day of fun.

Susannah saw the bright blue sky above Lake Michigan, the fluffy white clouds. She saw her father standing on the little platform at the back of the boat, his back to the water, knees bent, poised for takeoff. He pushed off and executed a perfect backflip, and she and Janie clapped. Jon tried to imitate him but spun sideways and made a crazy splash that made them all laugh. Their father climbed out of the water, his dark hair slicked back, laughing. He was so handsome, not like other people's dads. He had thick dark hair and bright blue eyes—Black Irish, he always said with pride—and a long torso that was still lean and muscular even now that he was in his forties.

He was in a good mood. He did more backflips. He stood on the platform, bent his knees, and launched Jon from his thighs, rocketing him into the water. Then their dad held Janie while Susannah swam. She slipped off her life jacket, as Jon had, so she could dive down into the cool, murky green water, and then back up toward the sun. It felt good. She and Jon took turns showing off their dives, telling Janie to clap loudly for the dives she liked best.

"Stay next to the boat where I can see you," their dad said. "No swimming off." Susannah was happy he was paying attention; it meant she could let her guard down and enjoy the day. She liked the feeling of the water rushing against her skin as she dove down, liked sensing the stream of bubbles that trailed behind her.

Their dad opened the cooler and pulled out a beer. He gave Janie a sandwich. He tore the sandwich into little pieces and pretended Janie was a pelican and tossed bits of it into her open mouth. She loved the game and flapped her imaginary wings with enthusiasm, crowing with delight every time she caught a tiny bit of bread or ham in her mouth. Susannah and Jon practiced their surface dives, and then Jon started mooning Susannah with each dive, his skin bright white against the dark surface of the water. Their dad made jokes about the sun shining on Jon's moon. At last she and Jon clambered back up into the boat and sat down, wet and satisfied, to eat their own lunch.

"My life jacket off," Janie said, tugging at the tie on her life vest. She pointed at Susannah and Jon, who wore only their swimsuits now.

"No, you've got to keep it on," their dad said.

"*No.*" Janie said. "Off!" She tugged and tugged at the bow Susannah had tied under her chin, and pulled it loose. She struggled with the buckle at her waist. "Take it off now!"

Susannah looked at her father. Five empty beer cans littered the floor of the boat. She was nervous about the beer. Her father was so unpredictable; you never knew when that particular drink, that last sip, might turn him suddenly from calm and pleasant into something else, something darker.

"Keep your life jacket on, Jane," she said. "See? I'm wearing mine." She quickly slipped her life jacket over her head and buckled it around her waist. "See?"

"No!" Janie began to cry. "Take it off!"

"Oh, for Christ's sake! Keep your goddamn life jacket on!"

Susannah and Jon exchanged glances, and Jon picked up his life jacket and put it on.

"See, Jane? We're all wearing them!"

But there was no stopping her now. "Take it off! Take it off!" She began to scream, a shrill, loud, high-pitched wail.

"You have to wear the goddamn life jacket!" their father said.

Susannah heard the edge in his voice. Janie screamed louder.

"You want it off? Fine! Take it off!" Their father leaned over and undid the buckle. Janie, surprised, stopped screaming and looked at him. Tears moistened her cheeks, clung to her long, thick eyelashes.

"Happy now?" he said.

Janie looked at him, put her thumb in her mouth, and nodded. She didn't even take the life jacket off; she just seemed happy to know she could if she wanted to.

"You know, Dad, we should go home soon," Susannah said. "We told Mom we'd be back by four." She wanted to avoid any more potential incidents, anything else that could turn his mood.

"We'll be back in plenty of time. Your mother's busy. She's off shopping. She won't notice if we're back late." He wiped his mouth with the back of his hand and tilted his head back, closing his eyes and letting the warmth of the sun shine full on his face.

"But we're going to Aunt Tessa's for dinner at five," Jon said. "Henry and I were going to go blueberry picking before dinner. I said I'd meet him before then."

"Jesus Christ!" Their father sat up and slammed the beer can down on the dashboard. "I take you kids out for a day on the lake, bring a picnic, swim with you—and all you can do is complain and beg to go home." He turned in his seat and switched the key in the ignition. "All right, we'll go home."

Susannah pulled Janie onto her lap and sat down in the cushioned seat at the back of the boat, next to the inboard engine. Their dad was mad, but if they just went home now, it would be fine. She didn't want to be trapped in the small confines of the boat with him if he really got angry. Jon sat on the other side of the motor.

Their dad pulled up the little ladder off the stern and started the engine, and pushed the throttle forward. The wind had picked up since the morning, and the lake now murmured with small waves and tiny whitecaps. The boat sped across the water, bouncing up and down over the larger waves. Susannah gripped Janie more tightly in her arms.

"No," Janie said. She pushed at Susannah's arm.

Their father pushed the throttle all the way down, and the boat picked up speed, flew across the water. Susannah saw another large speedboat cross a little ways in front of them, also going full tilt. It was white, she remembered, a big white boat. Janie waved, as she did at everybody. The people in the boat waved back. Susannah saw the white plume of water behind the boat, the surge of the wake. And before she had time to think about it, their boat slammed into the wake at full speed.

The impact lifted the boat into the air, lifted the bow up and up so that for one terrifying moment Susannah thought the boat was going to flip. Janie shot out of Susannah's arms. Jon rocketed into the air, landing on the floor by their father's feet as the boat came down. Susannah tumbled off her seat and hit her head against the cushioned edge of the chair in front of her.

"Stop!" she screamed at her father. Jon's cries mingled with her screams. And Janie—where was Janie?

"*Stop!*" she screamed. She lunged forward on the floor and grabbed her father's ankle. "Daddy, *stop!*"

Her father slowed the boat.

"I'm sorry," he said, over the hum of the engine. "I didn't see that wake coming and I took it a little too fast. No harm done. I—"

"I can't find Janie! I can't find Janie!" Susannah was on her knees now, scrambling frantically in the mass of wet towels and ropes and water skis on the floor of the boat.

Her father looked at her, at Jon, and then at the floor of the boat. His head jerked up and around, his eyes scanning the water behind them. Susannah pulled herself up and looked, too, and could just barely see a bright spot of orange bobbing on the waves: Janie in her life jacket.

"Oh, my God! How could you let her go?" he yelled.

He turned the boat in a wide arc and pushed the throttle down, zooming toward the orange spot.

"Slow down!" Susannah yelled. "You're going to run her

over!" She stood next to him, her hands gripping the metal at the top of the windshield, her eyes fixed on the bright spot of orange on the dark water.

"We hit so hard she flew out of my arms," she said. The horrible cold terror she'd felt when Janie first bounced out of her arms rose into her chest, flowed through her veins, made her teeth chatter. "I *tried* to hold her. But we hit so hard. But if she landed in the water she'll be okay, right? Right, Daddy?"

Her father slowed the engine as they drew closer. He didn't answer.

"I said she'll be okay, right?"

"You should have held on to her," he said. "I can't believe you let her go."

He swung the boat to the left and stood on his tiptoes to peer over the windshield and bow.

"Oh, my God. Oh, my God."

Susannah pushed open the glass panel in the windshield and scrambled onto the bow, kneeling against the little silver railing. She leaned forward. There, to the right of the boat, was the orange life vest, floating empty.

She stood up and dove into the water.

The water was cold, cold and darker than she remembered. She peered into the depths in front of her, but then her life vest, tightly buckled as Janie's had not been, lifted her up, up, up, back to the surface of the water. She struggled to take it off.

"Janie!" she yelled.

Her father was yelling "Mayday! Mayday!" into the radio and yelling at her to get back into the boat. Jon was frozen in his chair next to their father.

"Janie!" Susannah fumbled with the buckles on her life preserver. If she could get it off, then she could dive, could go under and find Janie floating, floating, and bring her up and pump the water out of her and make her cough, and then Janie's warm arms would reach up for her and encircle her neck, and she'd breathe her warm breath against Susannah's ear, and they'd all cry and laugh over the scare they'd had. *If she could just get the damn life jacket off.*

"Susannah!" She felt her father's hands grip her arm, looked up to see him leaning over the bow, pulling her back to the boat.

"Get back in the boat," he said. His eyes were red and swollen, his cheeks wet, a wet stream running from his nose. She stared at him, fascinated. She had never seen her father cry before. "Get in," he said. "I can't lose two of you."

"Janie's not lost!" Susannah screamed it at him. "She's not lost! I'm going to find her! Let me go!"

But he held on. He pulled her up by her arms, over the little silver railing, onto the bow next to him. She was no match for his strength. She lay there sobbing and sobbing next to her father, who didn't bother to move but just lay there.

He sat up and put his head in his hands. "Oh, my God," he said over and over. "Oh, my God."

He climbed back down into the boat. Jon rocked back and forth in his chair, hugging his knees, crying quietly. Their father looked at him as if he didn't recognize him; couldn't imagine what he was doing there. He looked at the floor of the boat.

"Gotta get rid of these," he mumbled, and Susannah sat up to see what he was talking about. She watched him pick up an empty beer can, and the four other empty beer cans, and put them in a plastic bag. He opened the cooler and pulled out the rest of the beer and put that in the bag, too. He opened the glove compartment and pulled out his flask and dropped that in. He held the bag with one hand, feeling its weight, considering. Then he reached for the heavy croquet ball that Janie had carried onto the boat that morning and put that inside, too, and tied the bag shut. He leaned far over the side of the boat and dropped the bag into the water and watched it sink down and down.

"The Coast Guard won't understand that I just had a beer or two," he said. "You kids are not to say anything about the beer. It could get us all in a lot of trouble."

Susannah stared at her father, disbelieving. He was worried about *the beer*?

"Go get her!" Susannah shouted. "You're bigger; you can dive down and find her. What is wrong with you? Go get her!"

Jon began to cry louder now, wails of terror and heartbreak that pierced the air, the soft murmur of the waves, that ripped open the clear blueness of the sky itself. Susannah didn't so much hear his screams as see them—bright streaks of grief shooting up and out and falling all around her, like the ashes from fireworks. But she didn't feel any sadness herself, not yet. *Because Janie was not dead.*

But their father didn't move.

"Go get her!" Susannah shouted again. "You have to go get her!"

Her father looked at her with vacant eyes and shook his head. "She's gone," he said.

Then he sat down and sobbed, his cries mingling with Jon's and then, finally, her own—all of it ashes, falling and falling and falling around them, grief without end.

Chapter 23

Betty 1968

The strangest thing about the accident was that Betty could not for the life of her remember what they'd been fighting about. She remembered the date: January 9. It was Jim's half birthday (twelve and a half), and she'd baked him half a cake the day before, and they were going to celebrate the half holiday and Bill's return.

She remembered standing on the dock and watching the mail boat come in. She remembered her first glimpse of Bill as he ducked to step out the door of the cabin onto the deck, his hair blowing back, his trousers whipping around his legs. She remembered her surprise at the silvery strands in his thick dark hair, even though it had been only six months since she had seen him last. Her treacherous heart still lurched at the sight of him, even though she and Barefoot had been lovers for three years now. Bill was her first love, the father of her only child, and because of their long shared history—as messy and complicated as it was—he knew her in ways no one else ever would.

His grin and green eyes were the same. He enveloped her in a hug and gave her butt a playful squeeze through her jeans.

"I missed you," he said.

"So much that you're here ten days later than you expected." Betty's voice was dry. She was still angry that he'd promised to be home for New Year's Eve and then called to say he'd been delayed. *Delayed, my ass*, she thought.

"Come on, Betty, I did miss you. Look at you."

He pushed her an arm's length away, his hand still resting on her shoulder, and let his green eyes travel from her boots to the outline of her hips and up to her throat, her lips, her eyes. He looked into her eyes and held her gaze. "I mean it. Look at you. Thirty-six and you've still got it."

"What I've got is a hungry almost teenager at home and a pen full of bawling goats that need to be milked," Betty said.

He threw his duffel bag in the back of the pickup and slid in behind the wheel. It had been an unusually dry January, and they jolted over the hard roads, the windows rolled down in spite of the cold so Bill could smell the Sounder air. Dry leaves rustled in the gullies along the side of the road as they drove by. It was a fine, clear day. Betty spotted small clusters of white snowdrops amid the brown at the edge of the forest. Bill kept one hand on the wheel and one hand clamped on her thigh.

They talked about Jim; she remembered that. She remembered telling Bill about the parachute incident in August. Jim had become fascinated with parachutes and experimented with making homemade parachutes out of old sails and plastic garbage bags and canvas tarps. For a while he'd had fun attaching his parachutes to apples or gourds and throwing them off the roof of the cottage. Then he'd gotten the brilliant idea of making a giant parachute for an old cedar log that had been lying up on top of Crane's Point for years. The parachute he constructed, with the help of two buddies, was huge. But Jim had forgotten about how much time in the air was required to build up enough drag to allow a heavy object to actually *float* from a parachute. When he and his friends attached their homemade parachute to the log with nylon cord and then rolled the log off the cliff, it dropped like a bomb right behind Bill Chevalier's boat as he was coming in from fishing.

"If they'd dropped that log two seconds earlier they'd have killed him," Betty told Bill.

She remembered how Bill laughed, his head thrown back, one hand on the wheel and the other still on her leg.

But then what? She had no idea. They started to argue about something just as they turned into the long gravel driveway of the farm. Maybe it was because he had come home a week late; maybe it was because he'd been gone so long. It might have been about missing Christmas, or the chores, or his next trip. She wondered later if she'd picked the fight because of her own guilt about Barefoot. Whatever the reason, when they got to the first gate, he put the car in park and hopped out to open the gate, leaving the engine running.

Betty slid over into the driver's seat. *You son of a bitch*, she remembered thinking. *You can damn well walk the rest of the way.* She meant to nose the truck through once he opened the gate, then speed on to the next gate, so she could pop out and open it and drive through before he could catch up to her on foot. But when she pushed the clutch in and shifted gears, the truck lurched, and then shot forward. She felt the thump and heard it at the same time. One second Bill was there, his back to her as he pushed the gate to the side, and then he was gone. The thump sounded like a ripe pumpkin hitting the ground.

She released the clutch and slammed her foot down on the brake and swung the wheel hard to the right, away from Bill, or where Bill had been. The truck rattled across the frozen furrows of the field, coming to a stop in a ditch at the edge of the woods. She struggled to push open the door, which wasn't easy because the truck was at an angle and the door was uphill.

"Bill!" She cranked the window down, climbed through it, and clambered out into the ditch. She scrambled on her hands and knees up the side of the ditch until she found her footing and stood. She saw Bill lying motionless next to the gate, his body sprawled at an odd angle, with one arm twisted behind his back. She ran to him.

His eyes were closed, but his mouth was open. She noticed a stream of bright red blood coming from his ear. She put her hands on his shoulders to shake him, to wake him up, but then realized she shouldn't move him in case he'd hurt his neck or back. And it was at that moment, with her hands gripping his shoulders through the thick wool of his coat, that she noticed the odd stillness.

His shoulders were still beneath her hands. His mouth was open, but his chest was still. She slid her hand up the side of his neck to the spot just behind the angle of his jaw—a spot she'd kissed often during lovemaking, when she'd trace a path of kisses from his ear, down along the line of his jaw, until she found his lips—but that spot, the spot where his pulse was supposed to be, was still, too.

She gripped his shoulders more tightly. "*Bill!*"

She shook him then, yelling his name over and over, willing his chest to rise and fall, his eyelids to flutter. He remained still, his head hanging back. Yet she kept shaking him and shaking him until her son, who had heard her cries, came running over the frozen fields and found her there, with his father's lifeless body in her arms.

It was January and the ground was hard, but one of their neighbors had a backhoe and they were able to dig out a grave for him in the small Sounder cemetery. Bill hadn't set foot inside a church since his boyhood in Massachusetts, but Jim wanted to make a wooden cross to mark the grave, and it didn't matter to

Betty. If it made Jim feel better to have his father buried under a symbol of God, so be it.

Ted Ross, who was great with cars and could fix anything with an engine, checked out the truck after the accident and found a mechanical malfunction that had caused the truck to slip out of gear. "It wasn't your fault, Betty," he said, holding out the guilty part for her inspection. "It could have happened to anyone."

"It didn't, though," she said. "It happened to me."

The medical examiner told her that Bill's death was bad luck. He'd been standing in such a way that when the truck hit him he'd been thrown forward and his head had slammed against the ground. The impact had fractured his skull.

Jim never blamed her for the accident with even a look. He grieved his father more than she had imagined, given how little time Bill had actually spent at home, but she understood he was grieving the loss of all the possibilities he'd hoped for as much as anything else. He tried to take care of her, in his twelve-year-old-boy way. He made clumsy grilled cheese sandwiches for dinner and put them in front of her, even though food had lost all appeal. He spent less time with his friends and more time at home, watching her. Bobbie begged her to come live with her in Seattle, but Betty refused. Sounder was the only home Jim had ever known. She had to stay here, where Bill had last been, where Bill was now.

With his death, much of the bitterness over his infidelities faded, as did the hurt over the months and years spent alone. She was left with the remnants of her love, her longing, and an all-consuming guilt.

While Bill was alive, she had felt little guilt about her affair with Barefoot. Barefoot loved her and nurtured her in a way Bill never had. She trusted Barefoot completely. She understood enough about herself to realize that without Barefoot her marriage would have collapsed under the weight of her anger and loneliness—something that would have crushed her son, who knew nothing of his father's infidelities. But now—now her relationship with Barefoot seemed ugly, opportunistic. She had, in some of her worst moments with Bill, wished Bill dead. And now he *was* dead, and she was responsible.

She was haunted by the *ifs:* if she hadn't been so mad and decided to drive on past the gate without him, if she'd waited for him to open the gate all the way and then pulled through slowly, or if she'd hopped out to get the gate herself . . .

Bill's presence had often hovered through her days and nights even when he was away. Now it was bigger than ever in this final absence. She couldn't sleep, because his body filled the bed; couldn't eat, because his face was always across the table from hers; couldn't sit on the porch, because she was waiting for the sound of his footsteps on the gravel drive. She told Barefoot, who had come to her as soon as he heard about the accident, that she couldn't see him for a while, not even as a friend. She needed time to think.

Barefoot tried. He came to her house and stood on the porch and talked to her through the door. He left herbs and tea and wine and food. He wrote to her, and she left the letters on the floor by the front door to gather dust. She did not deserve to be loved so.

When spring came, she threw herself into the physical labor of the farm. It was a relief to work to the point of exhaustion, to sleep for a few hours. She had to wait until the end of May to plant the corn and beans and squash, but she spent February and March digging out the blackberry bushes that were growing up next to the field, and cleaning out the barn, and repairing the chicken coop.

One day in April she was turning over the dirt in the garden and preparing the beds for the potatoes when Barefoot walked up the driveway. He stopped and watched her for a while. She could feel his eyes on her as she pushed the spade into the ground, lifted shovelfuls of dirt, turned the spade over to drop the newly turned earth back onto the ground. Finally she stopped and turned to look at him.

"Hello," she said.

Barefoot didn't bother to return the greeting. "Look at you," he said. "You're emaciated—stand there with your arms straight out and no one would know you weren't a scarecrow." He reached over and took one of her hands in his own and turned it over, studying the back of her hand and then the palm. Her knuckles were swollen and cracked, her palms covered in calluses, her fingernails chipped and broken. He dropped her hand and looked at her.

"Got a hair shirt on under that flannel?" he said. "Or do you just flog yourself before bed?"

"None of your business," she said.

He stepped closer and leaned in toward her until she could feel the rough stubble of his unshaven face against her cheek. It stirred something in her, a memory.

"Listen to me," he said into her ear. His voice was low, deliberate. "You keep at this, you keep letting all that guilt wrap itself around your soul like ivy, and soon your son will have lost both parents. Is that what you want?"

He pulled back and stared at her now, his blue eyes locked on hers in what Jim called Barefoot's "gunfighter stare."

"I take care of Jim," she said. "That hasn't changed."

"I'm sure you do," Barefoot said. "You want him to grow up confident and proud and believing he's worthy?"

She was too tired to talk. "Of course," Betty said.

"Can't give your kids what you don't have," Barefoot said.

She looked at him. She tried to remember what it felt like to care about something, anything.

"It doesn't matter if you work yourself to death or keep breathing. You're as good as dead now if you keep on like this." He paused, and leaned in toward her again. "If you've decided you're a worthless piece of shit because your truck slipped a gear and the fates were misaligned at that moment, go hang yourself and get it over with. But if not, if you can see it for what it was, a tragic accident with no one at fault, then treat yourself with the kindness you would show to anyone else in the same circumstances. *You* choose."

She turned her head so she didn't have to look at those eyes anymore.

He reached over and took the hoe from her hand. "Go home," he said. "I left some tea on the counter. Steep it for ten minutes. It'll help you sleep."

He put his hand on her cheek. "I love you and I will not give you up," he said. "You don't have to love me back or make love with me or do a damn thing other than stop torturing yourself. That's enough for me."

She drank Barefoot's tea after dinner that night, and slept for ten hours straight. The next morning she got up and went into the kitchen and started to mix up griddle cakes and fry bacon. She ate a big breakfast, then walked over to the post office and told Chet McNabb that she needed help with the plowing and could he please ask around and that she'd pay a fair price for the help out of Bill's life insurance money. And that night, before bed, she washed her hands and trimmed her nails, and rubbed some salve Barefoot had left into the painful cracks in her skin.

Within a week, the cracks had healed over.

Chapter 24

Susannah 2011

"I'm sorry," Susannah said to her scrap metal angel. "I'm sorry."

The grief she felt now wasn't for Janie, she realized, but for herself. She remembered that day sitting in the tree, talking to Betty. What did Betty say? Something about mourning the loss of possibility. The accident was so long ago. Susannah had no idea who Janie might be had she lived. She knew only that she herself would be someone else entirely, someone she would much rather be.

The door to the barn slid open and Matt walked in.

"Hi," Susannah said. She stood up from where she'd been kneeling, on the barn floor by her angel. "I'm sorry about what I said earlier. I didn't mean it. I shouldn't have said those things."

Matt shook his head. "I don't know what to say. You were really *mean* to your mother. She is not an evil woman, Susannah."

"I didn't mean to be rude to her. I don't know why she irritates me so much."

"Well, maybe you should figure it out."

"I guess I should," Susannah said. "It's like dominoes. My mother drives me crazy; I drive Katie crazy. I can't wait to have grandchildren so Katie can drive them crazy and continue the family legacy."

"This isn't a joke," Matt said. "Something is wrong with you."

"It's always *me*," Susannah said. "I'm rude to my mother; I'm too controlling with the kids; I'm I don't know *what* to you, since you never say anything about how you feel."

"Stop being a martyr," Matt said. "You do a million things right. But this whole thing with Katie that started last year has changed you—you've become this uptight, overprotective crazy woman, and you need to back off."

"Crazy woman?" Susannah said. "You tell me what's crazier: to love my kids with too much intensity, or to be so indifferent to danger, like my mother, like *you*, that I put their lives at risk."

"Oh, Christ," Matt said. He paced back and forth in the barn, then stopped and looked at her. "Now I'm 'indifferent to danger' because I don't see death around every corner? Sometimes that bear you think is about to devour your kids is really just a tree stump."

They faced each other furious, panting.

"I came here to protect Katie."

"You came here to run away from the reality that Katie is growing up. You can't protect them, Susannah. You can try. But you have to learn how to live with some uncertainty. You have to trust them. You have to trust us, trust that we've done a pretty good job of raising them. But you can't control everything that happens, at home or here."

"I'm not an idiot," she said. "I know that. But you of all people should understand why I'm overprotective, *if* I'm overprotective. The unimaginable does happen, Matt, and it happens to normal people like you and me, and my mother. And it happens when you're not even thinking about it, or prepared for it, or expecting it"—her voice caught now, but she sucked in her breath and continued—"and I'll be damned if it happens to one of *my* kids."

She stood facing him, the grief that had haunted her since she'd arrived on Sounder filling her soul.

"*Our* kids," he said. His face softened. "Susannah. *Jesus.* You've turned watching over our kids into some kind of penance, and it shouldn't be. It doesn't have to be."

"I don't want to talk about it," she said. She turned away.

"Fine," he said. "You know what? I'm done here." He turned and walked out of the barn, and she heard the door of the white cottage open and close. She followed him.

Matt stalked into the bedroom, pulled his duffel bag out of the closet, and ripped open the top dresser drawer. He pulled out his T-shirts and socks and boxers and stuffed them into the bag, then opened the closet and grabbed his pants and shirts and rolled them up, still on the hangers, and shoved those in the bag, too.

"What are you doing?" Susannah said.

"Leaving," Matt said. "This time *I'm* going to run away. I'm taking the mail boat out of here today."

"But you're supposed to be here until Sunday. We haven't seen you in more than a month. Come on, Mattie, be reasonable."

"Reasonable?" He stood up to face her, his face suffused with anger, the scar on his cheekbone glowing white in contrast.

"I've *been* reasonable. I agreed to let you take *my* kids and come to this fucking island for nine months, while I sit home alone. Just how reasonable do I have to be?"

She winced. "Don't swear at me. You know I hate that. Listen, coming here wasn't about you and me, it was about Katie, and Quinn, about doing what was best for them."

"Really?" He tugged at the zipper on his duffel bag. "Well, maybe if you worried a little more about you and me and a little less about Katie and Quinn, we'd all be happier."

Susannah felt a sense of panic so profound she had an urge to bolt from the room and run, across the meadow, into the woods, down the gravelly roads. And then what? She was on an island; she could only run so far.

"Matt. Please. Stay and let's talk about this. You're right; I know there are things we need to work on."

He stood up and slung his overstuffed duffel over his shoulder. He looked her in the eye. "We'll talk when you come home," he said.

"But I can't pull the kids out of school here now, halfway through the year, and bring them back to Tilton."

"I didn't say you should. I said we'll talk when you come home."

"But what am I supposed to say to them? How am I supposed to explain that you're leaving early?"

"I'll go find them now," he said. He looked at his watch. "The mail boat comes at, what? Four? I'll tell them I got called back for work."

"But—"

"Susannah." He stood across from where she stood in the doorway of their bedroom, still in her rain parka. "Whatever it is—Janie or your dad or Katie or your own mixed-up ideas about how perfect you're supposed to be—you need to figure it out."

"I thought I could figure it out here. I'm trying, Matt."

He shook his head. "I don't know what the answer is. I only know that being patient and letting you find your own way through it isn't working. At least, it's not working for me."

"So you're leaving?"

"That's what you've done when you couldn't cope, right?"

"Mattie—"

"I'm going to find the kids," he said. "I'll be back for Christmas."

He came over and squeezed past her in the doorway, his chest brushing against her shoulder, his breath warm against her face. "I love you, Susannah," he said. "But I'm not sure I can be married to you."

And before she had time to say anything, or to wrap her arms around him, he was gone.

Matt left on the mail boat that afternoon. Susannah drove him to the dock in the truck, silent, befuddled. He hugged her before he stepped on the boat, but he didn't apologize or reassure her, and she didn't know what to say to him, other than "I'll miss you. I love you. I'm sorry." She knew it wasn't enough.

The funny thing was that Matt's love was the one thing in her life she had never questioned. From the time they'd met on the beach at age seven, he had been drawn to her and she to him. Her emotions ran close to the surface; his were buried deep inside. She was focused and organized; he could never remember things, or find them. She knew how to talk and listen to draw people out; Matt liked to keep to himself. With Matt, she was creative and interesting and empathetic and generous—the version of herself she longed to be. She in turn was a touchstone for him, the emotional center of his life, and she knew it. But what did she know now?

The boat pulled away and she watched it disappear around the curve of Crane's Point. Thick clouds covered the horizon, and her mood darkened with the skies. Susannah got back in the truck and drove home. The white cottage was empty, and Matt's absence so large it filled every room, pressing on her until Susannah couldn't breathe. Katie and Quinn were with Lila at Betty's, making blackberry jam. Susannah felt in desperate need of a friend and decided to find Jim.

She saw smoke rising from the black stovepipe that jutted out of the roof of Jim's cabin, just over the rise from her white cottage. Jim had painted the cabin a bright royal blue that made Susannah smile every time she saw it. Cedar shingles covered the roof, and a rustic bench made of gnarled juniper branches sat next to the front door. The cabin was tall and narrow, with a main floor, a bedroom downstairs, and a loft upstairs. Susannah usually walked around to the side of the cabin, to the door that led into the mudroom, but today the front door looked so inviting, with a bright spray of huckleberry set in a jar next to the bench, that she was drawn to it, and decided to go in that way.

She didn't knock, but opened the door and stepped into the living room, which was at one end of the room that made up the main floor of the cabin. To her right was a small table, and across from her, near the woodstove, was a navy blue couch where, to Susannah's surprise, Hood lay on top of Katie, kissing her, one hand on her breast. Katie's shirt was pushed up above her ribs, and her arms were wrapped around Hood. At the sound of the door opening they split apart and Hood leaped up. Katie stood up, too, pulling her shirt down. The top button of her jeans was undone.

"What the hell is going on here?" Susannah said, although it was clear exactly what was going on.

"Wow. Oh, wow. I'm sorry," Hood said. "This isn't as bad as it looks."

"Really?" The iceberg that had been a distant point on the horizon now loomed in front of Susannah, huge, menacing.

"God, Mom, don't you knock?" Katie said.

"I thought you were at Betty's making jam with your grandmother."

"Quinn and Baker are there," Katie said. "It was boring."

"I guess so."

Hood reached for something on the wooden coffee table in front of the couch, and Susannah stepped forward.

"What is that?"

She saw it just before he picked it up and slipped it in his pocket.

"A condom? *My God*, making out is one thing. Being here alone with a condom is another thing."

"Mom! We weren't doing that. We weren't going to use it."

"Katie, you are way too young for this. I don't know what you're thinking."

"Susannah," Hood said. "It isn't like that, really. I had it as a joke."

"I don't find anything funny about it."

"I know. I know," Hood said. He stood next to the couch with his hands in his pockets. "But it's not like that. I really like Katie. I mean I wouldn't—I mean—"

"You bet you wouldn't," Susannah said.

"Listen," Hood said. He cleared his throat. His face was flushed with embarrassment, and he looked at the floor by her feet. "Katie and I have this running joke about how I'm 'always prepared,' like some Boy Scout. I always remember to bring stuff, like the binoculars or Swiss Army knife or flashlights, when we do things. So last time we were in Friday Harbor, Baker and I bought these, you know—" His blush deepened. "It was part of the 'always prepared' joke. You know, living here you can't run out to the drugstore if—oh, God. Never mind." He looked up at Susannah. "It was a joke."

Hood was a good kid; Susannah knew it. But seeing Hood and Katie together had called up something in her. There was the usual visceral fear—*Katie's in danger!*—but also, now, something more. *Matt.* She remembered herself with Matt when she was just a year or two older than Katie was now, remembered the heady rush of feeling that he—so athletic and loyal and smart and passionate—loved her and wanted her beyond all others. She remembered the vulnerability in his face and voice years later when he had said, "Do you ever think about getting married?" and the way his love and desire for her were so clear and direct. She remembered her joy at creating the little study for him in their Victorian apartment, his surprise and gratitude, their shared sense of purpose in those days. She wanted all that back and she wanted it right now.

"We're going home to Tilton," she said.

"What?" Katie said.

"You heard me. I need your father. You kids need your father. I'll go talk to the Pavalaks. We'll leave next week, when school ends for Christmas break."

"I don't want to leave!" Katie said.

"This is my fault," Hood said. "Don't leave. I promise Katie and I will just be friends. I'm sorry."

"I'm sure you are sorry, but this really has nothing to do with you," Susannah said. "I need to take care of my family. We're going home."

Chapter 25

Betty 2011

The Sounder cemetery was one of Betty's favorite places on the island. Set in a field at the side of the road, it had no formal sign or even a fence, just a variety of rocks, plants, wooden crosses, logs, stone lanterns, Mardi Gras beads, and other mementos marking the graves, which were laid out haphazardly across the field. At first glance it looked like a half-forgotten garden, with little plots of eccentric plantings scattered here and there in the midst of the overgrown grass and dead leaves.

Betty pulled the truck over to the side of the road and sat for a moment, looking at the cemetery. Then she got out and walked over and through the little gate that stood as a kind of entryway, even though there was no fence.

She wandered by the graves. Some graves were marked only with a scattering of shells, a tiny statue of a laughing Buddha, a blue-glazed ceramic bowl, and visited only by those who knew where to find them. She saw the grave of Joel Thurlow, a boat maker, who had been buried in one of his cedar and canvas canoes instead of a coffin, his hammer tucked by his side. Dorothy Watson, a teacher at the Sounder school for more than thirty years, lay in a grave marked with a cedar bench, the perfect spot to sit and read. Two stone cherubs marked the graves of the twin daughters of Andrew and Ella Burns, drowned in a boating accident in 1923.

Much of the cemetery was in shadow, but in a few spots the afternoon sun lit bright patches of gold on the grass. Someone had put fresh calla lilies, which must have been brought back this week by boat, in a white pitcher on one of the graves.

She found the handmade cross that marked Bill's grave and stopped to look at it. Jim had carved his father's name, William Thomas Pavalak, into the wood, and the years of his life, 1926–1968. Betty looked around for a place to sit and settled on Dorothy Watson's bench, about twenty yards away. The seat of the bench was a red cedar log split in half, sanded to a satiny finish.

A small patch of blue elderberry covered the ground near Bill's grave; Betty contemplated it for a long time. It wouldn't be too difficult to pull the elderberry and dig a grave there, next to Bill. She didn't want anything fancy, maybe a nootka rose or a mock orange, with its lovely, fragrant flowers. There would be a certain irony in spending the centuries there at Bill's side. She had told Barefoot once that she wanted to be buried next to him.

"I'm not going to be buried," Barefoot said. "Why? So you can come and weep over me? Burn me in the brush pile and scatter my ashes in the garden, where they'll do some good."

"But I love you," she said. It had been one of those moments when she felt a particular tenderness for him, a mix of gratitude and love that filled her and overflowed her soul, drowning her natural reticence.

"I love you, too," he said, "but in forty years it won't make a damn bit of difference to either one of us if I'm buried or cremated."

She had not told him yet about her visit to the doctor in Bellingham, about the spot on her lung and the two spots in her spine revealed by the CT scan. Five or six months, the doctor said. She hadn't told Jim, either. But she had called Bobbie. Betty wanted to stay home on Sounder until the end. There was a hospice program based in Friday Harbor. Bobbie had offered to move in with her, too. "Whatever you need," Bobbie said.

She would have to tell Jim and her grandsons, and she would have to tell Barefoot. But not yet. Betty had kept the secret of her illness for a week now, holding it close like a precious thing and taking it out to study it when she was alone, turning it over and over in her mind. It would be hard on Jim, no question about it. She and Jim had been a team for many years, the two of them together. Even her long relationship with Barefoot had not frayed the bond she had with her son. And she hated to leave Hood and Baker before getting further along in their story, as she thought of it, before knowing more about where their lives might go.

And Barefoot—she didn't know how to tell him. He was still fiercely protective of her, and it would be impossibly hard on him to see her suffer. Maybe she'd be granted the gift of an easy, quick decline. Barefoot had told her once that he hoped she would die first, so she didn't have to suffer the pain of losing him and being alone and grieving. He wanted to take care of her through everything, and now he'd be able to do exactly that. Betty sighed.

A movement caught her eye and she saw someone walk down the road and cut across the yellow grass at the far end of the cemetery. She recognized Susannah's red parka and long dark hair. Susannah put up her hand to shade her eyes from the sun, then spotted Betty on the bench and began to walk toward her.

"This is such a lovely place," Susannah said, coming up to

the bench. Her cheeks were flushed with cold, but there were dark shadows under her eyes.

"It is, isn't it?" Betty smiled. "I used to think I wanted to be buried back home in Seattle. I was so mad when Bill moved us up here, away from my family. I used to tell him, 'Don't you dare bury me here, or scatter even one of my ashes in that god-damned bay.' But now it's home."

Susannah sat down beside her.

"It doesn't seem quite so scary in a place like this, does it?" Betty said.

"No."

A comfortable silence overtook them.

"You know Hood and Baker are leaving next year for high school," Betty said. "Fiona's going to get an apartment in Friday Harbor and live there with them during the week. Although if they find a new teacher for Sounder, Jim may go with them."

"So you'll be here all alone?" Susannah said.

No, Betty thought. *I won't be here.* "Maybe," she said. "Life is full of changes and surprises." She tilted her face up to the sun. "I've never been particularly religious, but in this place, on a day like this, it's hard not to believe in *something*."

Susannah clasped both hands around one knee and leaned back. "I've never been particularly religious, either," she said. "As a kid I used to picture God as kind of like my dad in one of his rages—especially once I read the Old Testament."

"Did you go to church?" Betty asked.

"Off and on. More off than on. We went to the Presbyterian Church. All I really remember about church is the music, this very good-looking, dark-eyed boy named Felipe who always asked questions that really made the Sunday School teachers mad—I think because they couldn't answer him—and the view out the window of the sanctuary, which overlooked Lake Saint Clair."

Betty laughed. "That sounds about right."

"I have to tell you something Katie said once," Susannah said, turning to Betty. "I hope you don't think this is hokey, but it has always stuck with me."

"Fire away."

"We were driving someplace—to preschool, or the grocery store—and suddenly Katie said, 'Mommy, do you know what God looks like?'" Susannah's face grew animated as she told the story. "And I said, 'I'm not sure anyone knows what God looks like.' And Katie said, 'I do.' She was four at the time, all big dark eyes and dark hair. Anyway, so I said, 'Well, what does God look like?'"

Here Susannah paused, concentrating on something far back in the recesses of her mind. "And Katie said—I never forgot this, because she was so specific about it, and so *sure*—she said, 'You see, when a baby is born, God and all the angels are right there in the room. So when the baby comes out she sees them all. But then as the baby gets older and gets farther away from the day she was born, she starts to forget God's face. But I still remember.'

"Then she said, 'God has long, long hair he wears in a pony-tail. He wears a bright yellow sweater with purple polka dots, and tie-dyed pants. And he has big purple shoes. I'll probably forget what he looks like, too, when I'm old.' And she told me to write it down when we got home so she'd remember. And I did!"

Susannah stopped now, in telling the story to Betty. "But that always haunted me," she continued, "the idea that God and the angels are right there when a child is born, clear as day, and we spend our whole lives trying to get that close to the sacred again."

Betty smiled. "And who knew that God looked like Wavy Gravy? Isn't that his name? He was big in the sixties."

Betty looked up, watching the wind stir the trees. "I've never really believed in God or a hereafter; I just tried to live this life the best I could. My son is a good man; he found and married a decent woman, and I've been lucky enough to live near them and know my grandchildren. I've been able to live here"—she gestured toward the field, the forest, the looming sky. "In many ways, I've had a better life than I could have hoped for. But if there is a God waiting to judge me, I hope it's Katie's version. It's nice to think a kind man with a ponytail will be there to welcome us home."

The pale December sun broke through the clouds again. A bird hopped through the grass across from where they sat, looking for insects. Susannah sighed.

"I came to find you to tell you that we're going home," Susannah said. "I know I said we'd rent the cottage through June, and I'll pay you the rent through then even though we won't be here."

"You're leaving?" Betty couldn't believe it.

"I have to." Susannah's voice faltered. "Katie has been really difficult for me to handle alone. The pot poem and the cupcakes, and today I found her with Hood and they were—well, they're involved, too involved. And Matt and I are really struggling, and I don't know if he wants to stay married to me, and I can't fix that if I'm three thousand miles away."

"Aw, honey." Betty put an arm around Susannah's shoulders and hugged her. "None of us are perfect. You did what you thought was best for your kids. And it sounds like going home now is what's best for you and your marriage. You do what you have to do."

"But I've made some big mistakes," Susannah said.

"So have I," Betty said. "And I made a lot of choices in my life that seemed wrong in some ways, but I know now all these years later they were exactly right. And I've learned to forgive myself my mistakes."

Betty felt for Susannah, she did. She wished she could explain to her that as you grew older some of the angst faded, and the joys became sweeter. She thought of all the agonizing she'd done over Bill and his affairs and her miscarriages and the move to Sounder, and even over Barefoot and her own infidelity.

When Betty looked back on her life now, she recognized that she had married a man who stilled her restlessness, but in the end she wasn't enough to still his. She had put up with things she would have found unimaginable, but for reasons that were more important than her own yearnings. She had committed adultery—something she once would have deemed unforgivable—but she did not regret it. She regretted Bill's death with all her heart, yet she accepted that it was not an act of her will that had caused it, but a random cruelty of fate.

It was, as Barefoot said, all how you decided to look at things.

"I don't know," Susannah said. "I doubt you made any mistakes like mine. I made a mistake once that's the kind of thing no one can forgive."

Betty remembered something Barefoot had said to her, all those years ago. "Don't confuse guilt and shame," she said. "It's okay to feel badly about something you've done. But don't let it make you feel badly about who you are. You're a good mother. And a good wife and daughter. I've known you long enough to know all that. You're a good person, Susannah. A really worthwhile person to know."

Susannah's eyes filled with tears, and she laid her head on Betty's shoulder and cried as she had not cried in years and years.

Chapter 26

Susannah 2011

The following Saturday Quinn awoke with a stomachache. He pushed his eggs around on the plate with a fork at breakfast. "I don't feel like eating, Mom."

"Okay, sweetheart." Susannah picked up the plate, and put a hand on his forehead. Warm but not hot.

"Do you want some tea? You want to lie on the couch and watch a movie?"

He nodded. She set him up with a hot water bottle, blankets, the laptop, and a DVD, with a cup of ginger tea on the coffee table next to him. He lay curled on his side, his knees drawn up. Susannah looked at him and felt uneasy, but didn't know why. In some ways she was relieved to be heading back to Tilton next week, close to doctors and hospitals.

Katie came out of her room. "What's wrong with Turtleboy?"

Susannah shot her a look. "He's got a stomachache. Leave him alone."

Katie sat down in the armchair across from Quinn. "I have an English project due this week," she said. "I'm supposed to finish it this weekend. Which seems kind of pointless since we're moving—*again*—in ten days or whatever. This is totally messing up my grades for this year, as well as everything else."

"It's not messing up your grades," Susannah said. "You'll be fine." But her conscience pricked her. Moving the kids twice in one school year *was* a terrible thing to do. When she'd told Quinn they were moving home, he had shaken his head back and forth, back and forth, as she spoke.

"No, no, no," he said. "It's much better here. I don't want to go home."

"It's not better here without Dad," Susannah had said.

"It doesn't matter," Katie had said. "Being away from Dad for nine months totally doesn't matter."

"It matters to me," Susannah said.

Katie and Quinn had bonded over their desire to stay on Sounder and had spent the past week trying to convince Susannah to change her mind. She wavered. It was rare to see the kids so united—even more, it was rare to see them passionate about something the way they were about Sounder and all the things they loved here: Barefoot, school, the Pavalaks, working on the boat, freedom from supervision. But all she had to do was think about Matt, about the deadness in his voice when he said, "I'm not sure I can be married to you"—and she knew she had to go. The kids were the most important thing in her life, but Matt *was* her life, and had been from almost the very beginning. She wanted to be good to him; she wanted to be worthy of him.

Quinn's stomachache grew steadily worse throughout the morning. Susannah put on her rain parka and walked up to Jim's to see if he had any Pepto-Bismol, but the cabin was dark and empty.

"Jim and Hood and Baker and Betty left for Anacortes this morning," Katie told her when she came back. "I forgot. They're meeting Betty's sister for lunch or something."

"Maybe I'll see if Barefoot has something that might help Quinn," Susannah said. The nagging worry in the back of her mind would not go away. "Katie, will you stay here with him until I get back?"

"Yeah. But if he throws up I am not cleaning it up."

"Great. Fine."

Susannah drove out the driveway and along the roads to Crane's Point. The sky was dark even though it was not yet noon, and the wind bent the tops of the firs and pines and danced the leaves along the road. The wind was worse on top of Crane's Point, blowing the craggy branches of the old Garry oak and whipping the thick boughs of the shore pines. She parked behind Barefoot's farmhouse, stepped onto the porch, and knocked on the door. "Barefoot?"

She opened the door and stepped inside. It was dark, but she saw a half-full mug of tea on the chest in front of the fireplace. "Barefoot?"

She walked through the living room and into the kitchen and from there out the back door to the greenhouse, but couldn't find him. There was no sign of Toby, either, which meant Barefoot was out somewhere. She wondered if he could be in the boat, the *Gota*, in its perch on the cliff top. She walked around the side of the farmhouse.

A red-winged blackbird chattered in the distance, and Susannah heard the sound of the water, the waves bumping roughly against the sandstone cliffs at the base of Crane's Point. As she emerged into the clearing, the wind lifted her hair, reddened her cheeks and ears, stung her eyes.

I can't believe the boat doesn't blow over in this, she thought. She stuffed her hands into the pockets of her parka to keep them warm. But then she saw the elaborate system of scaffolding and ropes that anchored the *Gota*. Barefoot knew what he was doing.

"Barefoot?" she called again. But of course he wouldn't be able to hear her voice over the wind.

She stood and looked up at the boat. She was curious. Katie had never taken her inside or shown her the work she'd been doing with Barefoot here. She saw a stepladder set up against the side of the boat, climbed up it, and stepped onto the deck. She lifted the heavy canvas flap of the wheelhouse and stepped inside. To the left of the steering wheel was a small door, like a Hobbit door, that led into the cabin beneath the bow.

She bent her head, walked down two steps, opened the little door, and stepped inside. It was more spacious than she had expected. The cabin was triangular, with two berths that met at the head, making an upside-down V across from the steps. Immediately to the left was a wooden counter with a sink and hot plate, and to the right was a small closet with a toilet inside. A long narrow rectangular window stretched above each berth. Susannah remembered that Katie had told her about making the cabinets and shelving that stretched above the berths and windows. She had also refinished the counter, the beds, and the door to the "head," as Katie had called the little bathroom.

Susannah ran a hand over the smooth, glossy surface of the wood counter. It was lovely. Everything about the little space was clean and neat and perfect. She had no idea that Katie had learned how to do so much, and do it so well. The berths, which ran almost the whole length of the cabin, were covered in sunny yellow cushions. The little counter, the shelves, the door to the bathroom, and the inside of the bathroom were all finished in rich, glowing mahogany. Susannah looked at it all and thought, with some surprise, *Katie is an artist, too.*

A gust of wind rocked the boat and the little door slammed shut. Susannah grabbed the metal door handle and tried to turn it, but it didn't budge. She shook it, then pushed hard against the door with her hip, but nothing happened.

"Shit!" Susannah leaned against the door, fighting waves of claustrophobia.

She shook the door handle again, and then began to pound her fists against the door.

"Barefoot! Barefoot! Somebody! I'm stuck in the boat! Get me out of here!"

She paused, breathless. She took a deep breath and noticed she was shaking, her hands, arms, and legs quivering. She pulled her cell phone from her pocket, but of course it was unlikely to be working in this wind. Sure enough, the words "searching for service" flashed on the display. She punched in Katie's number anyway, but nothing happened.

She tried to think. The Pavalaks were gone. Barefoot wasn't home and didn't own a cell phone anyway; he'd never hear her shouting in this storm. Katie was her best hope, but she'd have to wait until she could get some kind of cell phone signal. But Quinn was so sick. She couldn't wait. She had to *do* something.

She paced around the tiny cabin. The windows were made of thick, solid glass and didn't open. She started opening drawers and closets and cubbies, looking for a spare key, or maybe a screwdriver or something she could use to jimmy the lock.

She bent over and opened a hinged door beneath one of the berths and found a sleeping bag. Another compartment held blankets. Above the berths, on shelves behind sliding wooden doors, were cans of food, spices, bottles of water. In one drawer she found a silver flask, like the one Barefoot had had on the boat that first day, when he'd made her drive the boat on the way to Friday Harbor. She picked it up and shook it and heard the slosh of liquid inside. She unscrewed the flask and sniffed it, and the strong smell of whiskey and oranges hit her nose. If ever she could use a slug of "heart medicine," now would be the time. She took a sip and felt the warmth run down inside her.

She took another drink and wiped her mouth with the back of her hand. She screwed the top back on and slid the flask into the pocket of her parka.

There was no key. Or hammer. Or even a screwdriver. She sat down on one of the berths. She was stuck. She looked out the narrow window above the berth, at the grassy brown meadow and the gnarled, twisted trunks of the windblown junipers at the edge of the field, perched above the sandstone cliffs. A large granite boulder—evidence of an ancient glacier—sat next to the junipers. The sky beyond was thick and gray.

I am failing, she thought. Here she was, stuck, at a time when her son needed her care and protection more than ever, and she was letting him down—the one thing she had sworn she would never do. Her father's words on the day of the accident echoed inside her head: *How could you let her go?* Her whole life was nothing more than a constant attempt to make up for that one moment, that one moment when she was thirteen years old. And now she was going to fail again.

"*No!*" she yelled at the empty cabin. "You were driving too fast! You shouldn't have hit the wake that fast."

How could you let her go?

"*No!*"

Susannah stood up and started rummaging again through the closet, the cupboards, the tiny bathroom, looking for a hammer, a hatchet, something she could use to *smash* her way out. She wanted to blow up the locked door, this claustrophobic cabin, her whole cautious, guilty life. It was like that stupid analogy about women at midlife being butterflies inside cocoons, waiting to burst forth with fresh confidence and creativity into the second half of their lives. Only she didn't feel like a butterfly, or even particularly confident or creative. *I am a pissed-off woman,* she thought, *and I hate this fucking cocoon.*

She looked around again and saw the metal fire extin-
guisher, hanging on the wall above the hot plate. She stood up
and reached for it, lifted it over her head with both arms, and
pounded it against the door with all her strength. She heard a
crack and, to her surprise, the door splintered down the middle. Before she knew it, Susannah was free.

Chapter 27

Susannah 2011

She walked to the truck feeling both proud of her strength and somewhat concerned about Barefoot's likely reaction to the fact that she'd destroyed the door of his beloved boat.

When she turned the truck into the driveway, she saw Katie standing by the gate. Katie ran up as Susannah rolled down the window to talk to her.

"Where have you *been?*" Katie said. "God. I've been trying to call you and you've been gone for like an hour. Quinn's really sick. He won't get off the couch, and I think he has a fever. He's been throwing up, too. He's really, really hot."

"Could you get through to the clinic?"

"No. The Internet and cell phones aren't working because of the rain."

Within minutes Susannah was kneeling on the floor next to the couch where Quinn lay curled in a ball.

"My stomach hurts a lot," he said. His face was flushed with fever, his blond hair damp across his forehead.

"Is it like before?" Susannah asked. "Like other stomach-aches you've had before? Did you try the hot water bottle?"

Quinn started to cry. "Yes. It didn't help. It really, really hurts."

Susannah took his temperature: 103.5. She got out the medical encyclopedia and thumbed through it. Quinn had all the symptoms of appendicitis.

Susannah's mind started to spin. The Pavalaks were gone; Barefoot was gone. She needed to get Quinn to the clinic in Friday Harbor right away. Jim had taken his boat to go to Anacortes. She could take Barefoot's boat, the *EmmaJeanne*, the boat he'd showed her how to drive. A boat in this stormy weather. It was everything she feared most.

She turned to Katie.

"We're going to have to get him to Friday Harbor."

"I can't drive a boat," Katie said, shaking her head. "I mean, I've been out with Hood a few times, but I didn't pay attention. I—"

"I'll drive the boat," Susannah said. "I can do it. Barefoot showed me how. Do you know where his keys to the other boat are, the *EmmaJeanne*?"

"He leaves them on the boat," Katie said. "This is Sounder. Everyone does that."

"Okay. Let's go, then." Susannah bundled Quinn into a rain jacket and a blanket, and walked him to the truck. Katie was helpful, ready to do whatever she asked, but wide-eyed, scared. Quinn lay down on the front seat, his head on Susannah's thigh. Katie hopped in the truck bed. Susannah started slowly down the gravel drive, but Quinn cried out with every rut in the road, every jolt of the old truck. She stopped and got out.

"Katie, you drive. I think maybe it will be better if I can sit next to you and hold Quinn in my lap. Maybe I can absorb the bumps and it won't be so bad for him."

Katie got behind the wheel without a word. Susannah held Quinn tight as they made their way down the driveway, with

Katie hopping out to open and shut the gates. Quinn was hot in her arms. Within minutes they were at the road by the dock.

"You did a good job driving, Kate," Susannah said. "Thank you."

"It's okay, Mom." Katie's eyes locked onto hers.

We are in this together, Susannah thought. *She's going to help me.*

The water of the bay was black and choppy, dotted with whitecaps and sprays of whitewater where the ocean crashed into the cliffs at the other end of the bay. The sky beyond was thick and low and gray, like an animal waiting to pounce. Still, she'd made the trip to Friday Harbor with Jim and Barefoot in worse weather than this. It was rain and wind, and boats were made to handle it. She tried to carry Quinn in her arms, but he was too heavy for her. So she and Katie made a chair out of their arms and carried him, one of his arms curled around each of their shoulders, down to the metal float at the end of the dock. Katie untied the green dinghy.

"I'll row out and get the boat started and pick you up here," Susannah said, with more confidence than she felt. She'd only driven Barefoot's boat the one time. What if she couldn't control it? What if she crashed into the dock and her kids? What if— *Stop. You can't think about that now.*

"I'll come with you," Katie said. "Maybe I can help."

Susannah gave her a grateful look. "All right. Thanks. Quinnie? Hold tight right here, sweetie, and I'll be back in the big boat in five minutes."

The *EmmaJeanne* was anchored to a buoy about fifty yards out. Susannah climbed into the dinghy and began to row, trying to keep the bow pointed straight into the driving wind. Katie sat across from her in the stern. They pulled up next to the *EmmaJeanne*, and Katie clambered up the side and then leaned down to grab the rope of the dinghy. Susannah climbed on board and looked back to where Quinn sat huddled his yellow rain poncho. He was counting on her.

Katie found the key right away, in a blue mug sitting in a mug holder just below the chart box, to the left of the wheel. Susannah had to give Katie credit; after months of working on the *Gota*, she knew boats inside and out. The *EmmaJeanne* was also an Albin, somewhat newer than the *Gota* but so similar as to be almost its twin.

Susannah tried to remember the checklist Barefoot had reviewed with her about starting the boat. There was the switch to turn on the battery, and the fuel shutoff knob. The knob was pulled out, so she had to push it in to start the boat. She closed her eyes and tried to picture Barefoot standing next to her that first day all those months ago. She flicked the switch for the battery, pushed in the knob, and turned the key in the ignition. The engine turned over and began to chug in a steady, reassuring hum.

Katie looked at Susannah in surprise. "Wow. You actually know how to start the boat."

"Thanks for the vote of confidence."

"Can you steer, too?" Katie said, but she smiled as she said it.

"Very funny. Can you row the dinghy back to the dock? I'll swing by and get you."

"Don't forget to raise the anchor."

"Thanks, chief. I'll remember that." Susannah realized that Katie was teasing her, but gently, trying to help her to remember all she needed to do.

Katie climbed out and began to row while Susannah studied the instrument panel. There was an indicator that displayed the engine's rpms, an oil pressure gauge, an engine temperature gauge, and a fuel level gauge. So far so good; it was just like a car.

She looked out the window. Katie was back at the dock. She pushed the throttle forward and the boat surged through the water. All the old fears rose up in her at the sound and feel of all that mindless power rising beneath her and around her. She stilled her thoughts and focused on one thing at a time, pouring all her attention into each step.

She turned carefully in a wide circle and headed toward the dock. The wind was coming from the southwest, so it would hit her broadside as she pulled alongside the dock. Better to keep it behind her and then turn at the last minute, so the wind and waves wouldn't rock the boat so much. It was harder to see than she remembered, with rain pelting the windshield. There had to be a windshield wiper switch somewhere. But she couldn't look for it now because she was steering the boat, trying to remember how it responded to the wheel in her hands, trying to see through the rain-spattered windshield to the two figures on the dock in their yellow ponchos.

The water and wind buffeted the boat. Susannah gripped the wheel with both hands. She was almost at the dock. Katie was standing and waving, while Quinn sat farther back. She turned the boat and angled it so she'd slip in alongside the dock, but the boat didn't respond as quickly as she'd expected. She cut back on the throttle, but not in time. The boat rammed into the dock with a thud.

"God, mom, you could have killed me!" Katie said, after Susannah swung the boat around. Katie had been knocked flat on her backside by the impact, but the metal dock and the boat were fine. So was Quinn, although he was moaning in pain.

"I'm sorry," Susannah said.

"It's okay," Katie said, wiping her hands on her damp jeans. "Although I'm soaking wet now. Just remember, it drives like *a boat*, okay? It doesn't respond as fast as a car."

"Okay," Susannah said. She clamped down on the fear in her mind.

Katie helped lift Quinn onto the boat. Susannah insisted

they wear life jackets, and put one on herself. She wanted Katie and Quinn down in the cabin, where they'd be safe, but when she went to open the cabin door it was locked and padlocked.

"Kate? Do you know if there's a key?"

"No."

"Why is the cabin locked?"

"I don't know. Maybe Barefoot keeps stuff down there he doesn't want anyone to mess with."

"But you kids have to ride in the cabin."

"We'll be fine here, Mom. See?" Katie helped Quinn up into the chair opposite the pilot chair, and then stood behind Susannah. She unrolled the canvas flap that provided a back wall, of sorts, for the wheelhouse.

"Okay. Everybody please hold on. I mean it, Kate."

"Don't ram into anything else," Katie said, after Susannah had backed the boat up and then started to move forward again, away from the dock and out into the bay.

"Lucky for you there isn't much to ram once we're out of the bay," Susannah said. "Except other islands, and I can usually see those before I hit them." *I hope.*

Katie peered at her mother's face. "Are you making a joke?"

"I'm trying to point out that I'm not as grossly incompetent as you assume, even if I did bump into the dock."

"Bump!" Katie said. "Collide, or crash, is more like it." But her voice was mild.

They moved out of the bay and toward the wide expanse of Governor's Channel. The currents were strongest here, Susannah knew, and the sea the roughest. She could feel the water like a live thing, swelling and swirling beneath them. Back along the shore, the trees leaned in the wind. The waves were bigger now. She kept the boat headed straight into the wind. It climbed each swell and then dipped back down, up and down.

Susannah held the wheel with both hands and tried to concentrate on the rise and fall of each wave, on keeping the boat steady, on remembering to keep track of the wind.

Katie picked up the radio. "I can call ahead to the marina in Friday Harbor and see if they can have a police car or ambulance meet us to get us to the clinic."

"Good thinking." Susannah had forgotten that once they arrived in Friday Harbor they'd need to get Quinn from the boat to the doctor.

Katie put in a quick call on the radio and then clicked it off.

"I thought you were afraid of boats," she said.

"I am. Or I was."

"Are you afraid right now?"

"No," Susannah said. She hoped it was true.

It was after four o'clock, and getting dark. Susannah switched on the boat's running lights, and peered at the radar screen.

"Kate, do you know how to read the radar?"

"Yes."

"Good. Then can you watch the radar?"

"Sure."

Susannah found a small manual switch for the wipers and was relieved to see them swish back and forth. As they entered the channel and the water grew wilder, Susannah grew more and more calm. Maybe it was the lingering effects of Barefoot's heart medicine, or just the realization that there was nothing more she could do right now to affect the outcome of whatever was going to unfold over the next few hours. She watched the water, held tight to the wheel in her hands, and tried to feel the boat respond to the swells beneath them, the shifting winds.

"You're doing good, Mom," Katie said. "We're right on course. It's maybe another forty-five minutes to Friday Harbor." She paused a minute. "I'm impressed," she said. "I mean I know you don't like boats, but you're handling this really well."

"Thanks. I never would have been able to do this alone."

Katie smiled, a small smile of self-satisfaction. "It's okay."

Quinn sat up and vomited.

Katie's calm cracked. "Oh, my God! Oh, gross!"

He moaned.

"Mom!" Katie said. "He's really, really sick. You have to do something. Call the Coast Guard!"

"The Coast Guard is for real emergencies, like when the boat is taking on water, or someone has a heart attack. We're half an hour from Friday Harbor."

"But what if we don't make it?"

Susannah stopped watching the waves for a moment, just long enough to lock her eyes on her daughter's face. "I can do this, Katie," she said. She was not thirteen years old and terrified, cowering before her father's criticism, his certainty of her incompetence. She *could* do it. "Quinn is going to be okay. You're doing great. Hang on a little while longer."

"Okay," Katie said. "Okay." She found a roll of paper towels in the glove box and threw them on the floor to soak up the vomit. She helped Quinn curl up in the cushioned chair across from where Susannah sat, and then came over to stand behind Susannah.

"Is Quinn going to die?" she said in a low voice.

No, no, no. "Of course not. I think he has appendicitis. It's serious, but once we get him to Friday Harbor they can tell for sure and get him to the hospital in a helicopter if that's what he needs. He'll be fine. I promise." *He has to be.*

The waves rose higher now out in the channel, but there was a rhythm to it, and Susannah was learning it. She could do this. With her confidence growing, she pushed the throttle forward. The boat picked up speed and shot up over the next wave, perched for a second on the crest, and then slammed into the trough after the wave with a heart-stopping impact. Quinn flew out of his seat, landing on the floor with a scream of pain and fright. Katie shot forward and landed on top of Quinn. As they began to climb the next wave, both kids rolled across the floor toward the thin canvas flap that covered the back of the pilothouse, toward the back of the boat and the open water.

"Slow down!" Katie yelled. Tangled together with Quinn, she rolled through the canvas flap and disappeared from sight.

Susannah pulled back on the throttle and the boat slowed to a crawl. "Katie! Katie! Katie!" She shouted her name over and over again. She couldn't let go of the wheel; she couldn't see her children.

"Slow down!" Katie's voice came through the canvas, and then her arm. She crawled back into the pilothouse, dragging Quinn, who was crying. "God, Mom! Are you trying to kill us? *Slow down.* You have to go slower in big waves or you climb the waves too fast."

Susannah could feel the frantic pounding of her heart against her ribs.

"I thought you fell out of the boat," she said.

"We didn't fall out of the boat," Katie said. "We rolled into that big bench in the back, and I probably have a giant bruise now."

Susannah couldn't breathe. She turned to Katie. "I can't do this," she said.

Quinn sobbed. Katie looked at him and then at Susannah's panicked face, and her eyes filled with tears, too.

"What do you mean?" Katie said. "You have to get us there."

Susannah shook her head. "No, no, no. I can't do this again."

"*Mom.*" Katie was angry now. "*Don't* freak out now. *I* don't know how to drive the boat! You're the one who said you could get us there. Just cause you went too fast over *one* wave, you can't quit."

The boat began to climb the next swell steadily, slowly. Susannah held her breath as they reached the top of the wave, but then the boat slid down steadily, slowly, and rode into the trough. She exhaled.

"Okay," she said. "Okay." *This is not that day.*

"How do you know to go slower in big waves?" Susannah said. The fact that the boat had raced up a wave and then crashed into the trough didn't mean imminent death and destruction to Katie; it meant time to pull back on the throttle. Susannah saw for the first time the upside to Katie's fearlessness.

Katie rubbed the bottom of her wet jeans with her hand. "Ew, now I'm even more soaked. From being on the boat with Hood. I know you think Hood is wild, but he's really careful about driving the boat. Jim is kind of strict."

"You're a smart kid." She turned to look at Quinn. "I'm so sorry, sweetheart. Are you okay?"

He nodded.

"I promise no more going fast over big waves."

Susannah glanced at Katie. "Here," she said. "I need your help. I can't see very well in the dark. Can you help me keep watch out the front windshield here? I want to be sure I turn at the right time to enter the harbor."

"Sure."

They were both silent, then, and didn't speak again until they turned into San Juan Channel and began to make their way slowly along the eastern shore of San Juan Island. Now that they were in the lee of the island the water was calmer, the wind weaker. Susannah took a deep breath and felt the tension leave her body. She took one hand off the wheel to flex her aching fingers. She'd been gripping the wheel so tightly that her fingers were stiff, bent into a claw.

Katie stood next to Susannah as they entered the harbor and approached the marina. By the time Susannah pulled up at the dock, an ambulance was waiting at the top of the ramp. Katie gave her quiet instructions, and she was able to pull the boat alongside the dock with only a slight bump. Relief rose in her chest, loosened her shoulders. Before Susannah had time to shut off the engine and make sure everything was in place, Katie had tied up the boat and was directing the EMTs down the ramp to where Quinn lay, curled in a ball in the boat.

Within minutes they were at the clinic, where the doctor examined Quinn and performed an ultrasound. Susannah called Matt as soon as the doctor looked at her and said, "Yes, it's his appendix and it's ruptured. A helicopter is coming to take him to the hospital in Bellingham for surgery."

"I'm on the next plane," Matt said.

In minutes Susannah was on the helicopter, strapped into a seat next to Quinn's stretcher, with Katie across from her and a medic on her other side.

At the hospital everything was brisk and efficient. Quinn was loaded onto a gurney, wheeled onto an elevator, taken down to the surgical floor. Susannah filled out forms and answered questions and talked to the anesthesiologist and surgeon. Before they wheeled him into the operating room, Susannah bent down over the small, sweaty form on the gurney, smoothed the damp blond hair back from Quinn's face, and kissed his freckled forehead.

"You're going to be fine, sweetheart," she said. "When you wake up I'll be here."

The big doors swung open, the nurse wheeled the stretcher forward, and Quinn was gone.

Chapter 28

Susannah 2011

Susannah sat down in the waiting room on a couch that was either beige or mauve. A volunteer brought sandwiches, which Katie devoured.

Susannah leaned back, weary to her bones. She could feel the salt crust on her skin from the ocean spray; feel the stiff tangles in her hair as she put her head back against the wall. Thank God there wasn't a mirror here. She probably looked like one of her own junk scarecrows. She closed her eyes but couldn't still her mind. She wondered if the surgeon had started yet, if right now tiny instruments were cutting into Quinn.

But it wasn't just Quinn. She couldn't stop thinking about Janie, about her mother, about the accident, about how it felt when she'd hit that wave, the force of the impact.

She looked over at Katie, who was curled up asleep on the couch across from her. Susannah knew she should try to sleep, too, but she couldn't. She stood up, rooted through the pockets of her jacket for her cell phone, and slipped into the hallway outside the waiting room. She punched her mother's number into the phone.

"Susie? How are you, darling?"

"Oh, God," Susannah said. "Where do I start?"

"I'm listening," Lila said.

"I'm at the hospital. Quinn is in surgery; his appendix ruptured." Her mother started to say something, but Susannah interrupted her. "He's going to be *fine*, Mom. The surgeon says we got him here in time." She paused. "I had to drive the boat to get him to the clinic. And now I can't stop thinking about that day."

"You mean the day of the accident." It was a statement, not a question.

"Yes. There's a lot we've never talked about."

"I know." Her mom's voice was low. "What happened to Janie was not your fault."

"Right." Susannah heard the bitterness in her voice and tried to temper it. "You couldn't even *look* at me that night, when we finally got home. I needed you to forgive me, Mom. I needed to know you still loved me, thought I was worth loving. But you wouldn't even look at me. You *went to bed*. How do you think that made me feel?"

She heard her mother's long, slow intake of breath, followed by silence.

"*Why* did you let us go with him, that day? Why did you let him take us out on the boat? You knew he drank."

Another long silence.

"You know what happened?" Susannah said. "Janie was fussing, so Daddy unbuckled her life jacket to get her to shut up. He was drinking. He got mad and decided we had to go back. He was driving the boat really fast. I was holding Janie in my lap. I had both my arms around her, Mom, I was holding her as tight as I could. But he hit the wake and she flew out of my arms. I couldn't hold on." She struggled to control her tears. She could hear her mother's jagged breath on the other end of the line, but went on.

"I couldn't hold on," Susannah said. "But Daddy said, he said, *'How could you let her go?'* It was *my* fault she died. *I let her go.*"

"It wasn't your fault, Susannah." Lila's voice was thick with emotion but emphatic. "It was *never* your fault. I have never, for one second, blamed you. If anything, I blame myself—blamed myself." Lila took a deep breath. "I let you down that day. And I am sorry."

"I just want to understand *why*. Because lately I've felt like I'm losing my own kids, losing my husband, losing myself because I can't let this go. If I could just understand what you were thinking—"

"Susannah, I was pregnant. Your father didn't want the baby. He promised me he would give up drinking and be a good parent, a good husband, if I got rid of the baby."

"Pregnant? You mean, after Janie?"

"I mean I found out I was pregnant about a month before the accident. I hadn't meant to get pregnant. It was a bad time. Your father was drinking even during the day, and he'd been threatened with losing his job if he didn't shape up. I got married at twenty-one; I never worked after college. I had three kids. I was *forty*. What was I going to do with another baby and an unemployed, alcoholic husband?"

Her mother's voice wavered. "I couldn't talk to you about it then; I couldn't. And once you were older . . . I knew you hated me for letting him take you out in the boat; I didn't want to tell you something that would make you hate me more. I was going to tell you; I just never knew how. Once you had your own kids—"

"Mom, I don't hate you." Susannah said it automatically.

"I don't blame you for being mad at me. I shouldn't have let you go. But he *had* given up the drinking. He hadn't had a drink in three weeks when he took you out that day. I thought he'd licked it; I thought he was going to keep his word. So I kept mine."

"What do you mean?"

"I didn't come with you on the boat that day because my sister took me to get an abortion." She cleared her throat. "We thought if you kids were out on the boat all day you wouldn't notice so much if I wasn't feeling well that night. There was a doctor in Traverse City—at least it was legal by then, thank God."

"You mean," Susannah said, her words halting, "you mean you had an abortion the day Janie died?"

"Yes."

The word hit Susannah with such force that it knocked the wind out of her.

"Oh, God. I am so sorry. Why didn't you tell me before?"

"I didn't want to give you another reason to be angry at me, another reason to think I'd failed." Lila paused. "For a long time I felt I didn't deserve you and Jon, that I shouldn't be your mother. I thought you'd be better off if I was dead. I couldn't bear it that first year after Janie died, when you gave me a Mother's Day card, as though I were some kind of deserving mother. And the pink crane—do you remember?"

Susannah thought of the crane, crumpled into a ball in the wastebasket.

"Of course I remember. You threw it away."

Lila sighed. "I'm sorry." She paused again. "It was beautiful. And you were so innocent and hopeful. I didn't think I deserved it— that innocence and hope and love."

Me, either, Susannah thought. *That's how I feel*.

"But my sister wouldn't let me go. Every day, she told me it wasn't my fault. Every day, she told me she loved me and admired me. She made me eat. She took care of you kids. And once your father left, I had to step up. But I had to lock the rest of it away."

Her mother's voice wavered. "If I thought about it, I'd go crazy. I thought taking Janie was God's punishment for the abortion. I stopped going to church, because I figured even God wouldn't want me there."

"*Mom.*"

"Susannah." Her mother's voice was clear now, and calm. "I know I should have told you this years ago. It's taken me decades, and five or six therapists, and a lot of pain to come to terms with this. I thought that by sending you to that psychiatrist right after the accident and then by just moving on with our lives, you'd be able to put it behind you. But when you moved to that island this fall, I started to wonder what was wrong.

"I wanted to come at Thanksgiving because I wanted to talk to you, in person. I wanted to explain it to you. I wanted to make sure you didn't still blame yourself. But then you got so upset with me," her voice trailed off. "You were so angry. I thought if I told you about the abortion you'd never speak to me again. But I knew I had to tell you. That's why I wanted to talk to you alone."

Susannah remembered her mother's plea over Thanksgiving: *I need to talk to you.*

"I carried the weight of that guilt for years," Lila said. "Everywhere I went, everything I did. It's only been recently I've been able to see it for what it was: An accident. Pure bad luck." She sighed. "I struggled for so long. Then Tessa gave me a book last year, by some Christian theologian. It annoyed me beyond end—Tessa always trying to help me get over it. But I opened the book and fell on one sentence that somehow clicked for me: 'To forgive is to set a prisoner free and discover that the prisoner was you.' I was tired of being a prisoner.

"Once I forgave myself, the weight was gone. It was a simple thing. That's what I want for you, Susie."

"It's hard," Susannah said. "I'm the one who let her go."

"You were *thirteen*," her mother said. "Your father unbuckled her life jacket; he drank; he drove too fast. None of us meant for it to happen. Your father never got over the guilt; I don't think he looked me in the eye again after that day. It's *enough*. We have all paid for it over and over and over again. If *I* can let it go, you can. I hoped maybe you'd figure that out. I hoped maybe this move was about that, about being kind to yourself.

"That pink crane?" Lila said. "That tiny, precious thing? I realized I *am* worthy. We all are, honey."

"I'm sorry," Susannah said. "I'm sorry you went through all that. I can't even imagine. It's not fair. You didn't deserve that."

"None of us did," Lila said. "Not even your father. He was sick. He loved Janie; he loved you and Jon. He loved me. And I know, *I know*, it wasn't my fault. I hope with all my heart, Susannah, that someday you'll realize it wasn't your fault, either."

Susannah thought about the wave they'd hit a few hours ago, about the force of the impact when they hit. "We hit a wave tonight, when I was driving the boat to get Quinn to the clinic," she said. "It felt like hitting a brick wall." She was thinking out loud now, no longer aware of her mother on the other end of the phone. "It really did. And ever since then I've been thinking about the day we hit the wake—" She stopped. It was too close. What if it had happened again tonight, with Katie or Quinn flying out of the boat into the black water?

"I didn't realize until I hit that wave tonight that it *could* feel like that," Susannah continued. "Like a car crash or something, with so much *force*."

"Let it go," Lila said. "It was never your fault. Your father was drunk and going too fast. He unbuckled Janie's life vest. It was never you."

Susannah's tears overcame her. "I was holding her so tight, Mom, because Dad was going so fast. I was holding her *so tight*."

She heard her mother's sharp intake of breath, heard her struggle to hold back tears.

"It wasn't you! It wasn't your fault, Susannah," her mother said again. "I'll tell you again and again every day of your life if I have to, until you believe it. *It wasn't your fault.*"

Susannah clung to the phone, pressing it hard against her ear. "I know," she said, and the weight of thirty years slid from her heart, seeped out her pores, dissipated into vapor—leaving her light, breathless, translucent.

"I know," she said. "It wasn't my fault."

And this time, for the first time ever, she knew it was true.

Susannah snapped the phone shut. She leaned her back against the wall and slid slowly down until she was sitting on the pale tiled floor, the phone still clenched in her hand.

"Mom?"

Katie stood in the doorway to the waiting room, looking at Susannah. "Are you all right?"

Susannah wiped the tears from her cheeks with one hand. "Yes. I'm fine, honey." She smiled. "I'm good, in fact. Tired, but good."

Katie came over and sat down on the floor next to her. "Are you crying about Quinn? He's going to be okay, right?"

"Oh, honey. Quinn is going to be *fine.*" Susannah took a deep breath. Even with Quinn still in surgery; even with Matt in the air somewhere over some dark state, rushing to get to them; even with the complete physical exhaustion of all she'd been through in the last—could it be just twelve hours?—even with all that, Susannah felt a strange sense of peace.

"We have to talk, Kate," she said. She put a hand up and pushed a strand of Katie's dark hair behind her ear, and for once Katie didn't pull away at the contact.

"I was not going to have sex with Hood. Seriously. It's totally embarrassing to be talking to you about this, but I want you to know that."

"All right." Susannah looked at her. "I believe you. I trust you." And, to her surprise, she did.

"Listen," Susannah said. "Sometimes grown-ups make mistakes, too. I may have made mistakes in trying to protect you too much. My dad made some terrible mistakes the day my sister died; so did my mom. We all make mistakes. We all have to learn to forgive each other, and ourselves."

"Okay."

Susannah studied Katie's brown eyes, reached out to run her hand through Katie's thick hair. "You remind me of my sister. I wonder all the time what Janie would have been like at your age, or as an adult. She had a lot of spirit, like you."

"You never talk about her."

"I was just talking to my mom about her."

"Was that her on the phone?"

"Yes." Susannah closed her eyes. "I needed to talk to her. I really needed to figure out some things about the day your Aunt Janie died. My poor mom—" Susannah shook her head. "Anyway, I figured out a lot. And everything, *everything* is going to be better from now on. I mean it."

Katie looked at her out of the corners of her eyes, her face cautious. "Okay." She tilted her head back and looked up at the white acoustic tiles of the ceiling. "You mean you won't freak out every time I want to do something?"

"Right," Susannah said. "At least, I'll try. I'm really proud of how you handled yourself on the boat. I couldn't have done it without you. When I got nervous, you were fine. That's one of the many things I love about you. You don't get scared easily; you're willing to take chances. You're very capable." Susannah reached over and put her hand on Katie's leg. "You could work a little on the whole thinking-before-you-act thing." Susannah held up her thumb and forefinger so they were an inch apart. "Just try to be *this* much less impulsive if you can."

"You mean like giving you a pot cupcake? I'm sorry."

"I know." Susannah shook her head. Her anger seemed to have evaporated along with her fear, and her guilt. "You could be nicer to Quinn, too," she said. "He's a good kid. He actually looks up to you, you know. You're a lot of the things he wants to be—brave, outgoing, adventurous."

"I'm not *that* mean to him," Katie said. "God, he's my little brother; it's not like we're going to be best friends." She put her hand up to her head and twirled a strand of hair, unconsciously echoing Quinn's own habit. "Quinn isn't that bad, really. I mean, he is way more interesting than most kids his age. He just doesn't get how to act, you know? How to fit in. And I hate that; I hate feeling like I have to protect him all the time."

"Yeah, I know," Susannah said. "What do you think it's like to be a mom? To feel like you have to protect your kids all the time?"

"Well, there's being a mom and then there's *you*," Katie said, but her voice was affectionate.

Susannah glanced at her watch. Quinn had been in surgery more than half an hour already.

"They should be done soon," she said. She looked at Katie again. "Do you want to go home?" she said. "I mean, back to Tilton?"

"No." Katie's answer came more quickly than Susannah had expected. "I wouldn't want to live here forever, but I'm glad we came. It's different here."

The doors to the waiting room flew open and a nurse stepped out.

"Mrs. Delaney? We've finished the surgery. The doctor is ready to talk to you about your son."

* * *

"Susannah!"

Susannah's eyes snapped open. She'd been dozing in the chair next to the bed where Quinn lay sleeping, his mouth slightly open. Katie was asleep on a folding cot across the room. Susannah had gone in to see Quinn in recovery, and listened as the doctor explained the surgery. The infection had spread, and Quinn would need to be in the hospital a few days for IV antibiotics. But he was fine, would be fine. She had kissed him and squeezed his hand, promised to take a picture of his scar later (which elicited a pale smile), and then collapsed in the chair when he was finally wheeled into the room.

"Susannah!" Matt stood in the doorway to the hospital room. He wore rumpled corduroys and a long-sleeved black T-shirt. Dark circles of fatigue bloomed under his eyes, and a rough stubble of beard covered his cheeks and chin. "He's okay?"

Susannah nodded. "I was with him in recovery and I talked to him. The surgeon said he had to make a three-inch incision, so I promised to take pictures of his scar. He liked that." She stood up, wincing at the stiffness in her back from sleeping in an odd position on the chair.

"You've been up all night," she said.

He dropped his duffel bag and parka on the floor.

"Yeah, I've been up all night. I've been on a red-eye, wondering if my son was dying of peritonitis."

He walked over to the bed and stood looking down at Quinn.

"He's so pale."

"He's fine. His fever's gone. He'll need the IV for another day or two for the antibiotics, but he's going to be great."

Matt put his hand to Quinn's forehead, stroked his lanky curls. His eyes ran from his son's face, down the IV in his arm, and over the blanket covering Quinn's thin frame, so small in the big hospital bed.

"He hasn't been in a hospital since he was born," Matt said.

He turned around to look at Susannah and did the one thing she had never expected him to do: his eyes welled with tears.

"Matt!"

She crossed the room to him in a step and put her arms around him and hugged him fiercely, fiercely, but he pushed her away.

"I want my family back," he said. "You need to come home and bring the kids home. I can't do this."

She stood across from him, her arms hanging empty at her sides. "I want to come home," she said.

"I finally understand things," she continued. "I don't know, these last weeks on Sounder I've been thinking about Janie all the time. And then when I was driving the boat today with Quinn and Katie I hit a wave, *hard*. The impact was like hitting a wall. And I realized that no one, *no one* could have held on to Janie through something like that: *It wasn't my fault*. I know you've told me that a million times; so have my mother and brother. It's just that tonight—I *felt* it. I finally understood it wasn't me."

Matt sat down on the edge of Quinn's bed, his eyes on her.

"I thought I couldn't survive it if it happened twice, if something bad happened to someone I loved again, on my watch. So I've tried to protect the kids—"

"I'll say," Matt said. He rubbed a hand across his forehead.

She ached to make him understand. "But it wasn't just making sure nothing happened to them. Katie is so impulsive—I had to make sure *she* didn't make a mistake like I did, do something she had to feel guilty about for the rest of her life. You see?"

Matt looked at her. "Yeah, I see." He rubbed his hand

through his hair, which was already wild and uncombed. He looked around the room, searching for the right words.

"Look," he said, and he gazed back at her. "You and I are very different. I am not a complicated guy. I like my work, I love my family, I like to drink a beer and watch a baseball game. It's hard for me to relate to worrying about stuff the way you do. But I love you, so that's all part of the package. You're the most generous-hearted person I know. And I never tire of your company. I can deal with the rest."

"Matt. I'm sorry."

"God! Don't be sorry! Don't you see—that's the point? *Don't be sorry*. I never blamed you for Janie. Sure, our family is messy. Quinn's a different kind of kid, and Katie can be a huge pain in the ass, and you worry too much, and I could probably be more involved. But the bottom line is, I'm fine with all that. I love all that. *It's us*."

She looked at him, his face tired and puffy after his long night and the long flight, but the beauty still there beneath it all, the high cheekbones, the straight nose, the broad forehead. She loved knowing his face now and remembering it at age ten and fourteen and twenty. All those years, and she had been part of them, too. She saw the scar from the hockey blade on his cheek and reached forward and ran a finger across it lightly. She gazed into his blue eyes, the color of the ice in glaciers, and he didn't turn away. And she felt as she had all those years ago in that little cabin by the lake in northern Michigan, felt something rise in her, swirling and full and warm. Even now, after all these years, he *still* loved her like that. And after it all—after this last hard year of everything—she knew she loved him like that, too, and herself with him.

"Thank you," she said.

Matt's eyes searched her face, and he smiled, a sweet, reassuring smile—so like Quinn's that her heart lurched. Quinn shifted again in the bed, rolled onto his side. Matt stood up at the sound, and bent over him. But Quinn slept.

Matt walked over to look at Katie, asleep on the cot on her stomach—one leg tossed wide, her dark hair tangled on the white pillow.

"She's okay?"

"She's fine. It's been a wild ride this past twenty-four hours."

"It's been a wild ride since the day she was born."

Susannah came and stood next to him and put an arm around his waist. He turned to her, and his arms encircled her, and she buried her face against his chest.

"I love you," he said. "I love you and the kids and our family more than anything."

"I know," she said. "I love you, too."

He held her tighter, and this time, for the first time she could ever remember, she was the first to let go.

Chapter 29

Susannah 2012

The day of the funeral was sunny and clear. After a long, rainy spring, the air was warm and loam scented, and now, in late June, everything was lush and green. At the edge of the cemetery, two hummingbirds sipped at a blooming tangle of morning glory, and bees buzzed in the wild nootka roses. Above them, a pair of flickers pecked away at the deadwood of an old white fir, digging out a nest.

Barefoot wore a clean pair of black trousers and a warm gray sweater and no shoes, of course. The trousers were the only ones Betty had been able to find that didn't need to be pinned together in the front, and while he probably had a pair of shoes somewhere, he had never worn them in life, so it didn't seem right that he should wear them now. Quinn and Katie had found him curled on the floor of his farmhouse, on a rug next to the woodstove, with Toby at his side. The medical examiner said he had probably died peacefully in his sleep; for whatever reason, his heart had stopped. When Susannah and Jim had arrived at the farmhouse in response to Katie's call, after frantically driving across the rutted roads and then running pell-mell to the farmhouse, they had found Quinn and Katie kneeling on the floor next to Barefoot, hugging Toby, surrounded by a dozen coffee cans filled with earth and little seedlings.

"Barefoot always kept his plants next to the stove at night so they'd stay warm," Quinn had said, raising a tear-stained face to Susannah. "How can they be alive and he be dead?"

Now more than a hundred people clustered around the grave, including every single one of the islanders and friends from as far away as Ann Arbor and San Jose. Betty, too weak to walk more than a few steps, sat on Dorothy Watson's bench, across from the grave, with her oxygen tank at her side. Jim had carried her there before everyone arrived. She didn't want the other islanders to see the extent of her weakness. She wanted to do Barefoot proud.

Susannah and Matt stood a few feet from her, next to the grave. Quinn sat several yards away in the shade of an aspen tree, petting Toby. Katie stood close to her mother. After Quinn's surgery and recovery, they'd decided to finish out the school year on Sounder. The life they had begun to build here was changing them, and they wanted to see it through, to give those changes time to become something tangible they could take back to Tilton. Matt had been back and forth to see them every month, and Lila had spent two weeks with them this spring.

Susannah pressed against Matt's shoulder as Jim began to read the eulogy he'd written for Barefoot. Jim's husky voice broke several times as he recalled the man who had befriended him as a child, who had taught him to swim and to love plants and growing things, to appreciate works of art and fine things—the man who had been, in all but biology, his father. He talked of Barefoot's work—the thirty thousand plants he'd collected for the University of Michigan's herbarium, the disease-resistant wild melon he'd discovered in Calcutta that had saved the California

melon crop one year, the medal he'd won for his contributions
to world agriculture. As he spoke, Toby got up and walked over
and sat next to Jim, gazing up at him with his head cocked to
one side as though he were listening, too. Quotes from Goethe,
Mencken, and Dumas, Barefoot's favorite authors, were sprin-
kled throughout Jim's speech, each one calling up such a vivid
image of Barefoot that Susannah almost expected him to sit up
in his casket and tell Jim to stop yammering on.

Jim read a quote from Mencken: "Every normal man must
be tempted, at times, to spit on his hands, hoist the black flag,
and begin slitting throats." The crowd laughed, and Jim talked
about the adventures of Barefoot's past, the wild ride on horse-
back across the plains of Uzbekistan in search of a rare variety
of wild pomegranate, the robber he'd surprised in Tunisia, the
wild boar—named Judy—he'd kept as a pet in Iran.

" 'Every day we should hear at least one little song, read one
good poem, see one exquisite picture, and, if possible, speak a
few sensible words,' " Jim read. Every day, Barefoot had wiped
his bare feet on a beautiful, richly colored, hundred-year-old
Baluch prayer rug, and eaten homemade apple pie from delicate nineteenth-century Minton porcelain plates, painted with
white roses on a rich dark blue ground. He had loved beautiful
things and surrounded himself with them and enjoyed them
every day.

One by one, the other islanders stood to share their favorite
remembrances of Barefoot. Evelyne Waters's mother, Andrea,
recalled that she had once brought Barefoot a bottle of fine
French wine as a thank-you for some seedlings he'd given her.

"He told me, 'Take that swill back home,' " Andrea said, as
laughter rang out.

"Because it wasn't a Riesling," someone called out. "He only
drank *sweet* wine."

Susannah shared the story of her first boat ride with Barefoot, how he'd taught her to handle the boat, easing her nerves with a slug of his "heart medicine." Fiona, back from India for six months now, told a story, too, about the gift Barefoot had given her when the twins were born: a book on Far Eastern birth control methods.

When the last person had had her say, Jim stepped back up to the head of the grave. He took a deep breath. "I can't finish talking about Barefoot Jacobsen's life without also talking about my mother, Betty, and what she and Barefoot meant to each other," he said.

Susannah looked at him in surprise, and then at Betty, who sat erect, her face glowing.

"Barefoot and Betty were lifelong friends," Jim continued. "Beyond that, they shared a love so rich and full that, honestly, it humbles me to talk about it." His voice grew thick, and he stopped for a moment.

Tears filled Betty's eyes, but she smiled.

"It is hard for me to imagine my mother without Barefoot, or Barefoot without my mother. It's not because they were inseparable—indeed, they spent large chunks of time apart. But they were so connected that you couldn't be around one of them without feeling and knowing the other. If a relationship is defined by what is created in the space between two people, then Barefoot and Betty created something filled with trust, acceptance, generosity, and passion." He looked at his mother, his own eyes full.

"I don't think it's an exaggeration to say that, in many ways, Barefoot saved my mother's life after my father died. But I believe she saved his life, too, by grounding him, and also by letting him bloom. They were both most fully themselves with each other. They gave each other joy, and said so.

"They showed me what it really means to love"—Jim looked

at his wife, and then at his sons, and his voice broke—"and I try every day to live up to their example."

Betty closed her eyes, and nodded—in thanks, in acknowledgment of the truth he had spoken.

"I found a quote Barefoot wrote on the back of a photo of my mother that he kept in his wallet," Jim continued. "They're words from Willa Cather's *My Antonia*, and seem a fitting way to close." He cleared his throat, and read: " 'I was entirely happy. Perhaps we feel like that when we die and become a part of something entire, whether it is sun and air, or goodness and knowledge. At any rate, that is happiness: to be dissolved into something complete and great. When it comes to one, it comes as naturally as sleep.' "

Susannah felt the wind pick up, rustling the leaves in the trees arcing overhead, lifting her hair. She heard the rattle of metal and turned to see the sea-glass halo on her Janie angel spinning in the breeze. A few weeks ago, at Betty's request and with the agreement of the other islanders, Susannah had installed three of her scarecrow sculptures here in the cemetery. The first, the Janie angel, stood next to a tiny, freshly planted rose bush near the entrance to the cemetery. The second, another angel, stood on the spot Betty had picked out for her own grave. And the third, Susannah's junk metal version of Katie's pony-tailed God, stood in the center of the cemetery, with rainbow-colored pants made of copper and legs that danced now in the wind.

The sculptures were beautiful—wild and free and exuberant, all the things Susannah had never felt herself to be. But looking at them now she thought, *They are me, too.* She was both happy and fearful about going back to Tilton at the end of June: happy to be with Matt again, fearful of falling into old patterns, old terrors. Katie would be in high school this

September, Quinn in middle school. They would face the same risks, the same temptations. So would she.

But the kids were different people now; she was a different person now. She looked at the sculptures and thought, *I could not have created those a year ago.* She thought about the words Jim had just spoken, about being dissolved into something complete and great. She thought, with her husband and children at her side, about letting go. *It's like falling without a net*, she thought. *But it's so much better than being bound up in one.*

Hood began to sing. He had a beautiful, pure alto, and sang the spiritual Barefoot had requested in his will: "Ain't Got Time to Die." Susannah saw Betty smile and shake her head as Hood sang the chorus. As he finished singing, six snow geese, which had been honking in the scrubby field across the dirt road from the cemetery, suddenly took off and flew overhead, their wide white wings and black wingtips flapping in unison, almost as if it were timed.

Susannah looked up, following the geese with her eyes as they became smaller and smaller in the distance until they were no more than tiny black dots against the cloudless blue sky.

"Did you see that?" Katie said.

Susannah nodded.

"It would be amazing, wouldn't it? To be able to fly?"

"Yes."

The crowd started to disperse. People clustered around Betty, their hands on her shoulders, murmuring words of comfort.

Susannah turned to follow the crowd. Matt was ahead of her, talking to Quinn. Katie stood still.

"You coming, Kate?" Susannah said. "The party for Barefoot at the Laundromat is now."

"I know," Katie said. "I'll be there in a little bit. I have to—I wrote something for Barefoot."

"You did? I'd love to see it."

Katie shook her head. "No. It's just for Barefoot. I want to go out in the kayak and read it, just alone. Then I'll come."

Susannah looked at her. Alone in the kayak with dusk coming on, with every soul on the island at the Laundromat, with no one around to hear her if she lost her paddle or got swamped by a passing boat or caught in the current.

"Go," Susannah said to her daughter. "Fly."

Acknowledgments

Thanks go to many people: Joel and Margaret Thorsen welcomed me into their lives and their home and made it possible for me to get some sense of what life in a place like Sounder might really be like; I couldn't have written this book without them. Ann Rittenberg, my agent, waited, read, waited some more, read some more, made brilliant suggestions, and finally pulled out of me the book she always believed was in there, even if I didn't. My husband, Paul Benninghoff, worked hard every day and gave me the freedom—and encouragement—to write. I also owe much to Jim Maya, who first showed me the San Juans, and whose love for the islands was contagious. Every one of you is part of this book.

Thanks to Gracie Benninghoff, who read several drafts and made key suggestions, and to Emma Benninghoff, who cheered me on. I love you both like crazy.

Thanks to my mom, Ann McCleary, and to my brother, Tom McCleary, who love and support me through good times and bad, and to the person who singlehandedly sold more copies of my first book than anyone in the world, Dot McCleary.

The pieces of the puzzle didn't quite fit into place until Tessa Woodward, my editor, suggested I write a second point of view.

I did, and I'm happier with it than with anything else I've ever written. Thanks, Tessa.

In addition, thanks to the many friends who read early drafts and hold me up, always: Stacy Hennessey, Debbie Alfano, Laura Merrill, Lori Kositch, Kevin and Holly Hess, Paul and Karly Condon, Sarah Flanagan, Anne Krueger, Wally Konrad, and Julia and Wiley Loughran. Thanks to the Fiction Writers' Co-op: I am so happy to be in such good company.

Finally, here's to joy, love, merriment and the incredible gift of grace. Don't know how I got so lucky, but here I am.